Storm Over Bakery Hill

Also by William Cotter and published by Ginninderra Press

Poetry

The Darkness of Swans

The White Blood of Moonlight

Cloud Gazing

Refractions

Light Within the Stone

Pen Points

Of Forms and Shapes (Pocket Poets)

Of Light, Shade and Half-light

Mirror: Collected Poems

Stories

Thoughts By a Window

Play for voices

Of Baiame and a Tree That Said, 'Dig'

William Cotter

Storm Over Bakery Hill

Storm Over Bakery Hill
ISBN 978 1 76041 438 2
Copyright © William Cotter 2017
Cover image: *Battle of the Eureka Stockade.*
J.B. Henderson [1854] Watercolour [public domain]

First published 2017 by
GINNINDERRA PRESS
PO Box 3461 Port Adelaide 5015
www.ginninderrapress.com.au

Contents

1   A matter of survival   7

2   The wider's store   26

3   Alone   41

4   Visited again   51

5   The coach, the iron pot and something new   61

6   Duty   77

7   Of a cannon, windlasses and a robbery   84

8   The hotel and the logs   99

9   There's trouble brewin'   111

10 Feathers   125

11 A mystery solved   134

12 Of news, roads and religion   148

13 A meeting on Bakery Hill   160

14 Guns   171

15 Bentley's Hotel   189

16 Meetings and a surprise   201

17 A December morning   212

1

A matter of survival

You could go past and not recognise it as a cemetery. It was really nothing more than a patch of troubled ground, hacked out from the surrounding bushland. A place where the kangaroos grazed at dusk and the citizens of the settlement deposited their dead during the day.

To many struggling farmers, this part of the continent probably seemed as if it had a will of its own. A malevolent will that must have terrified the women who came with them. In the long nights, one could well imagine them pining for a more gentle landscape, one that did not echo to strange sounds at night and did not bring nameless, disappearing shapes that might be hostile Aborigines or prowling animals. At times, even the silences were full of threats.

Some of the locals, those with vivid imaginations, or those wanting to deter their children from wandering around the bush after dark, said that at night you could sometimes hear a strange moaning that no one could explain. Many probably felt that, if the dead were taken elsewhere in the future, the trees and the grasses would quickly reclaim possession and the place would return to its peaceful state. Nature, some maintained, if left to itself, would heal its wounds. However, it was the closest thing to a permanent cemetery that Ballarat had.

While some of the diggers simply dug graves in a convenient gully, shrugged or grieved and moved on, most clung on to the belief that the dead should somehow be gathered together in one place. Somehow, words spoken around an open grave and a wooden cross placed at the head of the raised earth later gave a sense of completion.

And Mary Douglas, true to tradition, had insisted that her husband be given 'a decent burial'. So, co-opting four local labourers to help him, Dan Morgan, the bullocky, had knocked together a rough coffin, and the coffin had been brought here.

One or two of the travellers on the track paused to watch what was going on. Most didn't. Death was nothing unusual here. The curious would have seen the widow, a slight woman of about forty, dressed in obligatory black, her hair drawn fiercely back. They would have noticed a small child, a girl, clutching her mother's hand and looking quite bewildered. Her simple frock had obviously been washed for the occasion, though her worn shoes were already spotted with dust. And they would have seen the son, a young man of about twenty, who stood rather apart. They might have briefly wondered about that. So silent was he and so rigid. Looking out but seeming to focus on nothing, there was a dark inscrutability about his face that would probably have intimidated any who dared to approach.

And they would have noticed the bullocky, ready with his shovel at hand. And the minister standing at the head of the grave. But they would not have known what thoughts ran through the minds of the family members standing there, silent with the wind mumbling through the stringybark trees behind them.

Nor, indeed, did the minister, the Reverend Thomas Hastie, who had come across from Buninyong to conduct the service. He was well known throughout the area and Mary Douglas had no hesitation in asking him. He seemed to have the respect of many. The wealthy farmers accepted him. Probably because they believed a man of the cloth would instil in the poor a respect for hard work. And for their social betters. However, and perhaps to the discomfort of the fortunate few with wealth or property, it was known around the area that he sympathised with the poor and the disadvantaged. Had even spoken publicly about the injustices they experienced.

Yet, in spite of these concerns, he seemed to be accepted by Protestants and Catholics. The possible invasion of their land by greedy miners was seen as a much bigger threat. And there was no sense that he ever leavened his sermons with heretical beliefs in land distribution or socialism. His tall figure, always decked in pastoral black, was seen often, emerging from the bush in out of the way places. And he was welcomed by most.

You might well describe him as the traditional pastor. A man plucked from the green fields of Britain and transplanted, it seemed without change, into this alien land. Yet, like many infused with a genuine missionary zeal, he was often haunted by self-doubt. In his dark moments, and there were plenty of those, he feared that his theological training in Scotland had not really prepared him for life as a pastor in this strange land, inhabited as it was, by miners, cunning businessmen, ex-convicts, shepherds and wealthy graziers. Sometimes, when he travelled through the bush on his pastoral rounds, he was struck by the enormity of his task, endeavouring to bring comfort to people in a land where the harsh hills, the rapid swing between hot and cold, the brutality of flood and drought and the suffocating isolation seemed to fuse into a solid determination to sweep all human endeavour away.

He thought that the words he uttered from his rough pulpits must often miss their mark. But he persisted. His mission was to bring comfort and help to the men battling and dying below ground or on the long, lonely plains. More so, perhaps, to the women trying to survive in filthy huts and to the undernourished children. He also felt a sense of admiration for these settlers, though he wondered, many times, why they had ventured out here. And his sense of loyalty to them grew as he suffered and, at times, rejoiced with them. Faces turned towards him for reassurance if death leaned against some tree or peered in through a crack in some lonely hut on a freezing, wrenching night. And he did his best. Offering the Word and a message of hope – hope that the survivors might be given the strength to endure.

Triumph was not a word one used here. To endure was perhaps the most one could expect. And yet, he often thought, perhaps even endurance represented a triumph here.

So it was his curse or his blessing to continue, though he knew that, if he asked, he could probably be transferred to another parish. Amidst all of his self-doubts, his personal faith remained strong. As did his commitment to the education of the poor. He believed, without question, that the children of poor families could, even with rudimentary instruction, escape the poverty that imprisoned their parents. The children here were pretty much like those of his homeland, poor, somehow able to smile in spite of their hardship, often reduced to tears, but looking too often out over their world with a distressing, blank acceptance.

At fifty-years of age, he still retained a dream of seeing such children grow into robust young adults, able to take their place in society, uncertain though he was about the kind of society that awaited them. For this reason he had established a school in Buninyong. And was hopeful that the new widow might enrol her daughter there.

Grief, he knew, took many forms. Funerals were the stage upon which all kinds of dramas could be played out. Tears. Angry outbursts. Words of consolation. Regrets. Even relief.

But this one, even though the cast was very small, mystified him. There was nothing a well-meaning pastor could latch on to. Nothing, in the stillness and the silence, to give shape to the relationships between the family members. The widow, slight, almost fragile here on the edge of the bushland, was clearly protective of her daughter, holding her hand and occasionally looking down at her. Only very briefly did her eyes wander to the coffin. Or to the rigid figure of her son. Nothing about her face gave any hint as to what she might be thinking about the man whose body lay so close.

The little girl, though clinging to her mother's hand, was half turned away from the grave and snatched only the briefest glance at the raw pile of clay.

Deeply puzzling was the isolation of the young man, standing there with his arms tightly folded across his chest. His face betrayed nothing of his feelings. But, in his very stillness, there was, to the minister, a sense of waiting, a desire to take his emotions, whatever they were and disappear into the anonymity of the bush. Only once did he look intently at the grave.

As he began to speak from the impeccably kept Bible he always took with him, the Reverend Thomas Hardie imagined that his voice was sinking into a deep, dry well, returning like a hollow, meaningless echo. His mind was torn in two conflicting directions. To hasten. And to work harder to impress his listeners. Mechanically, he ran through the required words, all the while fearing that they had not had any real impact at all.

As he closed his Bible, to look beyond the grave and the fixed figure of the bullocky, a coldness ran through him, a sense that the land itself resented intrusion and was waiting for peace to return. Indeed, in one corner of the cemetery, that was happening already. A grave, much smaller than any of the others, already wore a thin covering of grass. He had committed a small boy, of about three, to this corner of the earth about a year ago and had been told that the parents, distraught by their loss, had returned to Geelong. Whether they had come back at any time to grieve before this small bubble of clay, he did not know. The condition of the grave would suggest that they had not. There were no wilting flowers, no simple wooden sign to signify that a child was buried here. It saddened him to think of the tiny occupant unidentified in any way and he wondered if anyone in the future, even if only out of curiosity, would pause here. To wonder and move on.

Yes, these bush burials perplexed him. Without the usual trappings of paths, headstones and neat fences, such funerals always seemed incomplete. But his mission was to do what he could to maintain the dignities demanded of the church and his own personal faith. He hoped, at least, that someone would erect a headstone to carry this man's name towards eternity.

With a brief sense of guilt, he admitted, standing there on this small, cleared island, that he would be relieved to pass on what words of comfort he could and then trace his way back through the lengthening shadows to Buninyong. The feeling was strengthened by the realisation that he knew virtually nothing about the dead man.

Nor did the bullocky. He had known him as a struggling storekeeper and had met his wife, son and daughter very briefly. That was all. But he did have some idea of what others thought about him.

'Glad to see the old bugger gone,' one digger had told him. ''Ad a good enough store here, on the Melbourne track, to be sure. But 'ard as nails, 'e was. Don't know 'ow 'is wife put up with 'im. Didn't 'ave much choice I suppose. 'Ard for women out 'ere. I know that.'

Another, a little more charitable in his assessment, had praised his determination. 'Had a hard time, did James. That much I know. But he was able to survive. Until now, that is.'

And there they stood. Minister and bullocky on one side. Widow, son and daughter on the other.

Soon the body of James Douglas was consigned to the earth and the minister, having made his brief, comforting remarks, set off. At one point, he stopped and looked back. There had been little movement, except that the bullocky now stood beside the widow. Around him gullies and slopes shimmered in the late sun, shadows, like him, trying to shake off something unpleasant. The distant slopes still rang with the metallic clang of picks and the shouts of men. And, strangely reassured by these sounds of normality, Mr Hastie, Presbyterian minister from Buninyong, set off.

Mary Douglas did not wait for the coffin to be completely covered. She took the little girl in both hands, hugged her briefly, placed her hand awkwardly on her son's shoulder, thanked the bullocky and left.

He resumed his task, shovelling slowly, rhythmically. Until he stood up to ease his back and was aware of a shadow and a voice. Startled, he looked round. Beside him now stood a stocky figure, decked out in a sergeant's uniform and cap. His face bore a thick, well attended beard, a beard that did not quite conceal a nasty scar. His hands were placed firmly on his hips. No statue could stand more comfortably. And, in another place, you might say there was something quite comical, piratical, about him. However, the bullocky did not laugh. Did not even smile. For there was something else in the stranger's appearance. A confidence and a warning. Here was the embodiment of authority. And the policeman's steady gaze reinforced this. On the troubled goldfields, where even ex-convicts had been drafted into the constabulary, one trod very warily when dealing with the law.

'Came a bit late. Black fella givin' trouble in a pub. But I wanted to be here. To see, to see the Great Survivor despatched. We called 'im that, you know. Here, I'll finish that for you.' His voice, too, was solid, authoritative. A voice used to being followed and obeyed.

Coming forward, he took the shovel and began heaving the clay down upon the coffin. Soon the dry crackle of earth on wood became a soft drumming and the job was done. Without any show of emotion, the policeman handed the shovel back. 'There. Finally the old devil's safely tucked up.' The coldness in his eyes now bore a glint of satisfaction.

'Thank you, sergeant. Not easy, burying a man in ground like this.'

'No. Still, 'is fate comes to all of us, don't it? Well, can't stay any longer. Bloody blacks givin' trouble. Them and the Irish. Nothing but trouble. Don't know what we'll do if many more Paddies turn up. Things'll get worse, I can tell you that. Still, that's not your problem. Stay well clear of it. That's my advice.'

There was a short, uncomfortable pause, as if the sergeant was wanting to say something else. Then, finally, 'Tell the widow I'll be out to see 'er when I can. Need support, they do. Women out 'ere.'

The authority, perhaps, had slipped, momentarily. And the bullocky summoned up a brief smile. 'Thank you, officer. I'll keep that in mind. Don't worry. My beasties give me enough problems. I don't need any more.' Then, as an afterthought, he added, 'I will let Mrs Douglas know that you'll come out to see her.'

Now, shouldering his shovel, he began walking back toward his horse. As he was about to mount, he looked back towards the fresh, clean grave. The officer, in spite of his earlier sense of urgency, was still there. Not beside the grave. But on it. As motionless as the body below him. Then, as if jerked into motion, he stamped his feet, spat upon the clay and returned to his horse, unaware that the bullocky has been watching him.

The latter waited until the policeman was out of sight, then mounted, also. Ahead of him the track was empty. Silent, apart from the steady hoof beats and the gravelly voice of a crow perched somewhere among the stringybarks. Probably, he felt a sense of relief as he wound his way through the trees towards his hut. Almost certainly a sympathy for the widow. And possibly also, a dull curiosity about the policemen's actions.

The curious traveller, pausing here a few days later, would have seen, scrawled upon a piece of timber, this simple inscription:

James Douglas: died August 1853

He might have wondered, like the bullocky, what kind of a man lay here, now, beneath this tortured hump of clay. Was he a soul at rest after life's labour? Did he leave mourners behind who might return, stand by the grave and spare a thought for him? Or would he remain forgotten with the bush grasses growing careless and free above him?

In fact, James Douglas's story was probably not much different from that of most men sent unwillingly to the colony of New South Wales in the early years of the nineteenth century.

He was born, or rather ushered unceremoniously, into the grey light of poverty-ridden Aberdeen sometime late in 1789. No one seemed to consider his birth as worthy of recording and, therefore, no knowledge of his actual birth date existed. He was born of a Scottish labourer and an Irish mother, both worn and hardened by the winds that rumbled incessantly through the tumbledown streets. Jobs for a semi-literate worker were hard to find and, when the young James was ten-years old, the family moved from a Scottish slum to an English one and settled in, or rather clung to, a tiny corner of London. Many, of course, took the same route, hoping to find steady work beneath the towering smokestacks of the city.

'Honest, the old man was,' James told his own son. 'But poor as a tinker. Poorer. Drank too much, though. Got 'im to the grave, that did. Mother outlived 'is drinkin' by two years. Then she died. Left alone, I was, lad. I 'ad to learn quickly, to survive. Either that or starve. And pretty close I was to that, too, often enough. You'll learn that, too, boy. Survival. That's what matters. Nothin' else.'

Sometimes, there would be variations in the narrative. However, at odd times, he would place his son firmly on his knee, and, fixing the boy with an iron stare that brooked no questions, reveal a little more of his early life. Each time there would be a sharp edge to his voice, as if he was burning to exorcise from his own spirit the malevolence perpetrated upon his childhood.

'So the streets was me 'ome, then, boy. 'Ot and lonely in summer. Cold and lonely in the winter. And I 'ad to turn to crime. Small stuff, at first. And there were 'undreds like me. Nothin' else if a boy wanted to eat. Not proud of that, boy. But I 'ad no choice. Honesty don't mean much if you're a lad starvin' in the gutter.'

After each narrative, he would repeat, 'Survival, lad. That's what matters.' It seemed that, if James Douglas had ever been companion to compassion or sympathy, the streets of London had eroded them. 'Survival, boy. That's what matters.'

Then, in January 1809, he turned to more daring, more dangerous crimes and was arrested and hauled before the court. And, with surgical swiftness, the might of British law fell upon him. Property must be protected, and a young man, one who had from his childhood turned repeatedly to crime, could expect little mercy. He was to be expelled from the fair island as a convict. And within two months he was sweating, rolling and pitching on board one of His Majesty's vessels, bound for the colony of New South Wales.

Some of the condemned men who shared his cramped space and his stench complained about the injustices being heaped upon them. Some wept like children, promising their guards that they would never offend again. Some wished for death. Indeed, one or two took the opportunity, when they were allowed on deck, to leap overboard, taking the weight of their suffering and their chains with them. A few planned escape when they reached land.

But, in the black centre of the nightmare, the young Scot remained, fixed in purpose. He would endure, untainted by the fears of those chained beside him. No nightmare would see him tipped over the edge into madness. And as the weeks stretched out, he came more and more to despise those who did go mad or offered their suffering bodies as penance for their crimes. He shuffled them from his mind as promptly as they were shuffled overboard.

Nine months were spent on the oceans separating England from her newest prison. But all journeys have their end and late in August 1809 appeared the name James Douglas among those recently arrived at His Majesty's prison, Sydney Town, New South Wales.

Then, on the first of January 1810, he took his place among the troops and fellow inmates to welcome the high-minded and high-handed Lachlan Macquarie. With the scudding clouds above and the gulls squabbling over the bay, the resplendently attired representative of George III rose to address his charges. In this, the first of his visionary addresses, the governor made clear that he would, with unremitting diligence, enforce compliance to the laws of England and ensure that order and good government prevailed.

To the ragged group of English subjects herded together on this desolate corner of the Empire, the intention was clear. He made no allusion to the corruption that had preceded him. However, some of the old hands among the soldiers and guards would probably have taken particular note of his warning.

James Douglas watched, listened and thought much. Here, displayed for all, were the forces that would twist men until they were compliant and malleable. The red uniforms of the officers, the glinting metal of the weapons and the clanking of chains were the outward show of a social order that would not be challenged.

Chained, often detesting one another and soon burnt by the foreign sun, men were expected to renounce all hope. Most would.

Many would give way to a dumb, resentful acceptance of their plight. Some who had survived the madness that stalked between the planks of their floating prison would surrender to it here. But he would tolerate all, obey without complaint. It was not hope that would sustain him. No. Something much deeper, more deeply ingrained in the human psyche. The need to hold on. To survive. And he nurtured this with an unflinching contempt: scorn for those guards who taunted and whipped; disdain for the men who shuffled with him each day in chains and lay beside him at night. And he trusted no one.

'Got to rely on yourself,' he repeated over and over to his son. 'No one else. Nobody saw me try to escape. Some tried, of course. Fools. What chance against guns and soldiers. It was sport for the guards, roundin' 'em up.'

Those recaptured were ceremoniously returned in chains. All were flogged, their backs turning red as the lash scored across their flesh. One, he remembered, had come back gibbering, made crazy by the bush or the blacks. He gibbered and screamed, then gibbered some more against the agony. And then he was still.

But he, James Douglas, transported from London, waited. 'Patience, boy. That's what you need.'

He remained the hardest-working and the most obedient. Finally, cunning and a stroke of luck gave him his chance. With ten others, he was assigned to a small farm, a patch of broken land between low hills. Three of them, young and unbroken, seduced by space or the intoxicating smell of wattles along a creek, plotted escape. Their scheme was clumsy and doomed. They would, as they were being returned to their hut, seize their guards, take their weapons and take to the hills. Such were the pathetic plans of men in chains, peopled still by delusions and echoes of freedom.

Their fatal mistake was to reveal their plans to James Douglas.

'And,' he said one evening to his son, 'before you judge me 'arsh, boy, remember this: a man's duty is to survive. And that means takin' the chances as they come.'

Under the cover of darkness, two days before the intended escape, he apprised the overseer of the plan. The latter, although distrustful of convicts, decided to reinforce the guard and sent James Douglas back to his cell, instructing him to say nothing.

As the three would-be escapees, unshackled earlier to complete their work, turned upon their guards, they were overwhelmed by others concealed in the bush. Punishment did not come immediately, of course. Such an outrage needed a public sign of disapproval. Three days later, the whole party returned to Sydney Town. There, they would be stripped, wrapped around the triangle and flogged.

As was usual on these occasions, the convicts were mustered to witness the event. Work was halted and the men trudged across the parade ground. Backs aching from hard labour were to gain respite only to witness pain being inflicted on other backs. Revenge heaped upon some nameless wretches was meant to act as a deterrent to all prospective escapees. And in most cases it did. A flogging toned up the general moral fibre, it was claimed, impressing upon the men assembled a realisation that here was a society governed by just rules and that disobedience to those rules brought well deserved punishment.

So, with the harsh bush in the background, a few anxious Aborigines on the perimeter and the prisoners assembled in the centre, all was made ready. There was much uneasy shuffling as men pictured what was to come. However, the towering figure of James Douglas, intimidating to many at times, remained fixed and unflinching. Only the sweat trickling down his back betrayed any sensitivity to the agony soon to be unleashed upon those other backs. And his thick, dirty shirt concealed even that.

As with all such displays, this flogging was traced through with great precision. There was always a pattern, an inevitable unfolding of events as the horror was slowly revealed. In fact, much of the impact imposed upon men forced to watch came from this careful orchestration.

Initially, as the troopers took up their appointed positions, there was a scattering of attention. Men looked out at the sparkling bay, then at one another and finally at the impassive faces of the soldiers. There was much kicking of dust and one heard little conversation. Then, as if directed by some unseen schoolmaster, all turned to focus on the trooper charged with the responsibility of raking flesh with leather thongs. Immediately conscious of the gravity of the task and the hypnotic effect his position cast over his audience, he was a figure apart, sensing the power hissing and writhing impatiently at the end of his arm. Complete with regulation uniform of red jacket, thick white trousers and black, menacing boots, he was the undoubted master of proceedings. And he would, in a few moments, plant those imposing boots at right angles to the victim, calm as an archer teasing out a distance.

Almost mechanically, events now began to unfold. The first of the miscreants was dragged forward by two fellow inmates, his back bared, smooth with its muscles quivering in anticipation of the pain to come. Quickly, he was bound to the rough timber of the triangle. Then, in a series of hisses, the lash arced towards its target, straightening delicately just before impact. Flesh was scored with stripes that were neat at first, then blurred with red. And, in spite of the gag stuffed in his mouth, the man grunted with each blow, his body convulsing like some upright, grotesque reptile.

Beside James Douglas, a man urinated, while he, impassive, looked out over the yard to the few troopers lounging against the distant barracks wall. Other men, confronted by this precise inflicting of pain sanctioned by an authority ten thousand miles away, might wish for an escape into madness. But he allowed his hatred to burn within himself, flinching not at all. He was seeing, in the flick of the lash, its deadly fall and the groan of a man, power unleashed in its most primitive form. And he knew that such strutting violence must never be challenged head on. His, the way of cunning and opportunism, was the only chance a man had.

Always, at a particular point in this ritual of terror and with half of the assigned number of strokes administered, the surgeon stepped forward from the ranks of the troopers. The extent to which a man could be subjected to the agony must be carefully supervised and assessed. For each wrongdoer there was a delicate point after which suffering slid irrevocably through to death.

Today, in the absence of the surgeon, one of the officers strode confidently to centre stage. His examination was quick, his nod to the flagellator reassuring, and the flogging continued. However, a minute or two later, there was a sudden slackening of the body and a silence that hung heavy and sick in the afternoon air. The thread of this particular victim's resilience had been broken. He was dead.

The second prisoner, perhaps because of his youth, was treated with more care. Moaning and covered with stripes, he was cut down before the completion of his punishment, inspected perfunctorily by the officer and carried off in a dream of red and pain. The heavy doors of the prison block closed and only his moans remained, filtering out through the rusty bars. Attention lingered for a moment, then drifted back to the dusty yard.

Already, the third, the leader who had apparently slashed at one of the guards with a stolen knife, was being brought forward. Spared the agony of the lash, he was hanged.

Thus was justice administered. It was unquestioned. It was simple. And blood would seal it.

He did not retell these events to his son. Nor did he reveal that a week later he was himself attacked by another prisoner, a thickset man who lunged at him with a spade. A man who claimed that the victim of the hanging was his brother.

'You bastard,' he had shouted. 'I'll make you pay for this. My God, I will, if ever I get out of 'ere.'

James Douglas, sensing the danger, ducked and felled him with a blow that left a deep scar down his cheek. He had little fear that the incident would be reported, though he was relieved when his assailant was transferred, later, to a distant farm.

The months passed and compliant, industrious and cooperative, he was brought before a visiting magistrate. Finally, with the happy coincidence of the noble King's birthday, James Douglas was released. Free, now, not to return to England or Scotland, but to tramp the colony in search of honest work.

'Yes. My doin', lad. That's what got me free. Nothin' from anyone else.'

Years before, Arthur Phillip had proclaimed that this corner of the Earth would prove to be 'the most valuable acquisition Britain ever made'. Lofty sentiments, indeed. But it is not likely that the convicts who sweated in their chains, or even men freed of them, would have shared such piety. Certainly, what mattered to James Douglas was simply to find work and get enough food to fill his belly. In a tight-fisted land populated by tight-fisted men, he knew that this would be difficult. However, he had already endured much and learned much. The slums of London, while dirtying his soul, had taught him cunning. Years of prison and exile had given him a fierce determination. And ruthlessness now came easily.

'Oh, no, lad. You might not like what I done. But survivin' don't always mean fightin' fair. I don't drink alcohol, never fired a gun. But there are many ways to fight. You'll learn that. And we aren't in no gutter. Don't you forget that, either.'

Through all of 1813 and most of the following year, he took whatever work he could get. Those who knew of his past incarceration were reluctant sometimes to employ him. But, as trade increased, merchants could not be so choosy and he found sporadic work on the docks, unloading cargo or labouring on construction sites in the town. Then cunning and luck combined and he became, amidst the sprawl and stutter of the streets, a seller of goods and chattels, a collector and disposer of objects. Grog, timber, old clothes, nails, anything that sold found its way in and out of his tent.

And, along with his determination, Sydney Town was growing, also. More free settlers were dribbling into the colony and, while most were still clinging to the skirts of the vast ocean, some were beginning to look inland, nibbling more and more at the edges of the bushland. And within the dusty or muddy streets of the town were beginning to turn the wheels of commerce: wheels that were stopping more and more frequently before his tent.

Then, in 1833, he collected and kept a wife, the daughter of a tailor, Charles Thompson, a middle-aged Londoner who had come to Sydney Town with his daughter, after his wife's death, hoping that the new colony might offer them something new. It didn't, of course. Poverty wore the same clothes here and he had discovered that soon enough. But he was failing – not because he was poor at his trade, far from it. He simply lacked the necessary aggression to compete in this rough, new world. Probably, James Douglas harboured little but scorn for a man like this. But he kept his feelings well hidden. And he was somewhat attracted to the tailor's daughter, an attractive, though slight little creature who seemed malleable enough. Besides, a man needed a wife, didn't he?

He guessed, correctly, that a father in Thompson's position would think twice about knocking back a man who could offer his daughter at least the possibility of some material security. He judged, also, that the girl, and for the same reason, might not object too much. He was right there too. And so, after what probably passed as a colonial courtship, James Douglas and Mary Thompson were married. The ceremony was short and simple. The only witness was a young labourer, Thomas Jones, a quiet, uncommunicative boy, who might, under other circumstances, have had his eye on the young bride.

Married, James could now turn his attention to the task of gaining a firmer place in the topsy-turvy world of business. And, although he showed little affection for his wife, he was surprised how efficiently, and obediently, she worked.

For a time, success came in fits and starts. But, through every difficulty, the young bride saw first-hand the fruits of her husband's long apprenticeship. Nothing eroded his determination, and gradually the tide turned. The tent became a small shop known in the area. And the couple struggled clear of abject poverty.

This gradual success was commented upon each time Charles Thompson came to see them. Not that that was often. Like many, he was easily intimidated by his son-in-law. Never once did he ask his daughter if she was content. Perhaps, seeing the sad, but resolute expression on her face whenever he left, he did not have to.

Early in 1835, Mary Douglas gave birth to a son, Thomas, the first of their children. She had wanted to name the baby Charles, after her father. However, James had scoffed at this idea and had insisted that the child bear his paternal grandfather's name.

Later, the family gathered their possessions and moved to the village of Melbourne, far to the south. There was no real need for discussion, of course. Traders had spoken of the potential there: new farming land, growing population all needing provisions. Just the opportunity for a clever entrepreneur. There was no objection from Charles Thompson or his daughter.

The Great Survivor never learned of the silent grieving or the loneliness of his wife in the years that followed.

For a time, the Douglas store, which was really only a rough canvas structure on the outskirts of the town, found a ready market among the settlers moving to Geelong and beyond. Then, in December 1843, a wind raked the western edges of the town with flame. Ugly smoke covered the area for two weeks and the flimsy structure was destroyed. Stubbornly, James refused to move from the area and soon the store was running again. Stock was purchased and, with the iron will that had sustained him all his life, he set about re-establishing his business. Mary's fear of sliding into complete destitution gradually lessened and, while she did not believe his actions were motivated by affection for her, she could not but admire his tenacity. She often thought that for him family was seen as property. And property had to be protected. How different from the love her father had always shown her. Yet, she had to concede, it was her husband, not her father, who had brought relief from poverty.

Only on one occasion did he attempt to explain his decision to stay. 'We have a son now, Mary. A man must think of 'is responsibilities.'

In the midst of their struggles, a second child was born, a girl they, or rather Mary, named Susan. Choice of a name to James was of little importance. So she had chosen her mother's name. For a time, she feared that her husband would neglect the baby's welfare completely. However, to her surprise, after a few weeks, he began to change, showing outward, if awkward, signs of affection.

Soon vast changes were sweeping the colony to prosperity and business quickened. Would-be farmers, canny investors and gamblers rumbled their way to Geelong and the store did well. As did the children, the son looking like his father and with the same resolute will, the daughter gentle and looking, Mary thought, like the mother she could remember.

Then, in August 1851, reports filtered back along the track that the southern bush had yielded its first ounces of gold. For a time, these reports were hesitant, cautious, and their impact was small. But in the coming months they became louder and more frequent. The roads were churned by many wheels and feet and a steady stream of colourful men passed the store each day. Quick to seize his opportunity, James purchased the gear these gamblers would need to dig and sift the earth.

A strange madness seemed to possess the groups as they crowded into the store, quickly made their purchases and moved on. Some knew exactly what they needed. Others did not. Some told him that policemen were deserting their posts, teachers their schools and sailors their ships.

'We might even have ex-criminals strutting around in uniform one day,' one man said, laughing as he called to his dog, gathered up his material and left.

James Douglas listened and took note. But he did not yield to the temptation of joining them. 'Madness, boy,' he said to his son one morning. 'They'll return, draggin' their tails behind 'em. Most of 'em, anyway. But they 'ave to eat, don't they? And they need provisions, don't they? That's our chance, me boy.'

So, gathering up his chattels, wife and children, he moved to the outskirts of the raggle-taggle village of Ballarat, setting up business on the road leading back to Melbourne. Although some distance from the chaotic happenings of the diggings and the frenzy of Main Street, the store was well placed to catch the passing traffic. Newcomers needed equipment. Old hands needed replacements.

Little prone to humour, he found the pretentious street name amusing. 'Nothin' main there, lad. Just men diggin. But they need what we 'ave. We'll 'ope that the madness goes on.'

And, in those early days, when gold was found close to the surface, hope ran high enough. Gold would bring three pounds an ounce and the miners had money to spend and a desire to exhibit their success. The burgeoning hotels profited and so did the Douglas store. The bargaining that went on intimidated Mary, although James revelled in the experience, knowing that eventually the buyer would capitulate. There were few opportunities for them to buy elsewhere.

And so, the Great Survivor had come and conquered. And now, here he was, buried in the cold clay that gave other men dreams of impossible wealth.

James Douglas. Born Aberdeen, Scotland, sometime in 1789.
Died Ballarat. August 1853.

2

The wider's store

Mary Douglas, newly widowed, was now the sole proprietor of the store. And she, like many who came in to the store, wondered how she would survive. Some came to see for themselves. The curious will always do that. However, there was little in her outward appearance to tell them. She remained, faithful in black, courteous and helpful, saying little about her feelings, even less about her relationship with her departed husband. But cope she did.

On one occasion, she was visited by a robust, wealthy-looking matron who, having delivered the usual expression of sympathy, began an inspection of objects on the shelves. Mary waited, expecting the woman's real interest to turn to her. And it did.

Coming to a small, inconsequential vase on a shelf, the woman stopped and pointed. 'What a lovely object,' she said. 'And full of such pretty flowers. It has some personal significance, I suppose.'

Mary knew very well it would have little appeal to anyone else. And her reply was quick, guarded and succinct. 'My father gave it to me as my husband and I were about to leave Sydney Town. Yes, it has great value to me. It had been my mother's. And when she died, he kept it. Each day he replaced the flowers. And now, as you see, I have it. It was,' she added, 'a present to me for my wedding.'

The woman, putting down the fabric she had made a pretence of examining, continued, 'And so thoughtful of you to keep it so close. With fresh flowers also. A fine tribute. A reminder of your husband.'

Mary was not sure whether this was a statement or a question. So she said nothing, but smiled when the woman said, 'I wish my husband would treat me like that.'

She was relieved when, satisfied at her own cleverness, the woman swept on, bought a couple of trinkets that she probably did not want or need and left.

So life rolled on. Sometimes in fits and starts. Sometimes smoothly. But there was a routine she had to follow to keep the store running and it gave her a level of security. Whether she missed the dictatorial figure of her husband would be difficult to judge. Certainly her black dress was that of a widow. But her non-committal smile and unswerving politeness revealed nothing about her feelings.

Susan was her constant companion, a darting nymph who stopped only occasionally to stare out through the doorway as if she expected her father to come striding through. Mary would sometimes stand with her and anyone passing by would have seen a widow and child, silent and still. The picture of mother and daughter, grieving. But Mary never asked about her daughter's feelings. Nor did she lay bare her own.

Sometimes, in the long hours of darkness, she did feel alone. And she would shed tears. Tears she shared with no one. Tears too quiet to be heard. Tears too deep to be questioned. And she grieved, less for her husband than her father. He who could never have built a store. But he who had loved her.

The store was both an anchor and a prison. It gave her a sense of purpose. A certain income. But she knew that she could not leave and return to Sydney Town. Her father, in time, might become nothing more than a cherished memory. That was all. And even memories fade. Life, for both her and her daughter, depended on the fluctuating fortunes of men on the goldfields. Her son, she felt, had inherited the steely resolve of his father. He would survive. But, in spite of her anxieties, the store, too, survived. Quite quickly, people identified it as 'The Wider's Store'. The Great Survivor would have been astounded.

It stood, seemingly quite secure on the busy road, a stopping point for travellers coming to the town or departing for Melbourne. And Mary was able to concede that distant and uncommunicative her husband might have been but he had left her a tangible legacy. A small island fixed in the fluctuating tide of miners rushing to and from the goldfield.

Its construction had been a laborious task, one that he had never turned away from. Hauling, hammering and chiselling by himself while his son was away scrabbling for gold on Poverty Point. Hiring a young shepherd who, afraid of going mad in the bush or being attacked by Aborigines, had come desperate for work. Cutting, splitting timber. Lining both the small cottage and the store with cheap canvas. Spreading tarpaulin for the roof. Scrambling up to strengthen the roof with bark strips before the weather broke. And taking on the Welshman, Daniel Morgan, to help him construct a chimney. Then, at the end, saying with only a slight indication of satisfaction, 'There you are. At least you'll 'ave a roof over your 'eads now.'

That they had. And Mary was grateful.

Her real concern was the life of her daughter. Susan, at some stage, would probably leave, wanting to make her own way through the world. Had her own father, years before, not spent hours in the fading light of an evening, teaching her how to read? And saying that she had a right to a life beyond a dusty tailor's shop? Did Susan not have that right?

However, the thought came often as she lay at night, unsettling, cold and persistent. A thought made more unsettling, a few weeks later, by a visit from the benevolent pastor, Thomas Hastie. She accepted his words of comfort, sensing that at some stage he would raise the subject of Susan's welfare and her education. She was not mistaken. But his approach was cautious, thoughtful, understanding.

'I do not wish to intrude at this difficult time for you, Mrs Douglas,' he said, quietly placing his impeccably clean hat on his knees, 'but I again offer your daughter the opportunity to attend my school in Buninyong. We could look after her most attentively, I assure you. And we could help her develop the skills she will need later in life.'

Good, clear advice. But the pause that followed was a chasm, deepening as she tried to find a response.

Finally, calling upon that non-committal smile she had practised so often, she answered. 'Thank you, Mister Hastie. I appreciate your offer and I will consider it.' Then, with a degree of confidence that surprised her, she added, 'When Susan and I are ready.'

It was not anger she felt. The inevitable she had long ago learned to accept. But rather relief when the impressive hat was placed back on the impressive head, tapped firmly into place and the minister rose to leave.

'Indeed so, my dear. I understand that.'

Changes were being forced upon Mary Douglas. Changes in attitudes. Changes in feelings towards her dead husband. Changes in responses to people. Changes to her feelings for the land around her. And it was the latter, perhaps, that surprised her most.

Initially, the bushland had intimidated her. Particularly at night. The sense of being hemmed in by the trees and the sharp-edged hills, the roll of fog or clouds and the maddening silences. At night, if she did venture out, which was not often, she would look at the creeping darkness, always seeking some small pinprick of light. Anything to link her with the world she knew. Perhaps huddled beneath that light there would be a woman? A child? Some lonely soul looking out through the heavy darkness as she was, wondering, thinking, hoping, fearing. As she was. Did that light shine upon a woman like her, alone, perhaps knitting? Were those moving lights lanterns carried by newcomers, hoping to establish a home?

But as the town grew, edging closer, and the lights increased in number and the distances between them decreased, she changed. Indeed, there were times when she could relax, let herself be taken by the beauty of the landscape. Dawns rising like spiked flowers with the early mist. Swans at dusk flying in ragged lines across the hills, with their wings turning crimson. Kangaroos hopping along the road and lurching away only as a single rider swept into view. Such moments of spontaneous joy rekindled the delight she had experienced with her father on the excursions they had made together. In a strange way, both town and bush seemed to be coming towards her. And she was learning to accept both.

Few of the shoppers she met ever had the time, or the inclination, to share her new-found delight in the world around her. Most were struggling from point to point, battling to make a living. However, one did. A young man who explained that he was an artist, hoping to become a teacher of art in the town.

'Fat chance of that 'ere, young feller,' one customer said, placing his elbows on a bench and almost dislodging the goods there. 'No time for art 'ere, lad. Folks are busy underground. Or tryin' to put food on the table. This isn't the town for you.' Elbows removed, and goods gathered up, he left.

Mary, embarrassed for the young artist, but curious, asked him about his subjects. Perhaps relieved, he unrolled three paintings and spread them before her. None was a masterpiece. Even Mary could see that. But there was a living vibrancy in the colours. One depicted a sunset over a small creek. Another followed shadows rippling over a bush clearing. The third, although the figure of the child playing in the foreground was rather clumsy, focused on a bright pool of morning sun. This, when she had commented favourably on it, he insisted on giving her.

'You might,' he said, laughing, 'become my patron, madam.'

She watched him leave, rather embarrassed by his generosity. But envious, too. God only knew how he would survive. But his excitement, even his naiveté, warmed her. So she took the painting, smoothed it out and pinned it beside the vase her father had given her.

Such simple acts can trigger a flood of memories. And she could see, quite clearly, her mother sitting, painting a small stream dissolving itself in the vastness of the Thames River. Where, she was not sure. But it was her mother. And the small, agitated figure beside was herself, bored and wanting to go home. But she remembered, too, the colours that danced from the paper: the world of enchantment brought forth.

Would her own daughter find and retain that same, child's delight?

So many changes. So many new situations. And so few people to share them with.

There were women, of course. More of them as time went on. But Mary became more a listener, seldom a sharer of concerns. And she heard many stories. Many women came ostensibly to buy, but, in reality, often to unburden themselves or air their dreams and hopes.

On one occasion, a middle-aged woman, the Australia-born wife of an American, stood fingering a piece of fabric and, in her storytelling, exhibiting the same anxieties Mary had experienced when she had first arrived. A short, plumpish woman, she was clearly doing her best to remain cheerful as her husband rummaged through piles of mining equipment.

Others came, bewildered by the strange world around them, hopeful that their husbands would succeed, one or two quietly determined. But most of the customers were men, strangers coming and going in the great frenzy that drove all before it.

Solitude was one thing. Loneliness was something else. But there was one development, the friendship with the bullocky, that both gave her pleasure and, for a time, a lurking sense of guilt. Still dressed in the expected black, she could not hide her pleasure whenever he arrived.

Unlike her husband, who had dominated those around him, by his size alone, the bullocky was tall, almost stooped, bent, according to Susan, because he walked such long distances behind his team. Where James had either flared at any difficulty or retreated into cold indifference, he would sit at her table, place large brown hands on his knees, puff lazy loops of smoke from his pipe into the air, talk about his journeys. Or, more importantly perhaps, listen to her. He also advised her about what things might sell well, and often brought back items from Geelong or Melbourne.

Sometimes, at least when Susan was not there, he would sit motionless and retreat into silence. Sometimes, Mary felt as if he was waiting for her to speak. Occasionally their eyes would meet and he would smile briefly, draw on his pipe, run his fingers through his dark, unkempt hair and gaze out through the door. What lay behind this, Marty had no idea. And her curiosity she kept hidden. The cold secrecy of her husband she had lived with, learning quickly not to venture into his past. His cold gaze had been a solid wall, the darkness behind it something she had been afraid to penetrate.

However, the bullocky's sometimes sad withdrawal was something quite different. More a veil that at some stage – not yet, of course – she might be able to draw back. At the moment, however, she knew very little about him. His name, yes, she knew that. Daniel Morgan. And his nationality. Welsh. He had arrived, apparently, about ten years ago. Why he had left the green, accommodating countryside of Wales for the wild unknown of the colonies, she had no idea. But here he was, hauling all manner of goods between Ballarat, Geelong and Melbourne. And, when he could, riding across to visit her.

He was not particularly handsome. The wind, sun and rain had turned his face to a brown, creased leather. He walked with an unmistakable rolling, a shamble that could probably go on forever. And, more and more, she found herself glancing out in hope of seeing that slow shamble or the team of his bullocks rumbling into view.

The arrival of the bullock team was always a source of delight for Susan. As it approached, clanking, grumbling and throwing out spasmodic bursts of dust, she would rush to the door and she and Mary would wait. Sometimes, as the team lurched closer, Mary would think of the clumsy ships picking their way to and from their berths in Sydney. She would remember her father taking her down to the wharfs and the moments of delight they shared. There was sense of mystery about those wheezing giants ploughing their way through the water. There was this same sense as the wagon came lurching towards the store.

Each time, the bullocky would wave, crack his whip and, as if by magic, bring the eight bullocks to a halt. Then, leaving them steaming and sweating under a clump of trees, he would come, almost always laughing, into the store.

However, it was not Daniel Morgan, the jovial Welsh bullock driver, who strode through her door today. It was the policeman, Sergeant Miller. And with him, handcuffed and silent, the grim figure of a young Aborigine. The officer, prim and commanding in his uniform, the young prisoner bare-chested and wearing dirty, patched trousers. His feet were covered in dust and his face wore that inscrutable mask so unsettling to many of the white settlers. Both hands hung limply, dark, dirty and submissive, the left clawed slightly as if it had been injured. In spite of herself, Mary retreated, uncertain, anxious, wishing that she felt otherwise. And hoping that the young, helpless captive had not noticed her reaction.

The policeman stood briefly at the door, introduced himself and came in. 'Picked up this young darkie,' he said, waving dismissively towards the crouched figure, 'for pinchin' tools from a farmer down the road. Denied it, of course. As they do. But we found 'em 'idden away. But a couple of nights in the lock-up'll cure him. For a while at least.'

The dark face of the prisoner remained unmoved.

Instructing his captive to sit on the floor, the sergeant turned his gaze on Mary, noticing, with satisfaction, the slight, restless movement of her hands. He was used to reactions like this. There was nothing like a uniform to command attention. And this attractive woman was no exception. He let his eyes linger a little bit longer, then turned back to his prisoner.

'Now, me lad, you just sit there and don't give me any trouble. Don't worry, my dear, 'e won't harm you, will you, Johno? We call 'im that. Nobody knows why. But it'll do.'

Taking the chair offered, he sat down, removed his gloves and placed them on the table. Yes. Pretty. As the commissioner had said. That hair would run free enough once the bonnet was removed. And those slightly defiant eyes could be tamed.

'I came across to offer my condolences,' he said, 'and to offer any 'elp if it were needed.'

Mary nodded but made no reply.

There was a pause and the sergeant looked more intently across the table. 'Didn't know your husband well, Mrs Douglas. Knew of 'im, of course. Most of us did. But, as a representative of the law, I felt it my duty to pay my respects.'

Mary nodded. 'Thank you. I'll let you know if I need any help.'

He nodded, picking up his helmet and gloves, aware again of the tinge of defiance. 'Yes, life can be difficult 'ere. I know that.' He was standing now, carefully putting on his gloves. 'What with the little one and your son workin' among the miners.' He spread his gloved hands. 'It isn't easy for the police, either, Mrs Douglas. Not easy at all, tryin' to keep order among men and 'alf of 'em don't even speak English. Ex-convicts, Irishmen who 'ave no respect for anything British. Even Johnny Chinaman's 'ere, now. Not many of 'em, yet. But more will come. Unless the government acts to stop 'em. Not to mention these poor beggars, roamin' round the town and the camps. Stealing. Drinkin' themselves silly and creatin' fights.'

The prisoner did not move. His gaze was withdrawn or focused far off.

'And they all blame us for their troubles.'

'Yes, sergeant. I understand.'

'Yes, my dear. I'm sure you do.' Now, standing tall as he rearranged his helmet, 'You 'ave a son, I know that. Keep a mother's eye on 'im, won't you? You don't want 'im misled by troublemakers. Too many of 'em 'ere. 'Otheads not afraid to get others to do their dirty work for 'em. Important for a lad to stick on the right side of the law. And I'm sure you know that.'

The slight nod in response gave nothing away.

'Madness, my dear. That's what we 'ave. The madness of men lookin' for gold, wealth most of them'll never 'ave. A woman alone should be careful.'

For a moment, Mary looked away.

And the sergeant, satisfied now, motioned to his prisoner. 'Now, me lad. Time to get you tucked up for the night.'

Mary turned her gaze to the pathetic figure slowly getting to his feet. His tongue flicked across his lips, revealing large, dirty teeth. His arms hung loose, coming together where the light caught a gleam of metal. What riveted her attention were his eyes, large, piercing, resentful, but disturbingly sorrowful. Perhaps it was abject despair that stared at her.

'Oh yes, 'is 'and. You've noticed that. Don't know 'ow he got that. Might be from birth. Or a fight. Never seem able to keep out of fights, these young bucks.'

Poised, almost ready to leave, the sergeant again focused on the young man. And his expression changed from the cold condescension Mary had noticed to something that might almost pass for compassion. 'It's not easy, Mrs Douglas, as I've said. You might think me 'ard 'aulin' this young lad away like this. But in fact I feel sorry for 'im. His brother was killed a year ago. By a drunk shepherd. I 'ad a man arrested for it. Packed 'im off to Geelong for trial. But 'e was cleared. Not enough evidence, they said. Evidence? I'd given 'em plenty of evidence. Enough to convict a black man, if 'e'd done it.'

He was looking hard at Mary when he said this. Was he expecting some response? She did not know, but simply nodded.

'The law 'as got to be followed, by whites and blacks. And it's my job to enforce it. 'Ard? Yes, I guess I am 'ard.' There was a surprising pause now. 'But I've not always been like this. Life's made me 'ard. And things've 'appened to me. Things others 'ave done to me.' His expression changed as he said this, from anger to a brief introspection that might have passed for sadness. Then, as if collecting himself, he looked directly at her, coldly, as if she was an object viewed from a great distance.

Suddenly Mary was afraid. Afraid that the sergeant, standing there, so close and towering, might reveal some dark secret, a secret that would somehow involve her. And she was relieved when he finally made ready to leave.

His voice had regained its hard edge. 'But the law 'as got to be obeyed, Mrs Douglas. This lad 'as become a thief and 'e must be punished.'

Any softening had gone now. Carefully, slowly, he was taking a short piece of rope and playing it gently through his fingers. There was something about the slow, liquid movement of those gloved hands that held her. As a snake might. The young prisoner mechanically extended his arms. The rope was tied around both wrists and looped round the wrist of the sergeant. She felt almost a prisoner herself.

'There. That should do. Quite a walk back for you, though, me lad.'

A quick jerk brought the prisoner into the light and the sergeant turned to open the door. Behind him, the young black man fixed Mary with his cold, dark eyes. His lips moved slightly, as if he wanted to speak. But nothing came. Only the silence conveyed the depth of his contempt, his suffering.

'Now, my dear. Don't forget we're 'ere to help should you need it.'

Her thanks, almost whispered, seemed to come from a great distance. And she had the wild idea of somehow setting the young prisoner free and watching him dash, relieved as an animal, away into the bush.

As the sergeant paused to survey a noisy group of men bunched together and trudging towards the town, the young black looked back into the shop and, unnoticed by his captor, spat on the floor. The spittle gleamed yellow and sickly, inches from her feet.

Had the sergeant returned a few minutes later, he would have seen her standing alone, arms clutched across her chest, struggling to hold back tears. Had he lingered, he would have seen her go through to the cottage, take her daughter in both hands and hug her.

She hoped, the following day, to see the bullock team trudging up the slope and hear the bullocky's 'He, ho. Mrs D,' ringing out above his beasts. But nothing came to relieve her loneliness. Except a small group of women with their husbands, newcomers to the town. Some were excited, like schoolgirls on an outing. Others were clearly anxious. What any of them would think after six months of living and working in huts or tents she could only guess at.

When the bullocky did come, a few days later, she asked him if he would take her down to the diggings. She had never done that and he had been reluctant to do it. However, she insisted. And, having left Susan in the care of an obliging neighbour, they set off, comfortably seated together in what the bullocky called his 'village chariot'.

Soon, having rattled and descended through a brown, churned gully, they arrived at what was boldly called Main Road. The hurly-burly of the diggings, the tents, the shanties crowded together and the muddied stream creeping between heaps of brown, uninviting clay startled her. What struck her most was the frantic, unceasing movement of men coming and going, rising, descending, cursing and laughing.

And this was the life her son had chosen. She pictured him descending deep into the darkness with a pick and a sputtering candle. And walls closing in upon him. Crushing him. Taking him from her. But this was the madness he had chosen.

She felt her hand involuntarily grasp the bullocky's. 'Daniel, I think I've seen enough.'

He looked out over the scene, than back at her. 'Aye, Mrs D. I think so.'

In the days that followed, a number of the miners came into the store and, in spite of her initial reaction to what she had seen, she took an interest in what they had to say about developments on the fields.

Some, in close-knit groups, looking like brightly coloured beetles, rushed in, regaling her with stories of other men who had stubbed their toes on quartz and unearthed nuggets of gold. These, she felt sorry for. She had seen enough to get a sense of the reality these newcomers would encounter. Some strolled in, made a few purchases and sailed off in impressive gigs. But there were few of those. More, grim-faced, would appear, buy what they could afford and trudge off, back towards the diggings. Some would talk about their back-breaking, fruitless efforts and their determination to leave or look for work.

And there were the hatters, the men who worked alone. They came, pushing barrows or burdening their backs with the few objects they needed. They were quiet men, used to the tramping and the loneliness. Few of them showed much enthusiasm, but in them the madness seemed to run deeper. They seemed to be tolerated by the more gregarious miners she met. Some, of course, she could see, were shunned.

'Looney, most of 'em,' an old hand confided, some months before. 'Be careful of 'em, Mrs Douglas. Trouble. If you give 'em a chance.'

But strangely she had not feared them. Rather, she had found herself wondering, often, what events had led them to this lonely existence. What their childhood had been. And what events had shaped their lives.

A few days after her visit with Dan Morgan to the diggings, she was approached by a rather drunk, leather-faced man of about sixty who introduced himself, as steadily as he could, as Joe. He bought a small quantity of tobacco, folded his thin legs under a stool, sat down and perused the clumps of men and women coming and going through the open door. For a time, he remained silent. Then, when the shop lay temporarily cleared, he began relating scattered events from his past. He spoke with increasing excitement of his coming two years ago and the frenzy the first discoveries had created. His eyes wandered and returned to her face, his thin, bony hands remained firmly on his knees, as if they held him stable.

'Some men found gold winkin' at 'em from the ground. They thought they was mad. Dreamin', you might say. But it was real. And they wasn't mad.' He paused, until the weight of his words had registered. 'Some did go mad, though, later, me lady. Draggin' dirt to the creeks, muddyin' the water and then draggin' out the gravel. Some of 'em found the yeller stuff, of course.'

His face lit up now, as if he had reached the high point of his narrative. 'Funny names, they 'ave, you know, them places. Poverty Point, it weren' poverty then, though, was it? And the others, Eureka, Golden Point, Canadian Gully. Sort of names that sound promising, don't they?' He paused as a group of Chinese miners appeared at the door, peered in and moved on.

'Dunno about them Chinks, though, missus. Celestials, as we call them. Mighty good workers, some say. But I dunno whether you can trust 'em. Talkin' as they do in a lingo we can't understand. Can't really talk to 'em at all, can you?'

Struggling to pick up his original narrative, he looked back at Mary, rummaged through his mind and went on. 'Some men died, o' course. Dirt. Mud and dirt. That's what we 'ad, me lady. Gold if we was lucky. Dirt if we wasn't. Then it was orf to some new patch o' ground. Bloody 'ard, though – beggin' your pardon, me lady. Dug like rabbits we did. Paupers and kings all thrown in together, you might say.' Now he rubbed his hand across his nose. 'Americans are comin' now, too, me lady.'

Then, gazing around as if to ensure nobody else was there to hear and in a voice that was only just above a whisper, he continued, 'I'm told three of 'em found six 'undred ounces in a week once. Then left, 'eading for Geelong. One of 'em come back to Buninyong a couple of days later, sayin' his mates 'ad been murdered. And the gold stolen. True story, that, missus. The Reverend Mr Hastie, 'e told me that. But,' and his voice now could not have been more conspiratorial, 'I don't think that's the end of it. I reckon 'e done 'em in.'

He spread his arms now, as if to verify the truth of what he had said. 'As for old Joe 'ere. I don't hold no grudge against the rich. Some's lucky, some aren't. But your 'usband, 'e didn't take much to those who was rich, I'm told.'

Mary was amazed at this reference to James but answered as quickly and as calmly as she could, 'No, he didn't. That's true.'

She had not formed an instant dislike for this quaint old hatter. Far from it. Apart from the smell of cheap grog, she felt quite sorry for him. After a moment of silence, she was aware of skinny legs doing their best to stand erect. The sight made her think of an unsteady mantis preparing to fly off. But he most certainly would not do that. Walking would be enough for him. She knew that as he stuffed his tobacco into his hessian bag and made for the door.

Then, bowing deeply, he said, 'Good day to you, me dear,' and left, perhaps not even hearing her final 'Goodbye, Joe.'

She stood for a few minutes, watching the lonely figure drifting towards the town. Then she stepped back inside, smiling and absent-mindedly playing a piece of delicate Chantilly lace through her fingers. Perhaps hers would be the only fingers ever to touch it. Certainly, her husband had scoffed at the idea of placing such items on the shelves. 'Waste of time, woman. Vanity for the wealthy, that's all that is. Who would want to buy stuff like that 'ere?'

Folding the fabric carefully, she placed it back on the shelf. 'I would,' she said quietly.

There was much to do, tidying, packing and cleaning. There was always much to do. But, for some reason, she stopped in front of a mirror hanging directly in front of her. A gift from Dan Morgan some months earlier. Together they had hung it above the small selection of goods in what he had called the ladies section. Already it was covered in a thin layer of dust and, as she stretched up to clean it, she encountered a face, her own, staring back at her. Perhaps it still retained something of the prettiness her father had praised all those years before.

Grateful, perhaps, that she was alone in the store, she paused a little longer. There was a directness in the eyes. And she felt distant, as if she was observing the face of a stranger. Then, without thinking, she reached back and released her hair. It flowed down over her shoulders, spreading its coolness and, with the coolness, a quick sense of freedom. And, with sudden delight, she saw her mother's hair tumbling and mingling with her own. And now, as she stood there, fingers, her mother's, were playing through her hair. And the face smiling back from the mirror was her mother's.

At another time, such memories might have moved her to tears. But not this time. Instead, she found herself smiling. What she felt was a quiet sense of pride. And it was with real reluctance that she captured the waves, imprisoned them and turned to the work to be done.

3

Alone

There was no question, now, about Mary's strength. She knew that she could survive. The harsh conditions and the difficulties had released a strength that, perhaps, had been dormant in the suffocating years of her marriage. But she had no companion, apart from her daughter. No adult, apart from the bullocky, and he had not come for some time. True, the long processions of miners and their families kept each day full. There seemed to be fewer departures now, and the population of the town was growing: all good for business. But, to her, most remained strangers, nomads who came, bought and moved on.

So, loneliness remained, a haunting shadow that came most days after business was finished. The distractions that the days provided she valued, often rekindling them and playing them, usually quite comfortably, through her mind in the evening. Some were disturbing. Others sad. And some amusing. All gave some relief. But only a few left deeper impressions.

Early one morning, just as she was opening the store, she was met at the door by two impeccably dressed men. They were journalists from Melbourne, come, they said, to report on the events simmering among the miners. Both had notebooks.

One, clearly the senior, took charge. It might well have been the sergeant of police, so assured was he, standing directly in front of her. He was not particularly tall. But his cool gaze and air of relaxation gave him a sense of importance, a sense he was obviously aware of. He began by commenting favourably on the neatness of the store and the variety of goods displayed. Then, smiling and spreading his hands reassuringly, he went on, 'We have come from Melbourne, madam, because our papers want to learn something about life here. And we thought, as a local businesswoman, you must be well acquainted with events here.' His eyes moved slowly around the store and lingered on her face.

Something inside cautioned her. 'No, sir, I'm not very knowledgeable. My business keeps me inside, as you see.'

'Of course. Of course.' Clearly disappointed, he nodded to his companion, who came forward.

More thickset, he, too, gave the impression of casual interest, as if he was not really fishing for information. But his question surprised her, both from its content and his accent, which was clearly American. 'But you have relatives, a son, perhaps, who could help us?' The eyes were gentle and the voice neutral. 'We're told in Melbourne that the authorities are treating the diggers roughly, unfairly. Our readers would be most sympathetic, I assure you of that.'

'You're right, sir. I do have a son. But I don't ask him questions about conditions on the diggings.'

Both were disappointed now, if not irritated. A few other questions followed. Harmless questions about running a business. However, she was relieved when they packed away their impressive-looking notebooks, mounted and rode off. A quiet victory, she thought, watching the two horses growing smaller. She had resented the hawkish attention the men had given her and their air of authority. Besides, she did not like discussing the troubles bubbling among the miners. It made her think of her son. And, in any case, newspapers had no business prying into the lives of citizens.

A happier meeting occurred a week later. The sun was beginning to shred the shadows and spread them across the road and she was about to close for the day when a cart pulled up and a young woman jumped down. She greeted Mary, almost with a breathless sigh of relief, dashed inside, rummaged through the items in the ladies' corner and triumphantly held aloft the piece of Chantilly lace Mary had placed there weeks before.

'Ah,' the girl announced, pushing her way back to the front of the store, 'I was afraid that it might have gone. My husband, bless him – you see him out there in our cart – has given me a little money to spend as I want. And I really must have this. I feared – yes, I was very afraid – that you might have sold it.' She paused momentarily, holding the lace in both hands. Had it been alive, it could not have escaped. 'I was here last week, you see, and I saw it then.'

Mary looked across at her round, plain face and her simple, unadorned clothes. Yes. Her husband, as a tradesman (and his appearance was certainly that of a tradesman) must have made some small sacrifice here.

The girl, with the prize now firmly in her possession, relaxed, pressing the lace against her cheek. Her face, flushed with success and surrounded by curly, resistant hair, was a restless, beaming flower. Mary remembered this same excitement on the face of her mother years and years before, when, on a shopping trip through London, she had picked up a piece of floral material from a stall, run it through her fingers, held it against Mary's cheek and whispered, 'Ah, perhaps, when you grow up, you will walk the streets of the city, covered in flowers just like this.' She had not forgotten that moment, the touch of her mother's hand, nor the sight of flowers flowing and tumbling back on to the counter.

'A tradesman, he is,' Mary heard. 'We've been married just six weeks. And I know he'll do well here. Very well. Yes, very well.' The repetition carried a sense of urgency and the girl's eyes dwelt on Mary's face. 'everyone says so. With so many people coming here. And I know we will be happy here. Together.'

The girl smiled, blushed and the lace spilled gently over her hands, spreading like a small stream. Was she waiting, now, for some kind of reassurance? There had been something quite touching, almost pleading here. And Mary rather envied the naiveté and the untested optimism. There had been no rejoicing at her own wedding, no surge, however brief, of excitement as she and James were joined together. No light beckoning over new horizons.

She knew she had to make some response. 'Yes, my dear,' she

began, 'he must be a very loving young man, your husband. And, yes, my son tells me there's plenty of work for hard-working tradesmen in the town.' Mary wanted her voice to carry conviction and the girl's quick smile indicated that perhaps it had.

Gathering her skirt around her and her precious parcel to her chest, the girl hurriedly paid, thanked Mary and left. The young man, seeing her bursting through the door, jumped down, laughed and lifted her up. Both waved as the cart lurched away.

Mary dwelt on the meeting long after the event. Not the sadness or the disappointment of her own situation. But the daring and the joy of the two young people. She hoped that, perhaps, they might return at some stage.

There were other encounters, too. Distractions. Most of them pleasant. And certainly, with the increased tempo of life on the diggings, business was good. But there were some encounters that were not so agreeable. Some that were difficult for a woman alone to handle. And a few that alarmed her.

Early one morning, for example, she was confronted by two down-in-the-mouth miners, men she remembered serving in the store about five months earlier. They had marched into the store and bought two picks, a shovel and a length of rope. Nothing more. Their confidence had swept them out into the road and they had left, rolling and lurching like two seamen who had suddenly been released to the shore. Now they had returned, looking anything but confident.

One, much younger than his companion, remained by the door, shifting nervously from one foot to the other and peering in both directions along the road.

The other, solidly built, bearded and rolling his shoulders as he came, stopped by the counter. In his hands he held two shovels and a pick. 'We've 'ad no luck,' he announced. 'Decided to give it away. So you can pay us back now. We got 'em here, as you'll remember. 'Ardly used, as you can see. You'll 'ave no trouble sellin' 'em later.' His eyes fastened on her face as he said this.

She felt her hands tighten on the counter. 'Oh, no, I'm sorry, but I can't do that.' The firmness in her own voice surprised her. But she waited with an inner anxiety for what he might say next. And she did not have long to wait.

The figure opposite stood erect, his hands fists, now. His face hard and his eyes narrow and intent. He repeated, almost word for word, what he had said. But there was sharpness now, a repressed anger that was close to bursting out.

Again Mary refused, sensing her throat tighten, but ensuring that her eyes remained firmly fixed on his face.

There was an explosion of anger now. The miner swept around the counter, gripping her by the arm. 'By Christ you will, lady. Give us our money back. We only want what we paid for 'em.'

Suddenly, there was a shout from the doorway. 'Mick! Traps is comin'. We better be off.'

The older man tightened his grip on her arm. 'Damn you to 'ell, lady. Me mate and me only wanted enough to get us some food between 'ere and Melbourne. 'Ere, you might as well keep these. We won't be needin' 'em.'

Picks and shovel clattered to the floor and she felt a sharp slap across her cheek. Then, trembling and feeling tears in her eyes, she bent down, picked them up and placed them mechanically among their fellows. Outside, she heard two horses galloping away and soon after Sergeant Miller and two constables entered.

'Good mornin', me dear. Called in with two of me boys 'ere. Just to see if all was going well with you and the little one.'

'Thank you, officer. Yes, all is well.' It was strange to feel both relief and dislike together. 'Yes. Quite well.'

'Ah. Good. We'll be away then. Off to arrest some young 'opeful who was diggin' without a licence. Or, my men tell me, 'e didn't have it on 'im, anyway. Think these devils would be able to pay thirty shillings, wouldn't you? If they kept their licences on 'em, there wouldn't be any trouble, would there? Took off, 'e did. Won't be far away, though. I think they see it as a bit of a lark, some of 'em, annoying the police like that. Want to be caught, almost. Can't see why, meself. Being locked up for the night don't seem much fun to me.'

Mary made no comment. But she was aware of the sergeant's quick perusal of the store and of his eyes returning to look, almost soothingly, at her.

'Your son, 'e has a licence, I suppose, me dear?'

Mary nodded. 'Oh, yes, officer. I'm sure he does.'

His eyes lingered for a moment and then he turned to leave. 'Good mornin', then. Wouldn't like to see the lad get into trouble with the law, would we?'

Mary noticed the scar half hidden under the officer's beard and she instinctively looked away. 'No, indeed not. Good morning.'

She watched as the police left, more concerned about the mention of her son than about the two angry miners who would have robbed her. Also, of course, she had no idea whether Tom had a licence, though she had heard disgruntled men complaining about having to carry one with them, even when toiling underground.

Finally, the bullocky did come. In fact, three times in the next month. The ritual remained the same. Hearing the clatter of chains and the booming voice of the bullocky, Susan would scamper out and scramble on to the wagon.

'He, ho, missus,' would ring out among the items neatly arranged around the store, and his hat would fly in an arc across to the counter.

They were not often alone on these visits. Susan saw to that. Perhaps she was jealous. Perhaps she was simply curious. Mary was not sure which. However, they would find some time while the child was playing in front of the cottage. The bullocky would tell her, in that slow, resonant voice she had come to enjoy, about the long distances crossed, the occasional loss of a beast and the fierce sunsets or raking storms that brought a day's travel to its end.

It almost became a habit for her to interrupt and say something like, 'You will be careful, won't you, Daniel?'

Usually, they both laughed at this point. He would then listen attentively while she unburdened herself. Initially, she had felt rather guilty: her husband would have seen this as weakness. But that was a long time ago.

Once, he placed his rough hand over hers. A simple movement, hardly a movement at all. And she did not remove it.

On his last visit, he explained that his next trip would be another long one, on to Melbourne, then on to Geelong and finally back to Ballarat. 'A couple of weeks, this one. Heavy equipment, from Melbourne to Geelong. Flour, timber, nails and canvas from Geelong to the men here. Yes, a few weeks this one, Mary.'

This was the first time he had actually used her name. Usually she was missus or Mrs D. and she hoped that she detected a note of regret in his voice.

'Weather less reliable, too.'

In her own voice, she certainly detected regret. 'I understand, Daniel. You will be careful, won't you?'

He did not laugh this time. His eyes fixed directly on her face, lingered and then wandered away. And was that shyness as he went on? 'Aye, lassie. And you'll see me as soon as I get back.'

On those few occasions that James had left to purchase materials in Geelong Mary had felt both relief and fear, relief that she would be able to spend some time alone with her daughter, fear that some situation might arise that she could not handle. But today there was a simple sense of sadness.

A few moments later, the beasts that had been parked like brown, heaving islands stuttered into life, the chains clanked and the tottering load lurched forward. Then, turning without warning, the bullocky took Mary in his arms and kissed her. No preamble. No preceding glance of enquiry. And Mary, whether through surprise or relief, made no effort to dissuade him.

'Now, lass, take care,' he said in his accustomed, cheerful voice. And he was away, following his beasts.

In the month that followed his departure, the weather changed and loneliness weighed heavily. June brought heavy bursts of rain. Grey clouds hung or caught among the hills and the slopes ran with yellow mud. For a time, the creeks were able to gather up the waters and rush them away. But finally the land seemed to surrender. Yarrowee, the creek that was small, ran fast and full, barrelling and tumbling across the bushland. The hill the Aborigines called the Mount of Emu Feathers groaned as it pressed its bulk into the thunder and the wind. There was nothing beautiful, she concluded, about the Australian landscape in weather like this.

Her thoughts strayed often to the bullocky trudging, cajoling and slowly making his way. He had never exaggerated the difficulties he faced. But she knew that these long wet weeks were the slowest and the most dangerous. Once, clearly troubled and unable to hide his feelings, he had admitted coming across, somewhere near Geelong, an upturned wagon. More like a shipwreck, he had said, half covered as it was by brown, swirling water. And when he had investigated further he had located the body of a man wedged under one axle. A man he had known quite well.

'We might be competitors,' he had said, 'but there's a kind of, well, comradeship when we're out on the roads, y'know.'

She could imagine Dan's tent, small and drooping before the wind, his silhouette, smoke seeping away from his pipe, the clumsy beasts plunging ahead each day towards Melbourne. She was not particularly religious but sometimes she found herself whispering a prayer for his safety. And she hoped that he would, perhaps, be thinking of her.

She thought, too, of her father. She had written many letters to him, letters that Daniel had taken to Melbourne for her. Whether they had been forwarded to Sydney she had no idea. Certainly, no answering letters had come. So, one evening, after Susan had gone to bed and almost as a test of her memory, she sat in the store and tried to sketch out his face. She was no artist and the folly of doing this struck her from the first tentative line. But, as she persisted, something of a likeness emerged. First the hollow cheeks, then the receding forehead, and finally she managed to suggest the sad, compassionate eyes. It was a relief to realise that she had not completely forgotten him. Then, for the first time in quite a while, she began to weep. And in her weeping there was a feeling that something of great value was being restored to her.

She also worried about her son, caught as he was, with hundreds of other men, on the slope. Ignorant of the ways of mining, she nevertheless knew that to go down into the shafts in weather like this was very risky. Miners had spoken often enough in her hearing of men being drowned as water poured out from underground streams or suffocating as wet, poorly timbered walls collapsed. She worried, too, when they spoke of others coughing their lives away, unable to withstand the onslaught of fever. She imagined them shivering and dying in some hideous gully, with not a single soul to comfort them. And occasionally, at night, her dreams were of bloating bodies or hands digging into clay that seemed to be incessantly moving. Sometimes she saw the face of her son, his eyes like dull lanterns and his mouth gaping like that of a grotesque fish.

She was very relieved early one afternoon when Tom actually walked across to visit her. The likeness with his father was striking, now. But there was something vulnerable about him as he sat warming himself by her fire

'Don't worry, Mother,' he announced cheerfully. 'We aren't going below now. Found enough gold to keep us eatin' for a week or two. Hard work, bottomin' at about forty feet. We might've cleaned her out. Not sure yet. We'll go down when things dry out. It won't be long. I can get work in the town, if I need to. But we should be back underground soon.'

As she had done many times, Mary reassured her son that she could help him, that he could come back here if he wanted to.

His answer was, as it had been many times, that he must make it on his own. That this was a test for him. 'Can't let me mates down. Good fellows to work with. We'll make out in spite of the problems the traps are givin' us.'

In the quick laughter that followed, there was both an anxiety and a defiance. But there was a change today. Something quite unexpected.

'And you don't need to worry, Mother. I won't turn out like my father. I know how he treated you. That won't be me.'

The surprise she felt was instantaneous. On the grey face opposite, so like his father's, there was reassurance but almost a sense of shame as he eyes looked quickly away. True, she felt relief. But at the same time an irrational desire to defend her dead husband. A desire that quickly passed and, although not knowing what to say in reply, she felt suddenly close to her son. Close enough to fold her arms around him. Yet something, something intangible but strong, held her back. And she didn't.

'No, Mother. No need to worry about me.'

4

Visited again

The wet weather persisted. Clouds tumbled over the hills each day. Water filled the ruts in the road. Mud spilled out under passing wheels or trapped them completely. And passengers and drivers would be sent scurrying for cover. But what is an irritation for adults can be a source of great amusement for children. And often, from the shelter of the store, Susan found real delight in watching groups of angry men endeavouring to extricate their trapped vehicles.

On one occasion, late one afternoon, she observed the antics of four Chinamen. Most Chinese arrived on foot, human packhorses almost buried under their load. However, these men came on a cart, pulled by an old, battle worn horse. Unfortunately, the cart had slid sideways and been trapped in the mud. It looked as if it might be eternally entombed there. But, with a great deal of laughter, pushing, shoving and cajoling, they were soon ready to resume their journey. One even waved cheerfully and shouted across to her as he took up his position. She laughed in reply, having no idea of his meaning. Their good-humoured reaction surprised her and she was disappointed that her mother could not explain why they remained so cheerful while the Europeans, caught in the same predicament, became so angry.

This group of Chinese was the first of many to trundle past the store. And, while the numbers might have alarmed some, the novelty of strange-looking men chattering in an alien tongue and dressed so differently, greatly intrigued Susan. On one occasion, Mary found her sitting outside, pencil and paper in hand, hastily sketching a large party of Chinese shuffling along the road. One of them, a short, thin young man, came across and looked at what Susan was doing. The pigtails, the slanted eyes and the wide grin staring up at him from the paper made him laugh and he motioned to some of his companions. Soon Mary and Susan were surrounded. Much laughter ensued.

An older man, who knew a little English, pointed at Susan. 'Your daughter, she may be artist. My granddaughter, in China, she paint, too. Better than this one.'

Again, laughter followed and Mary joined in. With that, the group left, purposeful, quickly lost in their own concerns.

It surprised Mary later, as she recalled the incident, that she had not felt at all intimidated. Nor, apparently, had Susan: in fact, she laughed about the old man's comments and dashed back inside, set herself on one of the benches and added length to the smiles on each of her faces.

Not always, however, were the encounters with the Chinese miners so cheerful. On another occasion, just beyond the store, a young Chinese man was dragged into the trees by three European diggers, punched, kicked and sent on his way, lucky to scramble off towards the town. The men then entered the store, still shaking with anger. But keen to tell their story.

'Had to be done, Mrs D,' one said, placing his hands authoritatively on the counter. 'Too many of them little wretches here now. Come walkin' through the bush. Nobody knows where from. Then drinkin', stealin' and gamblin'. They don't even work their own shafts, they don't. Go scramblin' through the workin's of honest men, instead. Same problems on other fields, too. If the powers that be won't act, we will and we'll get rid of 'em,'

Clearly these men had not come to purchase anything. And Mary was relieved when. parcelling up their righteous anger, they strode away. Anxious to check on the plight of the victim, she then hurried out onto the road. But there was no sign. Why she should feel guilty about the event, she could not say. But she did. And she was grateful that Susan had not been in the store to witness it.

Fewer people were using the road, of course. Those who did come into the store almost always voiced their impatience at this unchanging weather. It often seemed to Mary that only the land itself could remain patient through this. That and the Aborigines.

She saw them often enough, trudging to and from the town, wearing rough cloaks of skin or abandoned trousers and shirts. Few of them ever wore boots. Pathetic they might have appeared. But there was a stoicism in their slow, rhythmic walk that impressed her. Among a small band, late one afternoon, she recognised the young man who had come as Sergeant Miller's prisoner. His clawed hand attracted her attention first, then the bared chest and the cold, almost contemptuous eyes. He paused, stared across and moved on, deliberate and unhurried, a figure momentarily larger than life. She was relieved when he became just one shadow among others.

The land and its dark inhabitants might be used to waiting, but the miners certainly were not. Action was what sustained them. To be locked into inactivity made them angry, quick to lash out, and it seemed to her that their targets sometimes were chosen at random. She had heard of fights in the local bars – sometimes, her customers reported, without any real reason.

But there were real reasons for anger, reasons that had little to do with the vagaries of climate. And she had been made aware of these, by many of the miners who came into the store. There were repeated complaints about the cost of licences and the hefty fines men faced if they did not always carry their licences with them.

'And,' one bent old miner complained, pointing angrily at Mary, as if she was to blame, 'we don't even 'ave a vote. That ain't fair, is it?' Then, explosion ended, he hurried on. 'Sorry, missus. It ain't your fault, of course. But we ought to 'ave a say in what 'appens, I reckon.'

She had heard these words often enough, sometimes linked with a demand for land. Occasionally she was alarmed at their willingness to unburden themselves. And sometimes, she was simply confused. Why strangers would choose her, she could not work out. Perhaps the store was something solid, something that smacked of permanence. Perhaps some saw her as a family member, a woman like their sister or their mother. Some were clearly attracted to her; their lingering glances told her that.

Almost always she found herself wondering what Dan would make of the problems these angry men were depositing at her door.

It was not only strangers who did this, of course. Her son Tom also made the same complaints when he came across to visit. And with each outburst, she felt more and more alarmed. His set, tense body as he sat relating events and condemning the authorities was the set, tense body of her husband. But, where James had steeled himself to survive and overcome, she feared that Tom might lash out and be drawn into the gathering storm. There had been enough talk, even within the store, of potential armed revolt. Quiet talk, that was true. Almost as if the speakers were afraid the wrong ears might hear. But talk just the same. And the anger she heard in her son's voice concerned her.

Often he would sit by the fire, stare out at the drab landscape and mutter about water sliding down the slopes into the shafts and the wider unhealthy conditions of the camps. This, Mary understood. She had seen something of these on her few visits down into the town. But her son seemed more and more to lay responsibility for all of the hardships on the authorities.

Often, in the midst of a conversation, he would jerk himself to his feet and condemn the administration or graziers who held on to huge areas of the countryside. 'The miners have a right here, too, Mother. Hard working men, most of 'em. With families of their own, some of 'em. They're not gypsies. Nor am I. I have me rights here, too.' The words might alter with each visit. The message remained the same. 'But we'll go back down, Mother. When the weather improves. No traps, or toffs in Melbourne, will stop us from diggin'. And you don't need to worry. Joe Tyler and Andy Drew know minin'. They'll look out for me.'

But she did worry. And after he had left she was frequently haunted by visions of clay walls collapsing under the weight of water, bodies gasping for air, gaunt faces, dead, staring eyes. Too often the eyes of her son. And she worried even more when, on one occasion, a miner who had known her husband, commented favourably on 'young Tom's determination' and added, perhaps as a compliment, that he was 'a chip off the old block, Mrs Douglas, that's what I'd say.'

She thought, too, of the miners who were turning their backs on the town. Those for whom the privations and the lack of success had proven too much. Their stories seldom varied. But while their faces bore the same sense of defeat, she was often surprised by the lack of anger in their voices.

Her husband had glared at all privation, stiffened his resolve and pushed on. These men had cloaked themselves in a grey shroud of resignation. It was as if the rain and the hardship had destroyed even their will to curse. Sometimes she was pricked by a sudden admiration for James Douglas's ruthless determination. Then she would think of her own privations during their marriage and be filled with pity, perhaps for herself, certainly for these defeated miners.

Through all of this, her thoughts would return, particularly in the evening, to the bullocky. For years, she had rarely allowed herself to feel a sense of longing. Even for her father. She had wept at their parting, those years ago in Sydney, but when her husband voiced his irritation at what he called her weakness, she had trained herself to bury her feelings. Almost, but not quite, to deny their existence.

Not quite, indeed. The disappointment she felt at the lack of any news from her father had always troubled her. Letters she had given to her husband, knowing that he would pass them on to a coach driver in the town, had never been answered. And she could only blame the coach delivery north to Sydney, knowing, from what others had said, that mail deliveries were always unreliable.

But now, emotions long concealed were beginning to surface. For Dan and her father. For Dan, trudging along lonely tracks, pacing out the miles and then sitting alone in his tent at night, wreathed in smoke from his pipe. For her father, working still, she supposed, late at night. And, for both of them, sitting alone in the darkness. And, perhaps, thinking of her.

At night, she would close the store, cook tea and then she would sit with her daughter, playing games that Susan had devised, or reading with her. Not that there was much to read: a battered Old Testament that her father had given her, a copy of *Uncle Tom's Cabin* and a battered old book for children that had lost its cover. Not the kind of material to fire the imagination of a curious child. She knew that. But persistence was paying off and she was quietly proud of Susan's improvement. Perhaps she might not need to accede to the reverend's suggestion that Susan should leave and attend his school.

Three visits in the next two weeks broke the monotony. The last did much more than that.

The first was from the old hatter, Joe, the inebriate who had bought his tobacco months earlier and wobbled out of the store in search of pastures new. This time, early in the afternoon, he arrived on horseback, sitting bolt upright and looking extraordinarily sober. His horse, skinny and weather-beaten like its rider, deposited him directly in front of the store and then began to nibble at the rough grass that had appeared with the rains.

After tethering the horse, the old man greeted her and stepped inside. 'Come again for some baccy, me lady,' he said. 'On me way to Bacchus Marsh to visit a mate. And you don't 'ave to worry about old Joe, now. Off the grog.' As he said this, he swung himself onto an upturned box and looked directly at Mary, his self-satisfaction obvious, almost comical. His face still bore the same crevices and red blemishes, but his eyes seemed remarkably clear. Overall, he retained the appearance of some kind of skinny insect. But there was something rather likeable about him.

'Not drinking?' she cried, holding the tobacco in her hand and resisting the urge to ask, 'Why ever not?'

'No, me dear. No more "blow me skull off" for old Joe 'ere. Seen the light, you might say. Drunk as a lord one night. Locked up, I was, for makin' too much noise. And who should come by, but a young reverend on 'is way to Geelong. Sergeant Miller let me out in 'is care.

Gave me a real talkin' to, that young minister did. Strappin' young feller 'e was, too. Told me 'ell is full of drinkers like me. Grog, 'e said, was a' awful sin. Would send a man to per…perdition, 'e said. Spent all night talkin' to me. I 'aven't 'ad a drink in a month, Missus. Got this, now, to keep me out of trouble.'

There was a sudden shuffle, a rummage through his bag – and out popped a small Bible. 'Yeah. No more "blow me skull off" now. Done with it, I am.'

Mary handed him the tobacco, accepted the money and looked into the clear, if tired eyes. 'Yes, Joe. That's excellent.'

'Aye, missus. 'Aven't felt better in years. But,' stuffing the tobacco beside the holy book, 'still need this. Still need me baccy. Good day to you, me lady.' And with that, he left.

The second came a week later on one of the very few fine days. The sun had actually appeared, giving the landscape a sheen, almost a soft glow, and the wind was barely a ripple. She was about to close the store and retreat to the cottage when she was greeted at the door by a woman wanting to buy a few household items. Outside, on the edge of the road, stood a small cart, loaded to overflowing and occupied by two boys. One, who seemed to be about fifteen, was holding the reins and gazing ahead, as if he was impatient to move on. The other, probably about ten, sat beside him, looking down and playing nervously with a short piece of rope. The woman, Mary guessed, was about forty. She was short and thin. Her hair was drawn tightly back and there was a restless energy in her movements as she rummaged through the items Mary spread before her. An energy which, as she began to talk, transformed itself into open anxiety.

'I'm taking my two sons to be with their father,' she announced, running her hand quickly over a length of material. 'He has a job working on a large farm about ten miles further on.' She accompanied this with a quick, broad sweep of her arm, as if she was keen to dismiss its location. 'He has written asking me to bring the boys. I've never lived in the country and I…' She paused and for a moment Mary feared she might break out into tears. But she recovered quickly and continued, 'I do so want to succeed out here, you know. There was little work in Melbourne and John decided to look for work in the country.' Again she paused, not looking directly at Mary but down at the counter and then away. 'I do so much want to succeed,' she repeated in a voice that only just struggled across the counter.

For a moment, their eyes met and Mary saw the same fear that she had felt when she had left her father in Sydney. The woman's gaze lingered, as if she wanted Mary to offer some word of encouragement. So many, coming with this need.

And, again, she did her best. 'Oh, yes, I'm sure you'll be able to live happily out here.'

'At least,' the woman went on, laughing uneasily, 'at least he's not digging for gold. That would make me very afraid.'

'Yes, I quite understand that. That could be very dangerous.'

The woman made her few purchases, climbed back on to her seat, ran her fingers through the hair of her younger son, and the cart moved off. The older boy waved briefly, obviously relieved that the journey could continue.

Mary stood watching the late afternoon absorb the vehicle and then felt her daughter's hand nestle in her own.

'Mummy, do you think that lady wants to live out there, on a farm?'

Mary looked down. 'I don't know.' Then, as if jolted back, she added quietly, 'No, I don't think she does.'

'I don't either.'

Almost without thinking, Mary clutched her daughter to her chest and they retreated into the semi-darkness of the store.

The third visit came soon after, a Sunday when trading was frowned upon, and she was busy sweeping and arranging boxes on shelves that the bullocky had made for her. Susan was asleep and a cold, dry wind prowled among the wattles and the straggling yellow box trees along the road.

Just as she was struggling to heave a box of nails into its designated place, she was startled to hear a voice behind her.

'Ah, my dear Mrs Douglas. Allow me to help you with that.'

Turning, she saw the uniformed figure of Sergeant Miller. She had the uncomfortable feeling that he had been watching her through the half-open door.

'Oh, sergeant, you startled me.'

He stopped, close to her, then took the box from her hands. There was an intensity about him that troubled her. 'I didn't mean to do that, me dear.'

What followed was difficult for her to recall later. But, as she turned to pick up another box, she slipped, toppling forwards. The sergeant, more nimble than she would have expected, grasped and held her. She smelt the closeness of sweat. But, as she endeavoured to right herself, she became aware that he was holding her more tightly. There was a wildness, almost a sense of panic in his eyes, and he bent his face to hers. The scar on his cheek seemed to glow and grow larger.

'Don't need much thanks, little lady. Just a kiss.'

Revulsion hit her like a cold, inescapable wind. She was the captured animal struggling to escape. The drowning desperate to reach the surface.

'And I wonder when the Great Survivor kissed 'is little wife like this.' His face was closer now, and revulsion became suffocation. His right hand locked her firmly against his chest, the other was clumsily searching for her breast. 'And I wonder if 'e ever did this,' he whispered. 'No, no need to fight me. Too long since I 'eld a woman. Too long. And too long, too, I think, since you were 'eld by a man.'

She could see nothing now but his face. The dark, unblinking eyes, those eyes that had pinned the young black boy. Now, more closely, the beard and the scar. The lips half open. And finally, deep inside, the mouth with its dirty teeth. Her whole body rose in revolt. Desperation became a cold, fixed will, a determination to break free.

What followed was instinctive and worked perhaps because she was stronger than he had expected. Wrenching her arms free, she pushed him hard in the chest and saw him topple back. She might not have finally succeeded had it not been for a pile of potatoes that tripped him up and then collapsed around him.

She quickly fled behind the counter, aware at the same time that her daughter was calling from the cottage.

The sergeant, disentangling himself from the potatoes, was already struggling up. 'Oh, I would not've done that,' he muttered, clutching his cap and pointing at her. 'Would not've done that. I 'ad no intention of 'urtin' you. But it isn't a crime for a man to want to kiss a woman. Just a bit of fun for both of us.'

She waited, trembling, but alert. Wanting to scream out but unable to make any sound.

Whatever his feelings had been, they now erupted into anger. Perhaps he had a sudden sense of how ridiculous he must have appeared, fully uniformed, but sprawled there as he was, like an upturned frog among an unstable pile of potatoes. His face glowed and his eyes were riveted on Mary's face. 'But I 'aven't finished with the Great Survivor's wider just yet. Oh, no. I 'ave an old score to settle with 'im. And you, little lady, you'll 'elp me settle it. Oh, no. I 'aven't done yet.'

She had difficulty standing now. But suddenly he was gone. Only the smell of his closeness and the echo of his final words remained.

Trembling, fearful that she might be violently ill, she gathered up the wayward potatoes, returned them to their rightful place, locked the door and went through to the cottage. 'Coming, Susan.'

She said nothing to her daughter, but spent five minutes vigorously washing her face and hands. If it had been possible, she would have stripped off all of her clothes and washed her whole body. Only much later, when Susan had gone to bed, did she wonder what the unsettled score might be. Now, more than ever, she longed for the physical presence of the bullocky.

5

The coach, the iron pot and something new

Finally the weather broke, the clouds peeled away and the sun gave almost a crystal crispness to the landscape, dripping in little globes from the leaves and tracing the streams of water down through the gullies. The change brought more people along the road, too. Some of the travellers trundled or rode impressive gigs and carts. Others trudged with an air of depression, having waited for the weather to change enough for them to leave. The extremes of hope and despair could be seen rubbing shoulders, pausing perhaps and then heading their separate ways. Here, an old man might check his steps, watching with disbelief as two small children leaped like rabbits around a loaded cart. There, a young man might pause to watch a family set out, with little but a few belongings in a wheelbarrow, on the long return journey to Melbourne.

Other travellers were using the road, now. Men and women who called themselves townspeople. They were more leisurely as they came and went, but at the same time they moved with a sense of quiet purpose. When they passed a collection of miners, they often looked rather askance at them. If locals came into Mary Douglas's store, they sometimes spoke of the ruffians who destroyed the land, misbehaved in the shanties and were always in trouble with the law. A few argued vigorously that the governor should strengthen the garrison in the town.

One old man, arriving at the store late one afternoon and shaking his fist across the counter, as if confronting some imaginary miscreant, maintained in a croaky, high-pitched voice that all that was needed was a strong hand. 'A show of authority, lady. Uniforms and weapons.

There's nothing like steel glinting in the sun to dissuade renegades. You mark my words.' Then, nodding at his own brevity, he left, striding away, taking with him the loud approval of the few shoppers left in the store.

Clearly, not all within the community supported the claims of the miners.

With the change in the weather, Tom visited his mother less often. But when he did come, the stories remained the same. Licence hunts, more often now. The small size of claims. The lack of any voice in decisions that affected the diggings. The denial of land to the miners. The only discernible change was the level of anger.

'There will be trouble, Mother,' he muttered, almost through clenched teeth, on one of his visits. 'I can tell you that. Too much to expect honest men to put up with it much longer.'

Mary listened in silence, noting the icy tone and the tightened face staring at her. This was the old James. And when her son stood up, bracing himself as if in defence against a strong wind, raising his hand and looking almost accusingly at her, it was the figure of her husband who stood there.

She took care not to mention her confrontation with Sergeant Miller, but did advise him, hesitant though she was, to be careful in his dealings with the law.

He was quick to respond. 'Dealings with the law, Mother? I don't want any dealin's with the law. If the police leave me alone, they'll have no troubles from me. But they don't leave us alone, the traps and the troopers. If there does come any trouble, they'll only have 'emselves to blame. The miners only want a fair deal. For 'emselves. And their families. You can see that, can't you? There's little easy mining left, now. Men have to work deeper. And harder. And they don't need the traps houndin' them every day.'

'Yes, Tom. But you will be wary of…of…Sergeant Miller?'

She was not sure whether he had heard or not. And was probably relieved when he simply continued his assault. 'More police now, prowlin' and struttin' about the diggings. Been criminals themselves, some of 'em. Even the blacks are marchin' about in uniforms."

The conversation ended with the appearance of the coach from Melbourne. Thanks to the bullocky, it stopped here, on its journeys to Ballarat now, although that was against the company policy. She smiled inwardly, thinking that the fine weather would bring him back to the town soon.

'My beasties don't like tramping through the rain,' he had said. 'Get their feet wet. Spoil them, I do, lassie. They're like us. Like the sun shining on their backs, they do.'

Well, the sun was shining now and perhaps he would not be far away.

Susan had come out to join them and they stood in the gleaming world of sun and shade, watching the grand conveyance roll towards them. And grand it was, this Concord coach. Fresh from America: a gleaming, red giant turning its yellow trimmed wheels and swaying importantly. There were other curious onlookers, also, scattered along the road. Some were jealous, perhaps, of the fortunate few seated within; at twenty-five shillings one way, they would always be outsiders looking in. Others, perhaps, simply wondered who the occupants were. Sometimes there would be a few miners loafing around the store. To see the well-to-do arrive, irritable and uncomfortable after a long, bumpy journey, gave them, perhaps, a brief sense of social equality

Susan, however, was fascinated by the horses that came always in a rush, champing and snorting, with their coats uniformly black and steaming with sweat, their breath a rapidly approaching thunder and their heads straining forward. And stopping each time as if by magic, directly in front of the store. The bullocky had told her that the horses were changed every ten miles, so that those she saw were not the ones that had left Melbourne.

But the driver was always the same, a blustering Californian. He was a round, healthy man of perhaps sixty. So active was he, so intent on being the centre of attention, that Mary often felt he would be an excellent ringmaster in a circus. He always wore a multicoloured hat, enormous and bobbing with each sway of the coach, a hat that miraculously stayed in place. His jacket was always red. And his black trousers ballooned out and were tucked into large, impressive brown boots. How he maintained his impeccable appearance she had no idea.

And his voice had a springy, penetrating sound that often made people laugh. Once, he had confided to her – and to anyone within earshot – that he earned the princely sum of a thousand pounds a year. 'Far more than those poor devils diggin' below ground,' he had announced, with a theatrical wave of his hand and a tap of his boot upon the clay. 'Probably more honest, too. Still, I pity 'em. Pity 'em, my dear lady. Getting a rough deal from the authorities, they are. No doubt about that. And we in Melbourne and Geelong, we know about it.'

He had told her also, and almost in the same breath, that he had a wife in Melbourne and a girl in every town. 'Like a sailor, I am, Mrs Douglas. But I know that they're only drawn to me because of my money. Not Catherine, of course. A good woman, that one. The best wife a man could have.' He had paused then and a few wags who had come to the store had responded with a loud cheer.

She did not know how honest he was. But the general laughter that greeted his performances each time he arrived made it impossible for her to dislike him. Indeed, she rather welcomed his coming and the comical accounts he gave of his journeys and the descriptions he gave of characters he had met. In the good humour of those occasions, it did not matter whether the adventures were as remarkable or the characters as eccentric as he painted them. What she really hoped for, each time he came, was a letter from her father. But she had been waiting in vain for so long now that she had abandoned any thought of disappointment.

This afternoon, as always, his face beamed with self-importance as he held aloft his whip, flashing it above his charges. He was the undoubted master and the few people there were his audience. It had been said that often he would dismount before reaching his destination, run a quick glance over the coach and remove any offending dirt or mud. And today, as it rumbled towards the store, it glowed with colour, a giant beetle swaying above its leather springs and iron-clad wheels.

Pulling hard on the reins, standing on the brake pedal and shouting a quick instruction, he brought his exotic machine to a halt. No ringmaster could have performed better. Silence settled like a cloud, apart from the staccato breathing of the horses or the sharp tinkle of metal as one of them tossed its head. Then there rose vague sounds from within the coach, sounds of people moving. Faces peered out and the frame of the coach trembled as bodies stretched and eased away from the stiffness the long journey had inflicted.

Already the driver was preparing to swing down from his lofty perch to the humble earth. As he did so, his clean-shaven face broke into a smile, he winked conspiratorially at the widow and called into the coach, 'Now, ladies and gentlemen, the best store in Ballarat awaits. But remember, only ten minutes.' With that, he opened the door to help the passengers alight.

Tom and Susan disappeared quickly into the store, while Mary stood by the coach, still as a hostess, receiving guests.

The bedraggled collection of passengers set about disentangling themselves from boxes, cloaks and trunks. Mary sometimes met travellers she knew and they would often tell her about happenings in other parts of the colony. Indeed, there were some who saw her as a local and she was coming to feel that way herself. Occasionally, she envied the kind of freedoms that seemed to have, but at the same time she felt a quiet satisfaction. It was as if they were reporting back to her.

There was today, as always, the accustomed ritual. Blinking of eyes, sleeking back of hair, hasty adjustments to clothing, stretching of tired limbs. And then, from the anonymity of uncomfortable travel, the emergence of individuals.

At the head of it all, of course, was the driver, conscious of his position as star performer. 'Mornin', Mrs Douglas. I saw your son and daughter there a moment ago. Gettin' more like your husband, each time I see him, the lad.'

She nodded in reply, a mechanical movement that conveyed little, at the same time casting a quick glance towards the doorway, hoping that Tom had not heard. She then walked into the store, waiting for the newcomers to disembark.

Passenger number one was now stepping down, a girl of about eighteen, dressed in a simple grey skirt and blouse. Around her neck was a cheap-looking chain, probably imitation gold, and an equally artificial blue stone. Her face was pretty, with full lips and bright eyes that seemed to maintain a sense of naïve excitement. But there was also, if one perused those bewitching eyes a little more closely, a boldness, a glint of something else. A kind of challenge, perhaps. A something that would have attracted the attention of any male passenger sitting opposite on the coach. Women might have reacted rather differently. She introduced herself as Maria Smythe, smiled, first at Mary and then, as she entered the store, at Tom, letting those captivating eyes linger just for a moment on the latter. Soon she was strolling among the objects in the ladies' corner, looking, fingering, but always alert to what was happening around her.

Next in line were two young miners who spoke to one another in what might have been German. It was difficult to know; there were so many strange languages in the area now. Mary was surprised that they had come on the coach; few diggers could afford that. But there was certainly an air of opulence about their clothes. And their swagger. They were not new chums. Perhaps they had been among the fortunate ones who struck it lucky early. Both clean-shaven, they might well have passed for brothers, although there was about them the rough camaraderie one does not usually find among family members.

They spoke in surprisingly good English, making much of their knowledge about cradles, pans and puddlers. At the same time, they were obviously very aware of the pretty girl poised such a short distance away. She remained splendidly oblivious of their attention, pausing briefly, however, when they began to boast about their success. Her bright eyes swept over them with a childlike curiosity and then returned to the trinkets she was playing through her fingers.

A businessman stuck his head in through the doorway, readjusted his hat and retreated out on to the road, clearly anxious to move on.

The last person to descend from the coach and move forward into the store was a gaudy, robust woman of about forty, crowned with a mass of fierce red hair. Her costume, for that was what it seemed to be, billowed out in a blaze of colours, a cloud of red and orange that wrapped itself around her and swept her forward. A large bustle and matching ruffs gave her movement a kind of floating effect. And her bonnet rose up like a red pot plant that looked as if it might come crashing down at any moment. She sailed to the centre of the store, settled herself like a galleon under full sail and in a loud voice announced that she was Madame Hortense and that she had come to Ballarat to bring entertainment to its '*citoyens*'. All stopped to listen. Even the young miners looked up. Susan, who had been scampering between the boxes stacked in one corner, paused, wide-eyed.

'What a sweet little thing. *Quelle mignonne*,' emanated from the royal personage. '*Bonjour, ma petite*.' Expecting no reply, she then gave Tom a quick, dismissive glance and turned her regal gaze upon Mary. 'Ah, madame, I am sure that there may be acquaintances of yours who may like to attend my performances. This will give you some indication of my, my *carrière*. I can promise you audiences in this town, *cette ville*, will not be disappointed, *ma chère* madame.'

The foreign words, thrown in as they were at odd intervals, struck Mary as decidedly comical. Not just because she did not understand them. More because the woman paused so dramatically before using them. It was as if she needed to rehearse them in her mind first. This peculiarity had been noticed by the two foreign miners also. One of them was clearly struggling, and with only partial success, to restrain his laughter.

Madame Hortense cast him one contemptuous glance, gave Mary a sheet of paper, gathered her composure and marched out of the store. '*Et maintenant, monsieur le cocher*, your assistance, *s'il vous plaît*.'

Mary stood for a moment, holding back a smile and aware of the laughter beginning to ooze from the other passengers. Which of the many theatres, she wondered, would be graced with the presence of such a celebrity? None was identified on the scented sheet she held in her hand.

Could it be the famed Victoria? Certainly, the two thousand or so men who crammed between its florid red and gold walls would give her a rowdy reception. Oh, yes, they would do that. But as for showering the stage with coins and nuggets, as they apparently did if a particular female entertainer charmed them or was well proportioned? Ah, that was something else. Mary had seen them rolling and swaggering through its doors, their flamboyant Yankee hats, red serge shirts, hessian knee boots and scarlet sashes giving them the appearance of exuberant peacock,s and she feared for this stranger. And in which of the many new and expensive hotels would she seek accommodation? The George, perhaps? Or the Golden Fleece? Or the Criterion at twenty pounds a night? She watched the voluminous figure strutting out into the harsh sunlight and felt an acute pang of sympathy.

Put in the shade somewhat by such an extraordinary performance, the coach driver recovered himself as quickly as he could, encouraged the flowing folds of her red and orange costume to follow her aboard the coach and, turning his attention to the store again, urged the rest of Madame Hortense's entourage, for so the passengers now seemed, to board also.

When all were settled once more, with a final wink at Susan and her mother, he seized his whip, circled it cleanly twice and guided the vehicle back on to the road. Soon the coach, gleaming, clanking and jostling its cargo of mail, parcels and people, was dropping away in the distance. Taking, also, the renowned entertainer. To what cheap theatre or shanty Mary could not imagine.

At long last, the good weather brought the bullocky. First on his way into the town with his bullocks and their creaking, growling load, the next day on his 'village' cart. Each time kissing her with vigour and sweeping Susan high into the air. Mary felt the same rush, the same careless yielding to his embrace. And it relieved her that Susan showed no sign of disapproval.

She knew that she should be cautious and should learn more about this man who had entered her life. It surprised her, for example, that she had not even visited the small hut he owned on the western outskirts of the town. He had stables for his bullocks there. That much she knew. Whether there were secrets buried from his past she had no idea. He had told her so very little about his life before coming here. However, it did not seem to matter. Hearing Daniel Morgan talk in his low, lilting voice, sensing his interest in her and watching him cup his hands around his antique pipe were enough. For the moment, at least.

The store was closed early today. Mary and Susan were to accompany the bullocky down into the town. A rare treat. But necessary so that Mary could visit the bank and purchase a pair of shoes for her daughter. There was another reason also. But when the bullocky had asked what it might be, she declined, feeling a blush creep through her cheeks and at the same time acutely aware of a girlish excitement welling up inside her. He had peered through an exceptionally healthy cloud of smoke, smiled, nodded and made no further comment.

The sight of the cart approaching brought an excited shout from Susan. It seemed almost to be floating, bright green as it was in the clear air and preceded by its single, black pony.

Mary's excitement, only partly concealed, came more from the sight of the bullocky, beaming down upon her from his elevated seat. She allowed herself to be lifted up, watched as Susan was carefully placed on the seat behind, and felt the cart begin its glide down the slope.

At various points in their descent they passed groups of men who paused to stare or wave at them. Occasionally, from a tent, would issue a shout of recognition, which the booming voice of the bullocky would respond to.

The further they went, the more the land seemed to be under assault. Small, newly constructed islands of clay would rise up among wattles. Further on they would join into ugly, cone-shaped islands. And everywhere buckets scraped against rock, men rose and descended gaping holes, picks chipped away, windlasses turned, tents billowed and occasionally a woman would appear briefly at a doorway.

Surprisingly, amidst this frenetic activity, there were signs of things more settled, more peaceful and reassuring. Here a small hut. There a genuine footpath. And a well tended garden. Even children playing. In some places, a rush of flowers or puffs of yellow where wattles reflected the afternoon sun. And through this vast sprawl, this tangle of trees, tents and hastily constructed timber buildings, was the road, cutting its thin, tenuous line.

At one point, the cart was stopped by an untidy, angry group of men. They spilled around the vehicle, making advance or retreat quite impossible.

One figure, wearing the dark uniform of a police officer, detached itself from the group and stood firmly in front of the cart. 'There's a problem 'ere, driver, a disturbance. You'll 'ave to wait until good order is restored.'

Mary felt her body stiffen, recognising Sergeant Miller. Beside her, the bullocky took out his pipe, lit it in silence and sat, looking down. There was about him an air of apparent calm. However, she did notice that he had taken Susan on his knee.

There were perhaps thirty men, presumably miners, gathered here, many of them covered in dust. Around them hovered eight or nine uniformed officers, some clearly nervous, all carrying weapons. Three others were struggling to subdue a single figure, an old man Mary had seen occasionally in the store. He was wearing dark, torn trousers, heavy boots and a shirt that clung to his sweating chest. His face was red with anger and suddenly, wrenching himself free, he lashed out with his boot, catching one of the officers in the groin. There was a stifled oath, a crumpling and the man lay vomiting on the road.

The bullocky felt the little body tighten on his knee, the face buried in his chest.

Shouts of approval rang out as more miners joined the crowd, some clambering on mullock heaps to gain a better view. But reprisal was quick. Sergeant Miller advanced, took his truncheon from his belt and dealt the offender a stinging blow to his head. The action was precise, the sound sickening as the truncheon descended and the result instantaneous. The old man collapsed, was manacled and hauled upright.

'Now, sling 'im on that 'orse.'

Susan was quivering with terror now.

The truncheon was clipped back into place, the sergeant mounted his own horse and turned to confront the angry crowd. 'My job is to uphold the law. And the law says a man must carry 'is licence with 'im at all times. And I advise you men to remember that. And to disperse. Before more trouble comes.'

He watched as the anger coiled around him. The muttering and the upraised fists as the miners broke up meant little to him, now. The crest has been reached and past. Men would always respond to a decisive show of force.

Then, stopping just before the cart, he focused on the bullocky. 'Now, driver, you may proceed.'

Mary hoped that he had not recognised her. But she found herself pinned beneath a cold, unmoving stare.

'Some of these men would be better lookin' for honest work, wouldn't they? 'Elping their mother run a store, perhaps.' His eyes lingered for a moment.

Then he noticed, standing apart, the young Aborigine he had arrested earlier and displayed in Mary's store. There was a distant aloofness about this boy that had fascinated Mary. And his eyes showed the same contempt today. He returned the sergeant's gaze without flinching.

Beneath such obvious contempt, the sergeant was compelled to look away. First out over the bush, then at the figures silent on the cart. He seemed to need some target and eventually focused on the bullocky. There was clear dislike here. But the bullocky returned his gaze, knocked out his pipe, replaced it in his pocket and urged his horse into action. At the same time, he kept Susan on his knee and placed her fingers around the reins.

'There, little mouse. All's well, now. And you can help me and Milly here. That's the way.'

Her body slowly relaxed against his. He felt her hands grasp the reins more firmly and, as the cart moved away from the group, he turned towards Mary. 'You know that man?' he asked quietly.

'Yes, Daniel. I know him.'

Before they had quite cleared the scene, she noticed her son standing among the watchers. He had the same rigid stance, the same out-thrust jaw her husband had always displayed in his moments of crisis. And she wanted to shout out, compel him to leave and turn his back on the dangers here. But the cart was already gathering speed and he was soon lost among the crowd.

So they came into the town itself, a town moving rapidly towards respectability. Where Main Road reflected the turmoil, the struggles and the uneasy rubbing together of poverty and wealth, here, in Sturt Street, were neat offices, stables and shops. Where the dust of Eureka Street rolled in sickly clouds, filled the nostrils with its smell or clung to the boots of the miners, here the road was compacted beneath the shining wheel of imposing gigs, drays and coaches. To be sure, the dust persisted. But one felt that it could be controlled, wiped from windows and doors, and kept at bay. All around moved men and women, bent on important tasks. Children played beneath verandas, giving the whole scene a sense of lightness, the sense that here, at least, all was as it should be.

The bank was their first destination. Standing halfway along Sturt Street, it was known as the Iron Pot. The reason became clear to anyone coming upon it. It was small and coated with iron. In the summer, it creaked and sweated under the sun and the wind. In winter, it creaked and grumbled under the rain and the hail. Mary had seen the manager standing motionless behind his counter and still bathed in perspiration and on another occasion had had to shout to make herself heard above the clatter of hail on the roof. It had been robbed more than once and the locals were hopeful that it might be replaced by a building more fitting and more secure. Today it stood like a gleaming blister, advertising itself as 'The Bank of Victoria'.

Mary left the bullocky and Susan together on the cart and went inside. Her business was brief, but when she returned, she was smiling shyly. Susan smiled and nodded in return.

Picking their way between pedestrians, carts and wagons, they stopped, on Mary's request, before a large store. 'Wait here, Daniel, if you will.'

Smiling again, Mary jumped down, took Susan in her arms and together they entered the store. As she disappeared, Susan gave a quick wave.

The bullocky took out his pipe, lit it and settled down to wait. In the sun and the gently rising smoke, he let his thoughts float freely. To this woman who excited him and at the same time gave him a sense of peace. To his wife who years before had left him and had drowned with her lover while crossing the Bristol Channel. And then, with relief, back to Mary. And her daughter.

Perhaps had he wanted a child, his own marriage might have lasted. But that was long ago. His life had taken an unexpected turn, a turn that had brought a new woman into his life and also a small child for whom he had real affection. The warmth he felt for Susan surprised and sometimes unnerved him. He could handle the loneliness of long journeys. Responsibility over his own fate did not really trouble him. But the thought of caring for a small child? Well, that was something quite different. At the same time, he could not deny the pleasure he felt each time she clambered aboard the dray or sat confidently on his knee. Nor the growing sense of responsibility he did feel for her.

For about twenty minutes he sat, thinking and examining the movement around him. He noted the fashionable ladies, keen to show off their finery, and the businessmen who passed in suits. He watched, with a quiet sympathy, the few Chinese who had ventured into the town. As usual, there were no women, just men trotting along in close little groups, each wearing his traditional, loose-fitting clothes and his conical hat. They must, he thought, be very lonely, thousands of miles from their women and families. As lonely, perhaps, as he had been returning home from work to find his wife gone. What might happen to these strange, inoffensive Asians if violence were to erupt among the miners, he did not know.

His interest soon shifted to the tradesmen who came and went, carrying lengths of timber, tools and rolls of canvas. He caught the edge of a conversation between two young men as they walked past.

'A good thing we gave up minin',' one was saying. 'More money now workin' in the town. Safer doin' this, too. There'll be trouble over there. I ain't got any doubt about that.'

His companion nodded. 'Yes. Pretty soon, I'd say. And we can keep clear of it now.' He laughed then, pointing down the street. 'Even the old Iron Pot is going, too, I hear. The police say it's too hard to protect. A bit jumpy at the moment, they are.'

'Oh well, more work for us, perhaps.'

'Let's hope so. I want to bring me wife down from Geelong if the work holds out.'

More work for me, too, thought Dan, knocking out his pipe. Again, he found himself looking out over the people in the street. On one corner an elderly couple was engaged in a lively conversation about the misbehaviour of children. Dan smiled. Nothing new in that. Further along in a small alcove, half hidden by large crates, a prostitute was staring out at the pedestrians. Nothing new in that, either.

Further away, a black-clad figure, surrounded by a few curious onlookers, was performing, exhorting all to mend their ways. 'Old Joe 'ere 'as seen the error of 'is ways, friends,' he was saying. 'You, too, can avoid the flames by turnin' to God. And to this.' The 'this' was a rather battered old Bible that he brandished with a theatrical wave of his hand.

A few applauded. Others simply laughed. Only one or two seemed to take his words seriously. Dan felt a quick flush of pity as the crowd finally split up and the old man stood, silent but still holding aloft his Bible.

Suddenly, his attention was drawn to the store. Coming out were two figures, a woman and a child. And it took him a moment to recognise Mary and her daughter. Both were smiling. Neither looked the way she had half an hour ago. Instead of the obligatory widow's black, Mary was wearing a full, brown skirt that reached to the ground, a high-necked and pale bodice and a small collar that drew attention to her slender neck. Most surprising to the bullocky was her hair. No longer was it imprisoned, tied up beneath a bonnet. It now floated free, a black mass tumbling well beneath her shoulders. In her hands was a parcel, presumably containing her discarded clothes.

Susan was equally transformed. She now wore a short, yellow dress. The short, puffed sleeves contrasted with the brown of her arms, and a red ribbon held her hair in place. Nothing could keep in place her smile and the joyous agility of her steps.

Dan's shocked expression clearly amused them both. He jumped down, unashamedly admiring in his attention.

'I…I had a seamstress make them for me here,' Mary began. 'I had to wait until I could afford them.' She looked shyly away, then back. 'Do you…do you like them, Daniel? The hand-worked chain stitch embroidery she did for me. Just to make the dress a little bit, well, different.'

Knowing little about the mysteries of dress making, the bullock could only smile. 'Oh, yes, lass. Beautiful, beautiful.'

'And do I look pretty, too?' Susan asked, hopping colourfully in front of him.

'Yes, indeed you do. The prettiest little flower I've seen in all my travels.'

Relieved, Susan climbed up on to the cart. Carefully, so carefully that it made Mary laugh, he helped her up, climbed aboard and flicked the reins.

'Now, well, I suppose I'd better show off my two fashionable ladies to the other fashionable ladies of Ballarat.'

And that, to Mary's embarrassment, he did, driving slowly the length of Sturt Street and back again. He had seen other men do it, here in Ballarat and on the streets of Melbourne and Geelong and had laughingly dismissed them as pretentious dandies. Now he had to confess that he, however briefly, was joining their ranks.

At one point Mary noticed a woman she recognised – Madame Hortense, the flamboyant traveller from the coach. However, today she was much subdued. Her clothes were simple and with her was a girl, also unpretentious in her apparel. Both had red, striking hair. They might well have been mother and daughter. Mary was sure that thes girl had not been on the coach. She waved as the cart slid past. But there was no answering response from either of the women. In fact, Mary felt that the older one had seen her and had quickly looked away.

Finally, Dan turned the horse away from the town and back on to the Melbourne road, Mary with her hair still defiantly free, Susan almost asleep and the bullocky smiling to himself.

It was late when they returned. Mary prepared tea for her daughter, reassured her that those nasty men would not be coming there, folded her new dress, waited for the steady fluting breath that indicated she was asleep and then went quietly through into the store.

The bullocky and the widow sat for some time, saying little but listening to the creaking of timber and the distant call of an owl. A call that seemed to hang in the clear night air and then faded sadly away. At one point, a horse galloped past, the clatter of its hooves a brief and sharp intrusion into the quietness.

Then, with the silence returning, the store at peace with itself and the potatoes, those troublesome objects that had so upset the sergeant weeks before and saved her from humiliation, now quiescent in their boxes, Mary, at first with a degree of trepidation and then with mounting excitement, yielded to the embrace of the bullocky.

6

Duty

Freedom! How it fires the hearts in every time, in every place. Of men, of women and of children.

Susan, looking out over the spring, relishing the birds flung on the wind and the light now pouring through the bushland, was no exception. What, she wondered as the winter sank away, what lay beyond the safety of the store and her mother.

Thinking, perhaps, of her own childhood, Mary finally succumbed to her daughter's requests, giving her permission to visit the home of neighbours, a family who lived about a mile away.

As she watched the simple cart disappearing, with Susan only briefly looking back, she was aware of a number of conflicting emotions. A certain anxiety. But more, a certain pride. James would never have allowed this to happen. She could see him, spreading his arms across the table, breathing heavily and refusing. He had granted little of what his wife had wanted and often his speeches ended with a shake of his head and a loud snort, a kind of audible full stop that ended any kind of debate. Now, the memory made her smile. But, at the time. It had been anything but amusing.

'She's growin' up, Mother, isn't she?'

'Yes, she is, Thomas,' Mary answered, grateful, perhaps, that her son had abandoned his claim for the day. 'And nice, now, to see more families. More normal, don't you think?'

'Yeah. And there'll be more once those greedy landed gentry have to give up some of their land. More, then. I'm sure of that.' He was looking into the distance, Susan's adventure already lost in affairs much more pressing. 'There will be more,' he repeated, almost reluctantly turning his attention back to his mother. 'Things will happen. Things the miners will make happen. Things that will make their cronies think twice before they squeeze us any more. You can count upon that, Mother. Big things.'

She could not avoid his intensity. But her thoughts, edged now with anxiety, returned to her daughter. 'Yes, Thomas. But you will be careful, won't you?' The words came automatically, without emotion.

'Yes, Mother, I will. But we will do what must be done.'

The threat in his voice alarmed her. However, there was little point in pressing further.

Tom stayed longer, this visit. Perhaps to keep her company and to help in the store. More likely, and Mary realised this, to gather information from any miners who came in. One or two of them Tom would lead away and talk to in private, the slight bobbing of heads or outstretched arms the only indication of their conversations. And the intensity of their faces. These were men either unhappy or angry. One older man, not caring who heard his complaints, was waving his arms continually, as if tearing something down. Something or someone.

For most of the time, she felt she was watching the antics of puppets. However, at one point, and in the middle of an animated discussion, she noticed the men pause, as if frozen. Their eyes were unashamedly fixed on a newcomer who had arrived. To Mary, he was just another searcher for gold, young like her son, burnt by the summer winds and, like him, dressed in the drab clothes that resembled a uniform. He showed little interest in anything but the things he needed. However, conversation resumed only after he was gone.

So the morning unfolded, as it usually did. Quietly. At times, particularly towards noon, Mary looked out, knowing that the cart would return, either late in the morning, or early in the afternoon. Noon came and went. No sign. A further two hours passed. No sign.

And, by three o'clock, she was genuinely alarmed. Alarmed but also angry and guilty. Guilty at her original decision. Angry at both herself and her daughter. Although the sun still flooded the road and swept down through the trees, for her a dark shadow was descending and she asked Tom to ride across to the farmer's cottage and find Susan. Four o'clock came and she noticed in the distance a horse and rider. But no Susan.

Tom's alarm reflected her own. 'She left there about two hours ago. Determined to walk home. Foolish of her. Foolish of old man Smeaton to allow her. But it's done. And he's out lookin' for her now. He knows the bush well, travels through it each day. I'll go back now and help him. Don't worry, Mother, we'll find her.'

But she did worry. And the very bush that she had come to respect and enjoy was now a dark threatening force, glaring out even in this sunshine. 'No, Thomas. I want you to ride into the town and get help from the police.'

Her son looked down, wanting to reassure her that it would not be needed.

However, Mary raised her hand, her body shaking. 'No, Thomas. Do as I say.' Then, still shaking, she fell to her knees, unable to contain her tears. 'I shouldn't have let her go.' Then, she struggled to her feet, clinging on to her son. 'Please go.'

Not waiting for a reply, she turned and walked back inside, hearing her own heavy sobs and the clatter of her son's horse. Moving through to the cottage, she closed the door and sat down, unable to move further. If only the bullocky were here. He wasn't and for the first time in many months she wept uncontrollably.

Then, mechanically, every few minutes, she opened the door and peered out along the road. Each time, the shadows were cutting more deeply into its surface. Another hour passed. She would wait for the police and then go out with them.

At about five o'clock, she heard approaching horses. Quickly she composed herself and opened the door. Indeed the police were there. A young, uncomfortable-looking constable. And a sergeant. The composed Sergeant Miller. He did not dismount, but looked directly at her. She was clearly, now, a vulnerable woman. Her stained face and the fear in her eyes told him that. But whatever his feelings, he kept them hidden.

'Your daughter is missing.' The voice was hard, impersonal. Neither a statement nor a question.

'Yes, sergeant.' And she quickly explained what had happened.

The sergeant's eyes never left her face as she did so. Then, looking down, he pointed to a young Aborigine standing in the road. 'Might need this feller. Useful sometimes, these blacks. Eyes like cats, they 'ave. I never believed those stories about these trackers. Not until I saw 'em at work. And this young buck is the best, so they tell me. We'll find this little child, won't we, Johnno?'

A shadow became a figure. 'Yes, missus,' she heard, and a dark face lightened into a crease that might have been a smile. 'I'll find your daughter. We have good eyes, we black fellers. Not good arms, sometimes. But good eyes.' The raised hand, bent outwards, she recognised.

'Now,' the sergeant went on, 'we'll be on our way. And you, madam, you must stay 'ere. Don't want the little one arriving back to an empty nest, do we?'

Mary was about to interrupt.

But the sergeant's eyes were now hard, full of authority. 'I said, Mrs Douglas, that you will wait 'ere. We can't 'ave an anxious woman tramping through the bush and slowin' us down. We will find your daughter. You will stay 'ere.'

Although Mary trembled inwardly at this cold, measured voice, she managed to say, 'Thank you, officer. But please, please, find my daughter.'

Perhaps, for a moment, there was a glint of triumph in the sergeant's eyes. Then, nodding, he led the way back onto the road, the constable on horseback, the young Aborigine walking. All silent. All soon disappearing into the blanket of shadows.

For quite a while, she stood, mechanically staring down the road, then back towards the town. Creating in her restless mind dark shadows and a small wandering shape. When she retreated indoors, the shadows materialised into dogs, skulking and creeping closer. At other moments, in a patch of light, a man would be lifting a child, placing her on his saddle and turning for home. Too often, the scene would fade into blackness and a heavy pall of guilt would engulf her, She was too tired, now, to feel anger.

All night she sat, listening, fearing, hoping. The sounds of the night drifted in through the open door; sounds she had hardly noticed before. The whisper of a breeze, the chatter and spite of possums in the wattles, the distant, sad call of an owl and at one point, she imagined, the clatter of horses. But, when she dashed outside, three kangaroos sprang away and all was still again.

Never had she been so isolated. So deserted. Night was a nameless, threatening ocean. The candle and the seat she sat upon made up a small, desolate island. A few items flickered, like pieces of passing wreckage. The rest of the cottage was shrouded in darkness. As the night wore on, reality became blurred. Once, she imagined her father and mother sitting beside her, silent but looking out. Once, the bullocky came, sweeping aside the darkness and striding towards her. So real was this that she suddenly stood up, knocking over the chair. The sound was as sharp as a gunshot and, exhausted as she was, she managed a snippet of a smile, restored the chair and walked outside. She wanted to cry, flood the night with her despair. But tears would not come. It was as if she was squeezing a wet rag. How she wanted the bullocky, his robust physicality, the smell of his closeness and his rough hands on her face.

Once again, she heard the low, distant hooting of the owl. And she wanted to track it down, silence it with one, sudden blow. Shatter its feathers in a show of red. Such was the sense of hopelessness and betrayal she felt. Nature seemed, in that sound, to be mocking her. And the cold, glassy moon standing still amidst the floating stars was the callous observer looking down.

Dawn saw her again standing outside. The sun came slowly,

a careless paintbrush that daubed red on the tops of trees, dribbled orange down the gullies and finally on to the road. There was no beauty in this day unrolling around her. At other times, the magic of dawn had entranced her. But not today. So filled with dread was she that hope lay abandoned. She pictured the sergeant, aided by the black boy and Thomas, coming upon the small bundle of death she would recognise as her daughter. Such are the horrifying scenes our fears can unleash upon us.

The store remained closed. She sat as she had all night, waiting and occasionally venturing out. Sometimes, shadows would appear in the distance and she would jerk to her feet. But they would harden into strangers and move on.

So she waited, lulled temporarily by the warm sunshine, half asleep, half awake. And always fearful. Then, at one point, slowly, something began to emerge, a sound coming from far off. A something that became a knocking, a knocking that became louder. She felt as if she was fighting through a thick foam towards some partly lit surface. Behind her, the chair clattered once more. Trembling, she opened the door. The light swept forwards and with it the figure of Sergeant Miller. In his arms was a bundle. A bundle that slid down and ran towards Mary. As she gathered the child into her arms, an enormous, suffocating wave of fatigue swept over her, then a flush of relief. How long she stood there, with the sobbing child held so tightly, she could not say. Finally, she was aware of the sergeant, the constable and the black boy standing in the doorway.

Still holding the weary bundle, she turned. 'Sergeant,' she managed, 'I must thank you. Thank you for saving my daughter.'

The officer's face, though obviously tired, showed little emotion. 'I told you I would find your daughter and I'ave done so. Not,' he added pushing the young Aborigine forward, 'not without the 'elp of this lad. Tracked the lass this morning to a rock she was shelterin' under. She said she'd got off the track to look at an emu with its chicks and couldn't find it again. The bush 'as done that to plenty of people out 'ere, I can tell you. Your son's gone across to let the Smeatons know.' Again he looked at the tracker. 'Good for some things, after all, these darkies, eh?'

Perhaps there was the inkling of a smile on the dark face. But quickly the eyes were lowered and the clawed hand was drawn back, as if purposefully hidden.

The sergeant prepared to leave. But Mary found herself half whispering, 'I'm surprised, sergeant, that you would…'

'Come 'ere, to answer your call?' he cut in. There was irritation now. 'It is my duty to serve the community.' Now his face showed contempt. 'My duty. That's all. And I trust you'll take better care of your child.'

He seemed to loom larger as he said this. And she felt unable to look away, managing to say only, 'Yes, sergeant, I will do that.'

Apparently satisfied, he turned and left, followed by the constable. Before the young tracker could join them, Mary placed her hand on his shoulder, noticing the contraction, as if the boy was afraid. And the sudden shock she felt. Never had she touched a black man before.

'I'm most grateful,' she said. 'Could I offer you some, some money or some reward?'

The boy straightened, as if surprised. 'No. missus. We black fellers don't need anythin' for doin' things like that.' There was a pause. For the first time he looked directly at her. His eyes were suddenly firm, almost defiant. 'We have little 'uns, too, you know. Like you.'

And he, too, was gone.

Mary closed the door. For some time she sat, nursing her daughter, content with the togetherness, a togetherness which, a few days later, included the bullocky.

7

Of a cannon, windlasses and a robbery

Life returned to normal. Mary relieved, Susan recovered and Tom pleased to be back underground.

With his mates, Joe Tyler and Andy Drew, Tom was now working a claim on Canadian Gully. Any new claim was a gamble. But, finally, they had had some success. Their shaft had bottomed at about fifty feet and in the gravel that lay on the bedrock they had discovered a few small nuggets of gold. Not many, but enough for them to hope their drive, short as yet, might yield more.

Like all who were able to wrest success from the cold underworld, they were secretive and cautious. Miners were quick to ferret out information about successes, and thefts were common. Indeed, three weeks ago, a group working a few hundred yards away had been 'ratted' at night and left with nothing. All miners took care to keep their finds secret and the three had decided to place their nuggets in a small leather bag and recover them the next morning. So, before most of the miners had returned to their tents, they sat together, watching the fading sun throw its shabby blanket over the hills and waiting, as they often did, for the evening's entertainment, the firing of the cannon from the government camp. The three were well known among the other miners on the slope and they were often seen like this, yarning and drinking together.

Miners liked Tom, respecting his hard work, but they were wary of his uncertain temper. So fixed was he, once he had made up his mind to see something through, that some of those who had known his father referred to him as a copy of the old man. This was not something he liked and men working close to him were well aware of it. How much they actually knew about his father he could not say. Indeed, there were things about James's past that he himself did not know. But he had the uncomfortable feeling that there might well be dark corners and secrets stuffed away that he was better off not investigating. And, while he was sometimes curious to find out what others might have been informed about or had actually witnessed, he resisted the temptation to try and find out.

It was fairly common knowledge that the authorities were suspicious of Tom, Sergeant Miller apparently having referred to him in one of the hotels as one of those 'hotheads that needs watchin''. That did not bother him at all. Indeed, the knowledge seemed only to fuel his determination. But it did make him curious. There were plenty of agitators on all of the fields. So why had he merited this extra attention?

Probably, Joe Tyler was more popular. He was many years older, had come from California to try his luck and had teamed up with Tom Douglas a few months ago. His chunky, short frame, striding confidently around the slope, was easily identifiable. And his round, grinning face reflected an almost boyish enthusiasm. There developed between the two the kind of trust and affection that sometimes quite quickly cemented relationships between men working in dangerous situations underground.

Joe was one of the few genuinely unselfish men on the slope and while he gave little away in terms of information about happenings underground, he was always willing to help any miner he felt was in trouble. More than once, he had paid fines for men he knew. And on one occasion he had risked his life to go down into a shaft and hauled a semi-conscious miner back to the surface. There was universal respect for him. And, although Tom never confessed this to anyone, not even his mother, he often felt a kind of attachment to Joe that he might have wished he had sustained for his father. True, as a child he had admired his father's cold determination and the equally cold respect men gave him. But, with time, Tom had sensed that this respect was probably closer to fear. And for Joe there was something more than respect; a kind of warmth that carried across to most of the men who knew him. A mate for older men, a father figure for those younger.

Andy Drew was not popular. And men often wondered why Joe had taken him on. He did his work, worked the hours, as one digger said of him. But he was seen as a drifter, scorned by those who valued hard work and determination. Bitter experience had taught most of the miners that the days when an individual could stub his toe against a nugget were long gone. They knew that perseverance, the ability to work with others and the courage to face the dangers lurking underground every day were the qualities needed. Those were often seen as the measure of a man now. All hoped for wealth. Gamblers always do. But few carried around with them the delusion of finding easy wealth that he did. Often Tom compared him to his father. Unfavourably. No task ever deterred the Great Survivor. Where Andy Drew would baulk, James would roll up his sleeves and launch himself into action.

These observations perhaps made it easier for the participants and the watchers to explain what happened the following day. Certainly those events were to elicit genuine sympathy for Tom and Joe. Contempt for Andy Drew took a little longer to surface. But it came.

For the moment, they were partners, hopeful of finding more gold and protecting what they had. Their plan was simple enough. Joe would return down the shaft once night had fallen and stay there to watch over their find. Tom and Andy would join him in the morning and their gold could be safely removed. It would be easy enough to bring it up with the gravel from the morning's work.

It was almost dusk now. Weary men were trudging up the slope and in a few minutes the cannon from the government camp would boom out over the diggings. This was meant to mark the official ending of the day's labour. But why this meaningless ritual was carried out so theatrically and so meticulously each day, no one really knew. Officials, when cornered, argued that it was too dangerous for men to work underground after dark and that it was necessary for the administration to intervene and ensure that the work stopped at sunset. Few miners took this seriously. And, while presumably men could be fined for disobeying this order, no one had actually been fined or knew anyone who had. Many laughed, claiming that the police were too drunk to go out on patrol at night, fearing that they might fall down the shafts themselves. Others saw it as yet another attempt by the authorities to exercise power, a way of reminding free men that they were not really free at all. In any case, few saw a flash and a puff of smoke from an antique cannon as worthy of serious consideration.

But the camp itself, the source of these explosions, was taken very seriously. From its location, not far from the diggings, it stared down with a watchful eye. In earlier days, its ramshackle tents, stable and guardhouse were almost indistinguishable from the other buildings on the slope. And therefore appropriate fodder for the diggers' sense of humour. Not any more. It was now fenced, the administration buildings were permanent wooden structures and the staff tents stood in neat, submissive rows.

More and more frequently, too, on what could best be described as a parade ground, troopers could be seen carrying out precise military exercises. To many, now, the men inside the camp seemed more like an army of occupation than a force charged with the responsibility of maintaining good order and protecting the rights of hard-working and law-abiding citizens. Above the buildings floated the royal flag and many were coming to detest this object as much as they did the regulations flooding out from the camp. Once, the flagpole had been blown down in a raging storm and some of the wags among the miners had heralded this as an omen. But the next day the flag was riding high once more. A few, determined to prolong the joke, wore black armbands for a week.

All, however, like the three miners sitting now in the lengthening shadow of their tent, could always laugh at the firing of the cannon. And the ritual never changed.

Right on cue, with the sun dipping below the hills, the two

officers charged with disturbing the peace came forward. Leaving the central block of camp buildings, they moved with their habitual solemn purpose towards the squat cannon, settled as it was at the end of the compound and looking remarkably like a docile pig. Sergeant Miller, the senior of the two, walked easily. Clearly comfortable with power, he looked neither to right nor left and ignored the dirty faces of the few boys peering through the gaps in the palisade. The other, a tall, gangly young man, seemed to walk and lean in turn. He was a comical mixture of movements all coming and going together. So uncomfortable-looking and so ungainly was he that the locals had called him the Turkey.

Moving in unison, or as much in unison as the Turkey's extraordinary motion would allow, they reached the cannon, removed the canvas cover and prepared the antique weapon for firing. They prodded and fiddled, there was a sudden stab of light, the harsh metal of the barrel gleamed briefly and both men straightened and drew back. Almost immediately there was a flash, an explosion and a roll of sound that wallowed and spread over the gullies. Close by, a flock of galahs or whatever birds had settled near the camp scattered into the sky. Then, calmly and with real solemnity, the two officers replaced the cover and retreated, and the administration deluded itself that all work had stopped.

Some did obey, of course, feeling that they now had official permission to bring their hope or their despair to the surface and examine it by candlelight. Many, as could be seen by the candles disappearing down shafts, didn't.

This was the routine, and the ending never varied. A small group of Chinese miners, whose tents were closer to the camp, would tumble out, gesticulating wildly and shouting at the two officers. No one knew what their shouts meant, of course. But the sight of their pigtails waving and their bodies rushing out from their tent was enough to send the miners into shouts of 'Go to it, Johnny Chinaman.' They would then gather together, mutter among themselves and retreat to their tents, and the performance would be over. Sergeant Miller had once remarked that at least while the miners were making fun of this small wretched group, they were not taking to them with their fists. And there was clearly some truth in that. The Europeans disliked the sight of the Chinese fossicking through abandoned heaps and at least two of them had been dealt with behind a convenient shanty and sent bleeding back to their tents. Less trouble for the authorities if they could be simply treated as objects of scorn.

Tonight all was as it should be. After the evening meal, Joe and Tom went off down the slope to their shaft. Andy, as was his habit, departed for one of the local shanties to have a drink with his mates, 'And a bit of something extra if I can get it.'

Once they reached the claim, Joe was lowered down into the shaft. A few seconds later, the rope went slack, a candle spattered the lower timbers with a pale light and Tom knew that his mate was signalling for him to depart.

For about an hour, Tom lay on his bunk, listening to the usual sounds: men coughing, plates scraping together, even a song, and sometimes the clank of metal on metal. Then, restless, he strolled outside and looked at the strange transformation taking shape. Clearly, stories about Canadian Gully had spread far and wide. There were many more tents now. And on a clear night such as this they glowed like a field of mushrooms. Each had a character of its own. This one showed the silhouette of a man stooped over a table. Another revealed two figures moving in slow, flat relief, drinking in turn from a perfectly outlined bottle.

In places, he could make out lanterns swinging and small camp fires stuck like papier mâché to the slope. Darkness hung upon the distant bushland and he thought of that other darkness, the one that held hard-working Joe and surrounded him with the drip of water and the creak of timber.

When he returned to the tent, Tom found Andy sitting on his bunk, smelling, as he usually did, of grog and tobacco.

'Good time there, tonight, Tommy, me lad,' he managed to say. 'New barmaid. Maria, 'er name was. I can't think of 'er other name. Pretty little bitch. I'll have 'er on her back by the end of the week. Won't be able to resist me then, will she? When I'm rich.'

There was no reply and a few minutes later Andy managed to struggle to his feet again. 'Might take a bit of a turn round the camp. I'll see you in the mornin'. Not too early, though, eh? Don't want to raise any susp...suspicions, do we?'

Tom slept fitfully, drawn back, each time he woke, to the image of Joe crouched deep in the belly of the earth.

In the morning, he rose early and looked across at Andy's bunk. It was empty. 'Oh, the lazy bastard,' he thought out loud. 'Probably staggered into the wrong tent again or he's hauled up under a tree. Might've even snuggled up to that barmaid he was talking about.'

He waited for perhaps an hour and in disgust set out for the claim. The sun was already smearing the broken horizon with red as he set off, and men were about, pulling on trousers and boots, laying out lengths of rope, carrying buckets or swilling out their breakfast plates. Some were clearly curious, stopping to look across as he approached. This amused him and he wondered whether there was an element of truth in the story that some men had a nose for gold and could smell it out. Or had Drew tossed down one drink too many and shot his mouth off in the shanty? That was more likely.

The Chinese were already about, moving like busy mushrooms on skinny legs, shuffling from their tent to a small fire, muttering and laughing among themselves. Settling briefly on their haunches and then straightening and setting off for their claim. Always aware of the general scorn of the Europeans, they made as little fuss as they could.

Tom watched their departure and set off himself. Knowing that he needed help, he found an acquaintance he could trust, explained the situation and enlisted his help in operating the windlass.

The small kibble they used to bring the gravel up from below was swung out over the dark square. Tom clambered aboard, taking just a candle and a box of matches. He heard, as the windlass began to turn, a voice from among the curious watchers.

'Hey, darkie, careful there, or you'll fall over the bloody edge. Long way down. And with that bad 'and you'd find it 'ard work climbin' back up.'

There was a quick burst of laughter from the onlookers. Nobody had noticed the young Aborigine until now. He retreated quickly and the knot of watchers tightened.

The Chinese miners, who had gathered together in a small group and were also watching the proceedings, attracted little attention either.

At first, as he descended, Tom could see the faces clearly outlined above. But quickly shapes melted into a uniform grey and around him he could see just the close walls of the shaft, gleaming, clean timbers and long fingers of water. He identified quite easily the spot about thirty-five feet down where Andy had almost been suffocated by a sliding mass of sand and where they had almost abandoned the shaft.

Then he was plunged into darkness, a night in which he imagined, as he looked up, that he could make out the pinpoint sharpness of stars. Each time he descended, he clung on to them; they were fragile but visible connections with the world he knew. A man did not want to be completely alone, sensing around him nothing but cold, wet rock and the constant threat of water or sand pouring in on him. Always, coming down, he was filled with a sense of unease. His stomach muscles tightened and he could sense a pounding in his head.

His father had refused to descend into any of the shafts. 'If I'd been meant to go down there,' he had angrily said on one occasion, 'I'd 'ave been a bloody mole.' And Tom took a certain pride in the fact that, in spite of his own fears, each day he could confront the wetness, the creaking and the darkness. Something too frightening for his father even to contemplate.

It surprised him, also, that his father had seemed to need walls around him. Not these cold, treacherous and wet ones. But the solid timber walls he had erected. Should he not, because of his prison days, have welcomed open spaces? Instead, he had seen the bush, with its long meandering corridors of light and shade, as a threat. And when he had gone out, it was usually with an axe to bring timber home to build more walls. Or, not long before his death, a fence behind the store. James Douglas had revealed little of his thoughts to anyone. But he had confessed a few of his fears to Tom. And the confessions had made him seem more approachable. At least for a time.

Soon Tom was surrounded by nothing but black silence, a silence punctuated by the bumping of the kibble against the wall and the occasional drip of water. As he reached the bottom, the kibble grated on the loosened gravel. And the silence, now, was almost complete

He struck a match, watched it cough briefly and go out. The second one sputtered more boldly and its small star of white merged into the broader canopy of light from the candle. He could now see the sickly puddles at his feet, the streaks of mud on the rock and the slabs standing like broken teeth.

Turning, he bent down to enter the drive. The partners had laboured long and hard here, but it was only about fifteen feet long. One could not stand upright, and anyone clambering into it was protected only by the benevolence of the good earth and a few slabs of timber. Tom had lost some of his fears about working in drives like this. But sometimes at night he would still wake up gasping for breath, imagining thousands of tons of rock and clay were collapsing upon him. And he felt his stomach tighten as he entered now.

'Mornin', Joe. Had a good night, have you?'

No response. So he kept moving forward, half crawling, half walking. Light from the candle rested on the jagged thrusts of rock, the weeping timber and drops of water that stood out like eyes watching and then upon two eyes that were indeed open and watching.

'Mornin', mate. Didn't hear me back there, eh?' He placed his hand on Joe Tyler's shoulder and suddenly the body toppled forward, knocking the candle to the floor.

'Oh, Christ, what's happened here?'

Tom hastily retrieved the candle, lit it and looked around, first at the bland rock and then at the shape at his feet. Joe Tyler was clearly dead. One leg was thrown out in front of him, the other was curled under him. His arms were limp as if in a final resignation. His face was thrust out, while the mouth that had laughed so much in life, now wore an obscene, fixed grin. It was as if some monstrous hand had reached out from the middle of a nightmare and twisted it into a new, dreadful shape. From that mouth dribbled a dark globule of blood and on the right side of the temple a repulsive depression revealed red and a show of white, broken and sharp-edged. The eyes were stuck in a permanent look of surprise.

Tom felt the coldness of fear and loathing. He crouched, fascinated by that huge wound and the death stare of his mate. Then, before scrambling back, he checked the fissure where the bag containing their gold had been placed. Nothing. And, almost vomiting as he touched the man's clothes, he searched quickly through the pockets. Nothing there either.

Obviously, Joe had been murdered, bashed to death in the confined space, and the murderer had escaped with their find. As he crawled out, holding the candle unsteadily, he heard the silence of the shaft shattered with an enormous roar. It dawned upon him, as he reached the end of the drive, that this unearthly sound was coming from him. The candle spluttered and went out. A sharp bump brought him hard against the bucket. Unable to shout now, he clambered into the kibble and wrenched hard on the rope. Soon he was being hoisted up. Light gradually returned and he could make out individual faces. Hands steadied the bucket and the miner who had helped earlier, sweating already from his labour, beamed across.

'Well, laddie, there you are.'

Tom looked wildly around, blinking in the painful glare of the sun. 'Some bastard's murdered old Joe, murdered me mate, and our gold's gone.'

Grinning faces froze, then changed slowly to blank pictures of disbelief. Silence fixed itself around the shaft. The kibble, with Tom still suspended in it, rocked gently and other men, having heard the shout, scrambled up. Soon voices were tumbling one upon the other.

'Joe's been killed.'

'Who?'

'Joe Tyler.'

'Yeah, murdered, in the shaft. And this feller's gold's been stolen.'

One of the Chinese miners, an older man who understood English, translated quickly for his mates. All five stood, silent as statues. Their inscrutable faces for a moment registered surprise and briefly they became a small part of the audience, rubbing shoulders with the Europeans.

An old man spat into the ground, made as if to walk off, then returned, waving his arms helplessly. Another smashed his pick through a pile of rubbish. Some swore. Others simply looked down into the shaft. And then, with Tom still swinging in his kibble, there surged among the onlookers something else, a rage that coiled and hissed like a snake.

'He was a good man, was old Joe,' rumbled out from one digger.

A cry rang out among the watchers. A cry that grew, quickly, helpless but dangerous.

It was at that moment that the young Aborigine, who had watched so closely earlier, suddenly moved. It was only a step, back from the shaft, but it was enough. The men now had a target.

'That's 'im. That young heathen, there. I saw 'im 'ere with one of 'is mates last night. 'E'll 'ave done it. Miller's grabbed 'im already for nickin' equipment. And now you've turned to murder, 'ave you? And come back to gloat, you thievin' black bastard, eh? Well, that'll be the last thing you'll do, lad.'

It did not matter where the voice came from. Now anger and helplessness could be changed into action.

From his perch, Tom watched the events unfold. There was a trickle of movement towards the boy at first. But quickly the trickle became a rush as the boy began to run. Shouts rang out and the game developed its own momentum. Someone released a dog that joined in. No chase for a greased pig or a kangaroo could have attracted more excitement. But the quarry here was a boy, guilty of being black and having moved at the wrong time.

Only the Chinese remained, bewildered, looking from Tom to the mad dash going on around them. There was no need for a translation. Their wide eyes told clearly enough that they understood what was happening. They had been chased often enough themselves by angry European miners. Fear was something they knew very well.

On all sides, men were erupting. Jaws of a trap were inevitably closing. In desperation, the escapee turned and hurtled back through the tents. Too late, he saw the shaft with Tom perched above it and too late he tried to scramble away. The lip crumbled and, with Tom frantically clutching his hand, the young Aborigine hung like a giant, convulsing spider.

'Hang on!' Tom shouted. 'Damn you, hang on. I can haul you out.'

Two hands clung to him now. One sweating, the other like a dry tangle of branches.

'I can haul you up,' he repeated.

But it was not to be. Hands were too sweaty, other hands too reluctant to help. There was a high-pitched scream, a series of bumps and then, silence.

Panting after the chase, the hunters gathered around the shaft, staring down into its mouth. A few voiced their satisfaction. Most, clearly uneasy, were subdued, standing in small knots and then dispersing. Some were thinking, perhaps, of the slim body lying beside the other fifty feet below.

Soon afterwards, two of the older, more hardened diggers went below to check if the Aborigine was indeed dead. He was, of course. The few who had lingered around the shaft sidled away and for a while an unnatural silence prevailed along the slope. Slowly, activity returned and with it the rhythm of work burying the incident under its usual hammering and rattling.

That night, any curious or guilty miner drawn back to the site would have seen something extraordinary – Tom Douglas endeavouring to fill in the shaft. A hopeless task, and he knew that. But anger, frustration and guilt can drive any of us to act in strange ways.

One or two of the men did come past. They stopped, hesitated, muttered and moved on.

Another, more curious, stopped him. 'Why the 'ell are you doing this, lad?' he asked. 'You could 'ave the body of your mate brought up and given a proper burial. And as for that thievin' black, well, you could dig a hole for 'im anywhere out in the scrub.'

Tom's anger was immediate. 'No. I don't want to go down that shaft again. If there's any more gold down there, it can stay there. My mate can rest where he is. And that other one, too.'

The miner shrugged, looked down and laughed. 'It'll take you a bloody long time to fill it in. That's all I can say.'

With that, he left, picking his way through the tangle of timber and equipment back to his tent. Lanterns flickered, fires burnt peacefully along the slope and from a distant corner there came the discordant sound of someone singing. The moon yawned above and the world seemed blissfully unaware of the single figure at work.

For a while, Tom worked alone, carting and tipping rubbish and clay down into the shaft. Then, at about ten o'clock, he was joined by the five Chinese miners who had stood by the shaft earlier. They came with barrows and shovels and stood like ghosts beside him. One of them, the one who habitually railed against the firing of the cannon, placed his hand on Tom's shoulder, nodding and pointing down into the black square hole.

'I had to bury me mate,' Tom said wearily. 'And, and that other feller.'

'It is good you do that. We Chinese, we understand. We know death. And memory. We send the bones of our brothers back, back to China. When we can. Back to their families. Yes,' the old man went on, vigorously nodding, 'it is a good thing you do. Your friend, he was miner. He returns to the earth. And the boy, he with dark skin and bad arm?'

'He saved my young sister.'

'Then we must give him peace as well.' He motioned to his companions and they set to, silently loading, carting and unloading.

By three o'clock, only about a third of the shaft had been filled.

The older Chinese again placed his hand on Tom's shoulder. 'It is enough. Your brother, he is safe now. We will place timber over the top now.'

That was done and soon the shaft was completely sealed.

Tom, weary like the others, sat down for a few moments with them. 'I thank you,' he said, his voice choking and slow. 'Nobody else would help me. Only you.'

There was a simple nodding and the Chinese rose to leave. Probably only the older man, sitting closest, would have noticed the tears streaming down Tom's face. Eyes met for a moment and he, too, was gone.

What happened afterwards did not seem to matter very much. Purely by accident, two days later, a wheelwright who had known Andy Drew came upon his body a few miles along the Geelong Road. Apparently, he had been thrown by his horse. Beside the body lay a small leather bag, open and empty. The name stood out quite boldly, Joe Tyler. Whoever had worked with Andy Drew had obviously escaped with the gold and would probably remain forever nameless. Clearly there was no honour among thieves.

Until now, Mary had never seen her son weep. But as he sat telling her what had occurred, tears ran down his face, turning the dust on his cheeks to small grey rivulets.

'He was like a father to me, Joe was, Mother. And he's gone. And as for the black boy, there was nothin' I could do, nothin'. It all happened so fast. His hands were too slippery. I tried, Mother, believe me, I tried. It all happened too fast. I couldn't save him. But I tried. One of his hands was like a claw but it had no strength. If he'd had two good hands, well, I would've got him up, I know. But I tried.'

She could not remember when she had last placed her arms around him. But she did so now and he did not resist. 'Yes, Tommy, I know you did. I know you did.'

A vision came to her of the young prisoner, his contempt for his captor, the dignified refusal to accept money as a reward and the deformed hand that had probably cost him his life.

8

The hotel and the logs

Virtue is a strange and complex illness, the causes of which seem to be largely unknown. We fall prey to it, some will say, because of our parents. Others will blame religion, pointing to dicta set down in sacred texts. Some will identify fear as the prime suspect, usually of eternal damnation if we do not mend our ways. A few, usually those who have been afflicted themselves, will say that virtue came upon them as a result of a particular experience. Saint Paul was a case in point, confronting enlightenment as he did on the Damascus Road.

The one common feature about virtue, and most seem to agree about this, is that, whatever its causes, it leads to a change in behaviour. And that probably explains why, today, Dan Morgan sat in this noisy pub, surrounded by avid drinkers, drunken conversation, and yet remained quite sober, drinking nothing more harmful than lemonade.

The reason for his sobriety was quite straightforward. Bullockies are not, in general, struck down by sudden blasts of light. Nor is it common for them to meet flying angels who, without wish of reward, pause and politely point out the error of their ways. Oh, no. Dan's visitor was decidedly terrestrial, a con man on the track east of Bacchus Marsh, who, having induced him to drink too much beer, waited until he had succumbed to sleep and then robbed him. Enlightenment, and abstinence, came to him through painful experience.

Sobriety gave him the opportunity, also, to keep his finger on the pulse of things. He could visit hotels such as this one and keep a clear head for information that might be useful. He was familiar with the *Ballarat Times* of course. Most people were. The clever, fiery editor, Henry Seekamp, kept everyone on their toes, particularly with his attacks upon the administration of the goldfields. But the place to be for up-to-date news was the bar of a hotel. Here, men from all over the area rubbed shoulders and swapped information. In the hurly-burly of business, any news of possible opportunities was invaluable, particularly now when competition for haulage contracts was so keen.

So here he was, sitting by himself, quite sober and listening to the convoluted exchanges going on around him. He would have preferred the quietness of Mary's store. But sometimes business had to take precedence.

Today, the bar was crowded and most of the customers were drawn to a lively performance given by three Irishmen. Apparently, they had come across from Bendigo. With things as they were on the goldfields, any voices raised in condemnation of general conditions would be listened to most enthusiastically. And complaining they certainly were, vociferously and with appropriate gestures.

The chief performer was a short stump of a man. Plying himself and his two companions with ample quantities of alcohol, he held the floor, his voice becoming louder as the audience increased. Red-faced he might have been, but it was clear that he understood the impact his words were having on this motley collection of miners. 'Oh, yes, lads,' he announced, throwing his arms towards the heavens, or at least as far as the roof, 'the English sent the noble Governor Hotham all right. Sayin' 'e'd set things right on the fields. But nothin's 'appened, 'as it? Except more injustices from Toorak. That's all. Plenty of those. But we'll beat 'em in the end, lads. Our Bendigo boys are ready for the fight, as I'm sure our comrades 'ere are, too. Those English lords will wish they 'adn't tangled with honest men on the fields.'

Such rhetoric could well land him in real trouble. The authorities knew, only too well, the agitations on the diggings. And also, some of the troublemakers. But the momentum of his speech only lessened when he paused momentarily to regain breath. And to enjoy the wild chorus of agreement rumbling up from those around. He made a few more verbal assaults on the camp and its occupants, adequately reinforced by his two companions and then by the assembled diggers. Finally, satisfied and spreading his arms once more, he sat down.

Feelings continued to run high. Anger, fuelled by alcohol, does not dissipate quickly. But then, slowly, conversation stuttered back into life, sometimes a fading echo of what had been said.

Dan was clearly an outsider here, an observer, but one steeled against the barrage and the chorus of support. He had seen men inflamed like this before. Wild-eyed miners in Wales, exhorting their colleagues to strike. There was always the same rhetoric. The same gesticulations. The same fists clenched as if about to tear apart the very air men breathed. And often the end result was a violent retaliation by those with power. Men injured or killed. Curtains closed and the thin, distant wailing of a grieving family. These were the fruits of violence. Had he not seen his own mother trying to dissuade his father from taking part in clandestine meetings? And had he not stood beside her as the body of his father had been brought home after a violent demonstration? No doubt, her weeping had been that of women everywhere, grieving and helpless. But it had been his mother. And he remembered, even as a boy, the guilt he had felt, being unable to save his father or ease her pain.

His moment of contemplation was interrupted by the sudden intrusion of a most unlikely-looking character. One more likely to arouse amusement than revolutionary excitement. Pushing his way forward and planting himself firmly on one of the stools, was a thin, leather-faced man, wearing a large, black hat and holding aloft a small Bible. Some might have remembered him as the mad old hatter they had seen often enough, prowling and muttering around the shanties and tents. Others, perhaps newer comers, would recognise him as the mad preacher encountered on street corners. Both groups, loosened with copious amounts of cheap grog, could see him as a humorous diversion. And they did. Two drinkers, putting their glasses down on the shelf that acted as the bar, came forward, grasped the old man, lifted him up and, to a wild chorus of encouragement, set him on his feet atop one of the tables.

'There you are, Moses,' one of them shouted. 'Now, go to it. There's plenty 'ere needin' divine 'elp, I can tell you.'

The old hatter, the miraculously reformed alcoholic, rose to his height, insignificant though it was, and explained the miracle of his new life, thanked his Maker and called upon his listeners to repent. And to call upon God. 'He will sustain you, my friends. He will avenge the evils done to you.'

They let him go on like that for some time. Some shouting encouragement. Others laughing. At last, perhaps to spare him further ridicule, the two miners came forward again and, to a burst of applause, carried him outside. Two others, hastily removing their hats, dashed around, gathering coins from the audience and hurried out, intent on rewarding the old man.

It took an effort, now, for Dan to refocus. As it did for all assembled in the bar. Once the general uproar had subsided, he noticed, past the bobbing and nodding heads and the arms raised and falling, two men who, like him, were taking a less passionate interest in the proceedings.

One, thickset and with a half concealed scar on his face, was the sergeant who had thrown the last clay upon James Douglas's coffin those many months ago. And who had, that day on the road into the town, found so much satisfaction in showing his authority. Dan knew that he was feared by many. Also that by some he was respected as an officer who would not be swayed from his duty and who would ruthlessly pursue any wrongdoer. There was something troubling about the man, seated there as he was, casually playing with an empty glass and looking out, quartering the hotel and yet seeming quite at ease. Not just because of the uniform, although that would be intimidating enough. Something else, something hidden, lurking beneath the surface.

The other individual he had not seen before, a tall man whose only distinguishing features seemed to be a bald head, ever moving eyes and a well cultivated beard. At the end of the Irishman's diatribe and the comic diversion, he leaned across and Dan heard him say quietly to the sergeant, 'Yes, sergeant, nothing new here. We had the same on the Californian fields. The same firebrands. Most of 'em harmless in the end. There are others we need to watch more closely, I'm sure of that.' The sharp twang in his voice gave him away as an American. Then, as if satisfied, he stood up, glanced around and left.

The sergeant remained seated, again scouring the bar.

Dan himself was ready to leave, but just before he did so, he noticed the sergeant stiffen and stare past the milling men. There, in animated conversation, were Tom Douglas and his new partner, Martin Jacobs. Dan had introduced the two, after the death of Joe Tyler.

Mary had been pleased to learn of this: she knew little about mining but understood that it was impossible for a man to work alone. But her gratitude had weighed on Dan's mind. Indeed, he had the strong impression that she somehow trusted him to be able to keep her son from trouble. God alone knew how he could do that. Anyone caught up in the conflicts on the goldfield was courting trouble. And anyone hot-headed and principled as Tom was would not be easily dissuaded from action. More likely he would be drawn to it. Probably his own wife had trusted him once and he had seen that trust slowly erode away. To the point where she had left him. He did not want to lose Mary in the same way. So he made a promise to himself that he would do what he could.

After a few minutes, the sergeant rose to leave. He looked once more at the two miners locked in conversation and paused in front of the bullocky. 'Morgan,' he muttered, nodding and looking down.

'Good afternoon, sergeant.'

Two days later, the police descended on the diggings, bent on arresting those who did not have their licences with them. There were more of these raids now, one or two a week, and the police came in larger numbers, were well armed and quite ready for any show of resistance. Those who did not have the scrap of paper on their person were unceremoniously hauled off to the camp.

The cry of 'Joe, Joe' rang out as it always did and the miners, like unusually well disciplined rabbits, scuttled for their favourite hiding places. Some headed for the nearest shanty.

One clambered into a hollow log, only to scramble out and stand, like a schoolboy caught in some naughty act, before the advancing officers. 'Bloody snake in there,' he bellowed.

Even the police laughed at that point and let him go.

Another scrambled up a tree. There he hung for three or four minutes while angry miners and police officers bickered below. But suddenly, nature betrayed him, a branch cracked and he was delivered, along with a shower of leaves, into the arms of the amazed officers. They shared the joke, although one of the horses reared up in alarm, almost throwing its rider. And the digger, the luckless one who had fallen from heaven, took his chance and, wrenching himself free, took off like a startled 'roo. Amidst shouts of encouragement, he made a brief, bold show until he was ridden down and perfunctorily manacled.

In these situations, the Chinese were often the butt of humour. They would almost always stand together, as if too terrified to move. With their heads bobbing and their arms gesticulating, they looked like agitated scarecrows. Today, as on most days, the police questioned them and then moved on. Again, as was usual, the miners broke into a loud squawking of hens as they departed.

Sergeant Miller, who seemed to be leading most of these hunts now, remained aloof from all of this theatre. He neither dismounted nor smiled. Stony-faced and intent on the seriousness of the occasion, he was directing his men from on high.

He finally stopped, along with his contingent, directly in front of the shaft begun by Tom and Martin. Looking down, he focused on Martin, who was standing by the windlass. 'Licence with you, me man?' he asked, with disarming politeness.

'Yes, officer, here.' Martin drew out the necessary sheet of paper.

The sergeant gave it one quick glance and handed it back. He was more interested in its owner. 'Jacobs, Martin Jacobs, eh? We know of you, my man. Californian, aren't you? Well, keep your Californian ways out of 'ere. We don't want trouble from you. Or the bloody Tipperary mob you seem to be keepin' company with. It's difficult enough tryin' to keep things calm 'ere without anyone makin' trouble among the men. Decent enough. Most of them.'

His gaze lingered and Martin felt his hands tighten around the handle of a shovel. He returned the gaze, unflinching.

'And your partner, the young Douglas boy. Let's 'ave 'im up 'ere, too.'

'Ah, he's out, gone to see his mother.'

Laughter broke out among those nearby.

The sergeant froze and his hand closed into a fist. 'If I send one of my constables down that shaft and find 'im, you'll wish you 'adn't even appeared yourself, today. Get the lad up 'ere.'

The officers closed ranks, eager now for a confrontation, their weapons menacingly ready.

'Tom, lad, you'd better come up.'

The rope tightened and Tom was winched up, cursing under his breath. His licence remained where it always did, stuffed under his bunk. They had only gone down to about thirty feet as yet in their new shaft. However, he winced in the acid sunlight as he reached the top. Scrambling out of the kibble, he was confronted by four police officers who closed quickly around him. There was to be no bolting for the scrub this time.

Quietly, methodically, the sergeant dismounted. His eyes remained fixed on the young miner and his voice was controlled, purposeful in its smoothness. 'I've seen you before, I think. Douglas, isn't it? Knew your father, too. Tough man 'e was. But 'e 'ad to be, didn't 'e, doin' what 'e did?' Then, after a short pause, he went on, his voice losing just a little of its smoothness. 'Know your mother, as well. Might get to know 'er better, too. Given time.' He stood, now, fingering the truncheon at his belt. 'Got your licence, lad, 'ave you?'

One of the constables laughed as Tom confessed he didn't.

'Pity that. You know the rules, my boy. A miner must 'ave 'his licence with 'im at all times. And back in 'is tent is not with 'im, is it? We might not like the regulations either, lad. But I'm 'ere to serve the orders of Sir Charles Hotham. And when those orders is given to my superior, Commissioner Johnston, and then to me, well, boy, I 'ave to enforce 'em, don't I?' His voice now had the smoothness of oil. There was a lingering eagerness in his eyes, the scar on his cheek seemed to glow and his face tightened into a rigid smile. 'And you don't 'ave the money to pay the fine either, I suppose?'

'No.'

'Ah, well, that's too bad. A night at the logs will certainly 'elp your memory, I'm sure of that. Pity we don't 'ave a real prison yet. But it's coming. Slips those 'andcuffs on, lads, and we'll be on our way.'

A raw mixture of panic and anger descended as the constables came forward.

Tom threw his fists into the first officer's chest and pushed him away. 'Get your bloody hands off me.'

The others were ready for this. Two threw themselves on him, forced him to the ground and pinned his arms behind him.

'That's right, lads. Get those 'andcuffs on. Sometimes lawbreakers 'ave to be 'andled rough.' Gone now was the mocking smile and the smooth voice. This was distant ice, the voice of authority. 'It's not wise to attack men who are doin' their duty, my boy. I thought your father would've taught you that. Your companion, I'm sure, will bring the money for the fine tomorrow. If not, well, lad, you'll stay until 'e does.'

Martin was quick to affirm that he would and the procession moved away. Some of the men watching booed, others remained sullen and silent. He remained, motionless for a few minutes, thoughtful as the cavalcade set off. He had seen violence on the Californian goldfields. He had witnessed men driven mad by the heat and the dust. He had seen miners ruthlessly take over claims, having driven others away. He had heard men coughing away their lives. And others, delirious from success. There was nothing new among these miners. Except that to those hardships they could now add indifference and cruelty by administrators and police. He had witnessed the police at work on the Bendigo fields. It would not take much to tip the miners there into open revolt, he felt sure of that. The same indignities were being perpetrated here at Ballarat. Time would come. A new order could be set in place. But only after the men had taken up arms. The important thing would be to stand in the gathering storm and when it broke, as break it would, be ready to harness its energy. A revolution could crumble into chaos without a firm hand at the top. Only ruthless direction could ensure that one form of corruption was not simply replacing another, one malignant growth flourishing where the old had grown and festered.

The thought had come to him, more and more often in the last few weeks, that he could supply that leadership. Not that he wanted it. Rather that it was being thrust upon him by circumstances. And the knowledge that he had experience that others did not have. He sensed, also, that others were coming to respect him and that his views were taken seriously. Yes, he would go to the camp, humbly pay the fine for his mate. But, by God, when the fire was finally lit, there would be no humility then.

As he trudged behind the mounted officers, Tom pictured the night ahead. He had peered through the fence surrounding the camp a month ago, attracted by the rattle of metal, and seen three Aborigines there. Shadows rather than men, they had huddled together, chained to stumps the miners called 'the logs'. Nobody bothered about the fate of Aborigines. Nobody really cared why they were being punished. What mattered was that they could be separated from European prisoners, even though that involved leaving them like dogs outside. Occasionally, if it was cold, a sheet of canvas might be thrown over them. That was all. Probably the rough hut, thrown up as a temporary jail, would offer him limited comfort too.

The procession entered the camp, the police contingent broke up and he was taken past the row of tents, past the neat commissioner's office and through to a shabby hut that was clearly the temporary guardhouse. A few officers lounged close by, smoking or watching with little interest.

Clearly, this was a scene they had witnessed many times. Another stubbed a cigarette and opened the door as the prisoner was led forward.

Tom blinked as he entered. The closeness and the darkness took him back to his descent into the drive and the discovery of Joe's body. A man could just as easily die in a hole like this too. He was drowning and wanted to reach up for air, to lash out as the handcuffs were removed. But something from his past restrained him. Some distant voice that warned him. 'Patience, boy. That's 'ow a man survives. And survival's what matters. Nothin' else.'

Once inside and alone, he felt the same claustrophobia he faced each time he descended a shaft. Only the window, small and barred about head high, revealed any real light. The rest of the cell was a dirty grey. Above, he could make out the heavy beams supporting the roof and on all sides the rough timber of the walls. The floor, covered in foul-smelling straw, lay like turgid water. A rat took time to stare up at him, swish his tail and leisurely disappear. Temporary it might be, but the bars looked real enough. He found himself clutching them and looking out.

He could identify all of the camp. The buildings and tents, the commissioner's office, the stables. All there for a prisoner to peruse and think upon. Above, high on its mast, floated the Union Jack, free as some mocking, exotic flower with its red, white and blue petals glowing in the sunset. All the trappings of power were here, and outside he could hear and see troopers marching in line, practising to exercise power over other men.

Sometimes, in the evening, his father had told him a little about his incarceration. Not a great deal, but enough to rouse in him a dark interest. Until now, barred windows, walls and forced solitude had seemed remote. Things he could toss around in his head. Almost like objects, harmless curiosities. But not now. The shame he had felt about his father's imprisonment and his own fears suddenly erupted and he began shaking the bars and shouting into the yard, knowing all the time that it was futile. The rat reappeared at his feet and without thinking he grabbed it by the tail, swung it round his head and hurled it against the wall. It exploded like a piece of rotten fruit, its guts spilling down the timber.

'Oh, that won't help you, laddie.'

The voice came like cold water and he turned sharply, amazed that anyone should be there with him. Sitting in one corner was a man, a grey shape only just separating itself from the darkness. All that stood out at first were a bald head, two sharp eyes and a beard.

'Frank Burgen, at your service.' The voice might have been American. 'Brought here, not for my health, I can tell you that. And you, you are?'

'Tom Douglas.' His own voice sounded weak, as if it had to be coaxed from the silence.

The other rose to his feet. He was tall and as he came forward, he limped slightly. His clothes were as ragged as Tom's. 'Douglas? Douglas? Oh, yes, I know that name. You work with my mate Martin Jacobs, I think.'

Tom nodded. 'That's right.'

Their conversation was cut short by the boom of the antique cannon out in the yard.

'I don't understand why they do that. Didn't have nonsense like that on the Californian fields. A good man, Martin. Believes in fighting for his, our, rights.' The stranger was quite animated now. He bent down, scraped up a fistful of straw and held it out. 'Ah! No way to treat honest men, this. Makin' 'em sleep on horse piss.'

'No. You're right about that.'

Tom's caution slowly melted away and the two compared grievances through the damp, cool night. They both knew that the same complaints were being aired that very night in any camp or cheap shanty on the goldfields. Unfair arrests. The lack of land. The refusal of the authorities to grant the diggers a vote. Lack of consideration and general harassment. Those were the festering wounds afflicting all of the diggers. And the two prisoners agreed that the wounds were becoming more serious as the weeks went by.

Neither slept. For a time, both fell silent. Then, at about two o'clock, the moon poked its head against the bars and Tom was aware that his fellow prisoner had moved to the bars and was standing there, peering out. He seemed almost relaxed, thoughtful and it might well have been the bullocky standing there, pensive and withdrawn as he was.

But then, as if sensing Tom's presence, he turned, his arms tightened and his voice cracked across the dark space. 'Can't expect good men to put up with the way they're bein' treated here, laddie. I saw darkies in America treated better than this. And Christ knows, they were miserable enough.' There was a brief pause. 'And good hard-workin' white men won't put up with this, I can tell you.'

Again the gaps between the bars were filled with shadow and silence returned. 'Laddie' irritated Tom, but he felt that here was a man who would be in for the fight. One who could be trusted. And he knew that some of those claiming to be with the miners could not. It was common knowledge that the authorities had planted 'ferrets' among the diggers – spies whose job was to report any troublemakers. Anyone supporting the cause of the aggrieved miners had to be careful. But the man sharing his anger here in this hole that smelled of horse piss was no ferret. When trouble came, as it would, the American would be there.

Dawn ushered a sickly, muddy trickle of light and, soon after, the door was unlocked. Two troopers entered and, ignoring Frank Burgen, they hauled Tom to his feet.

'Come on, young feller,' one of them muttered. 'Don't you want to be clear of 'ere?'

As he struggled out, he turned and looked at the figure sitting in the semi-darkened corner. 'No doubt I'll see you again, Frank.'

The reply came almost in a whisper. 'Oh yes, lad. You'll see me again.'

Officers were already out in numbers, some lazily moving in the early light, others alert and ready to march down the slope.

In the commissioner's office, Martin Jacobs stood waiting.

9

There's trouble brewin'

Three days had passed since Tom's incarceration and he had come back resentful and threatening trouble for the traps. But Martin Jacobs knew about young men's anger. It tended to bubble up or burst out and be gone. Older men, like Frank Burgen, were often better for the long haul. They knew how to feed their anger, control it and let it out only when the time was right. And the right time would come. But not yet.

Clearly, however, now was the opportunity to put his young partner to the test. Not that he couldn't trust Tom Douglas. He could certainly do that. But even men who saw themselves as seriously aggrieved might baulk at taking arms against powerful, well armed enemies. It was time to find out whether Tom was one of those. He chose his moment carefully, at night, in their tent. Shanties and public place were watched by the authorities and he knew that he was under suspicion also. His involvement in activities on the Bendigo fields had seen to that.

'There's trouble brewin' here, Tom,' he began, lighting the lantern and sitting down. 'Not yet. But it's comin'. You can see it, like I can. And hear it in the pubs. But mutterin' in shanties or making fun of the police don't make for a revolution.' He noticed the raised eyes and the quickening of attention. 'Oh, yes, lad. Justice will only come with a push. And that push will mean knockin' the commissioner and the royal lackeys in Toorak off their perches. There's no other way. Our comrades, those men who I know will be loyal to me when the time comes, aren't ready yet to throw down their picks and take up arms. It's a small group, but it's buildin' up. I'm workin' hard getting more men to join. Men like me, and you, who are sick of puttin' up with things as they are. And want to see a fair deal for all. Those I have will fight when the time comes. They'll follow. And you can be part of that, Tom. A cause, a crisis and leadership. That's all they need. With the stout lads from Creswick, we can give these corrupt officials somethin' to think about. Frank's confident, like I am.' There was a pause. He spread both hands before him, staring across the rough table between them.

Tom's surprise was evident in his fixed stare and his seeming reluctance even to move. 'Martin, I didn't know that...'

'That I was more than talk? That I'd been involved with the boys at Bendigo? And that I'd fight here, if I need to? Come on, laddie. How else can we change things? The lads in Toorak aren't goin' to listen to reason. You can see that.'

He paused again, watching the face opposite. Gradually that face was relaxing and perhaps there was even the hint of a smile.

'Now, Tom, it's up to you to decide. There's no risk in me tellin' you what I have. I know that. But no man can force you to join the cause. And, even if you don't fight with us, you'll keep quiet about what I've told you.' This was not a question and Martin made sure his voice betrayed no anxiety.

Outside, a horse snorted, a drunken man cursed, another laughed and noisily hauled his mate to his feet. But there was no reaction from within the tent. Martin waited, keeping his hands flat on the table.

In fact, Tom's decision came quickly. 'I don't need to think it over, Martin. I'm in.'

The older man stretched out his hand. 'I thought you would be. You're a lad of principle.'

In silence, they stood up and walked outside. On all sides, tents glowed like bottles along the slope. Outlined against canvas walls, the silhouette of men could be seen, and by one or two of the tents, in the glow of small fires, women were cooking.

Tom gripped his companion by the arm and in a hesitant voice went on. 'It's the, the ordinariness of it all, Martin. That's what makes it important, isn't it? My feelin' that this,' pointing to the settled camps, 'this is worth fightin' for.' He stopped, then, almost in a desperate whisper, concluded, 'And perhaps me father really wanted this, too.'

Nothing more was said until they returned to the security of their tent.

Once inside, Martin was clear to move on. His voice was confident. 'Now,' he said, leaning forward as if he was mentally rolling up his sleeves for action, 'you need to know a few things. We can't beat these bastards, as I've told you, without help from outside. And our real mates are on the Bendigo and the Creswick fields. We all know of the Red Ribbon lads at Bendigo. Our mates of the Reform League know 'em, too. There are good men in both. But I have me doubts as to whether they would take on the troops. No, our real hope lies with the Red Hand, a small band I know well workin' the Creswick field. Willing to fight, they are. I've no doubt about that.'

Martin gave these words a few moments to sink in. 'The commissioner and his men expect violence to come at Bendigo. Let 'em think that. Less snooping around here. If we have success here, then miners from other fields will join us. The Reform League boys as well. Now, Tom, your job is to go across to the boys of the Red Hand tomorrow. When you get to Creswick, make yourself known to a Ben Logan. He's our man. Irish. And the Irish are always spoilin' for a fight. You'll find him in the Tavern, a lively pub on the track in to the town. You can't miss him. He's a short feller. Thickset with a body like a tree trunk. Face like an old shoe. Let him know that we're close to somethin' big happening and that we will call on his men when the time comes. But be careful. The traps are pretty edgy at the moment."

A handshake and they lay down to sleep. Or at least Martin lay down and slept. For some time, Tom thought of the enormity of the task ahead. He remembered one occasion, on the edge of the town, standing with his father and watching the arrival of a detachment of foot police. There were ten of them, young, inexperienced, but trying to march. Their advance was so uncoordinated that a group of diggers began beating time for them. Tom had laughed along with them, but his father had gripped by the arm and muttered angrily, 'Ah, yes, boy, you may laugh now. But they're not clowns, I can tell you that. Nothin' funny in men wearing uniforms. They'll turn nasty enough when the time comes. So, laddie, you put stone in your bones, as my father would say. Stone in your bones and keep clear of men like that. I've seen too many men broken for takin' action against troops and police in my time. A man's got to survive, boy. Don't you forget that.'

And his son had not forgotten. But other men needed to survive too. And Martin had planted in his brain a way by which he could help them. A dangerous scheme, no doubt about that. But the chance to prove that life could be better. That life could be bigger than nodding at authorities and injustices.

So, in the darkness, he had committed himself to a plot to assault the might of the English Crown. A Crown long used to dealing with recalcitrant colonists. A Crown whose armies had suppressed revolts and fought successfully against other European armies. And against such power, a band of miners – labourers, sailors, teachers, clerks, unemployed, fortune hunters, all manner of people, linked only by a common sense of injustice – would be called upon to take arms.

Such are the desperate measures the desperate will advocate.

Martin did not want any unusual attention from prying eyes. Even among the hurly-burly that took place every day, he knew that spies were able to spot irregularities. He knew also that his own movements were somehow being watched. Possibly, Tom's movements might be under scrutiny as well. Better to be cautious than to be sorry later.

So they worked together through the day. Then, as the ludicrous cannon coughed out at dusk, Tom set out. He was not a confident rider and was relieved that his mount, hired from a nearby blacksmith, seemed to be quite docile. He rode slowly at first, noting the clutter of tents, huts and shanties that jostled and fought among themselves the length of the three miles of Main Road. Piles of clay and windlasses spread out like broken spokes of an abandoned wheel, showing where men had dug deep to find the buried streams perhaps one hundred feet below. He wondered whether those streams had once gleamed in the sunlight. Certainly the creeks visible now were not gleaming. They struggled under the burden of mud thrown out from puddlers or crept into foul channels created by the miners.

He was about to turn away and out to the country when he was met by Frank Burgen. Tom wondered whether Martin had paid his fine also. But the other was so quick to engage him in conversation that he did no have the opportunity to ask.

'You're out late, laddie.'

'Yes, I'm off to Creswick to meet one of Martin's mates.'

'Ah, and who might that be?'

'An Irishman, Ben Logan. Leader of the Red Hand.'

'The Red Hand, eh? A good group of lads. Take care, now.'

Tom might have worried, giving information like this to a stranger. But Martin had spoken about Frank Burgen before and his own conversation with the American had convinced him that he could be trusted.

The two parted and Tom found himself moving into land relatively undisturbed. Wattles bristled in the gullies. Long patches of open ground spilled flocks of kangaroos and soon he was surrounded by lengthening shadows and the first stars.

At one point, noticing the weak glimmer of a fire in a clearing, he stopped, dismounted and moved quietly forward. A group of Aborigines was seated around the fire, some poking at the coals, others simply staring into the slowly turning flames. Two children were playing nearby and, seeing him, they scuttled back to the group. A man rose quickly, bristling with hostility. Tom waved, mounted and moved away. The forest of gums and box trees closed around him.

Darkness came slowly and for a time he let the horse go at its own speed, while he watched the sky begin to sprinkle its collection of stars. At about eleven o'clock, he dismounted, led the horse away from the track, tied it up, wrapped himself in his heavy coat and tried to sleep.

At one point, just before he did slide into a fitful kind of sleep, he imagined he heard a horse trotting slowly on the road to Creswick.

Dawn saw him on his way again. Above the diggings of Ballarat the sky was rarely clear and he took time to enjoy the appearance of the sun. At first it was nothing but a tumble of red, a drifting mass of ribbons caught briefly in the branches of trees. But soon it shook itself clear and rose as a fierce disc, too painful to look upon.

Later, he came upon a small swamp and disturbed a flock of black swans. Their drumbeats startled his horse and he had to pacify it before stopping to watch them rise into the sly. Their wings beat rapidly in a blur of black and white. Then movement steadied and they formed into a wavy line, knitting together the sparse white clouds. Soon they were gone, hidden by the low ridges to the south.

The bush was a source of escape for Tom. Not so much because of the beauty, although he had taken time to enjoy the dawn this morning. More because of the sense of freedom. His father had never been at ease here. 'Men used to escape out into the wild, lad. Thought they could survive in country like this. Came back, most of 'em, 'alf starved or dribblin' madness about the blacks. They was flogged, chained and slunk off like dogs. Others died, their bodies found later. Better the walls of a prison than madness and death, I can tell you.'

Tom was not intimidated by the isolation. Nor did he fear black shadows erupting from the long shadows. He felt in some way superior. And he pressed on, thinking of the grand cause and the part he was to play in it.

Later, he met a solitary shepherd anxiously watching a flock of sheep as they drank at a muddy pool. He was surprised, as he approached, to see that the stranger looked to be only about sixteen years of age. They spent about half an hour together and all the while, Tom was aware that the boy's gaze seldom left his sheep.

'I've got to make sure I arrive with all of 'em safe,' he said in a reedy voice. 'Me boss 'll sack me if I lose any this time. Last week ten of 'em in a flock I 'ad disappeared. Took off through the bush. I dunno whether the blacks took 'em. Or wild dogs. But 'ell broke loose when I returned with 'em gone. Lose any more, me lad, 'e said, and you'll be gone.' The boy faltered for a moment. 'And I can't not 'ave a job, you see. Me mother and me are left by ourselves now. Since me dad took off for the diggin's.'

Tom's sympathy rose as he watched and listened. But he was relieved to be able, finally, to leave. Bloody squatters, he thought. There were too many stories like that.

It was late in the afternoon before he caught sight of the town, covered as it was by a smear of dust. Dust he knew well. Sounds he knew well, too, as he went further. Puddlers, barrows and whining windlasses have a common sound and he felt strangely at home as he came upon the tents and shafts of Creswick.

For a while he rode, almost at leisure, asking those he met whether they could direct him to the Tavern. Nobody seemed to know. The comments by one old man he came across were echoed, with slight variation, the length of the streets he rode through. 'Tavern, laddie?' he said, displaying a wide grin and few teeth, 'why, they're all taverns 'ere. Most don't even 'ave a name. Don't need one, do they? We all 'ave our favourites, don't we? Places we can get drunk with our mates. Find 'em in the dark we can.' He laughed again. 'Our problem is findin' our way 'ome afterwards. But keep lookin'. Somebody'll 'elp you.'

As he dismounted, to make enquiries in a small cottage, he was surprised to see the Reverend Thomas Hastie being ushered out.

'Ah, Tom, my boy,' he exclaimed. 'Strange to see you here. How is your mother? Well, I trust. It must be difficult living by herself, with a store and a daughter to take care of.'

Tom had inherited his father's mistrust of men in uniform and he was wary in his reply. 'Yes, thank you, sir, she's well. And so is Susan.'

The minister appeared different today. More comfortable than he had appeared the day of the funeral. He stood more upright and even his voice had a greater resonance to it. 'I have come today,' he went on, 'because I am concerned about the welfare of children. Too many of them cannot read or write. And God needs people who are educated, Tom. Girls as well as boys. And I know I must do my part.' He was serious now. His eyes rested comfortably on Tom's face. 'I have spoken to your mother about her daughter. Girls need the rudiments of reading, writing and calculation, as I have said. I trust she will consider my offer to take the child into my charge at Buninyong. Women who have some training will always make for better wives, or servants, won't they? A cultivated husband will appreciate a partner able to converse with him, won't he?'

Tom mumbled his agreement, anxious to move on.

'And,' the minister continued, 'it is possible that the fairer sex, as you young men like to call them, may even take a larger role in our society. But it will only be possible for those young women who are our intellectual equals. You can see that, I am sure.'

Tom nodded.

'Yes, my boy. You do. Perhaps you might mention our meeting to your mother? And let her know that there is still a place for her daughter in my school?'

Again Tom nodded. The minister bowed slightly and mounted his horse. Tom was surprised at the skill and the confidence he displayed. He did not expect a black-clad man of the cloth to show such facility. Given Susan's brief disappearance earlier, he was not sure what their mother's answer would be.

He knocked at the door and a woman answered, a stout matron who took exception to his request for information about a drinking house. 'My husband, young man, does not consume alcohol,' she announced. 'Not since our marriage anyway. Nor,' looking directly into Tom's eyes as she went on, 'nor does my son.'

He waited, expecting to hear 'And neither, young man, should you.' That did not eventuate. Her point had clearly been made. The door was slammed and he was left standing, embarrassed and annoyed, on the path.

Time was dragging on and he wondered whether finding Ben Logan would be as easy as Martin had insisted.

A few minutes later, he heard a sound that he was very familiar with, the hammering from a blacksmith's shop. This gave him new hope. Blacksmiths knew almost all there was to be known about small towns. Why had he not sought out the local smithy earlier? Laughing now, he rode down a slope, following the sound.

Finally, he dismounted before a rough structure giving off smell and smoke. It was no different from countless other blacksmith shops he had seen in Ballarat and neighbouring villages. No different, either, from the one his own father had taken him to see as a boy on the outskirts of Melbourne. And the hammering took him back to that day, too. And the bare arms of the smith, rising, falling, hammering now before him, were no different in their motion from those of the man his father had pointed out to him those years before.

For a few minutes, Tom believed himself to be in the company of ghosts. Smoke rose in a great cloud, hammering went on and the fire cast its glow. But he could see no one.

Then, from the darkness, there emerged the blacksmith. He was smeared in dust, stood square, almost as wide as he was tall and greeted Tom with a handshake and a wide, accommodating grin. His hand was rough and sweaty and his arms, muscly as they were, seemed more like legs. 'Now, me lad,' he beamed. 'It's a good day to you. And what can I do for you?'

Tom repeated his request and, to his delight, the blacksmith was able to give him directions.

'Yes, I know Ben, Know 'im well. And the Tavern. I drink there meself, me boy. Go straight ahead. When you get to the baker's, turn left and you'll be upon it. Or in it, dependin' on your thirst.'

Tom thanked him and turned to leave. He had not noticed a small boy, coated in dust like the blacksmith, who had entered, carrying an armful of thin metal sheets and almost collided with him.

'Ah, that's me man, Freddie. I call him that. Don't know what 'is real name is. Come in, lad.'

The boy shuffled forward, grinning. As he approached, Tom was astounded to see that he was only about ten years old and that he was an Aborigine.

The blacksmith placed his huge hand on the boy's head. "E come in 'ere about six months ago. 'Im and a wee girl 'e said was 'is sister. They both looked like they was starvin'. Couldn't turn 'em away, could I? Well, they've stayed. Both of 'em. 'E 'elps 'ere, as you can see. I don't make 'im work too hard, though. As you can see, 'e's pretty small. And 'is sister, well, she's learnin' 'ow to cook. Only simple things, mind you. But she's learnin', Freddie, isn't she?'

The boy grinned, shuffled, nodded, put down his load and disappeared outside.

'A good boy, 'e is. They just need a chance, these blacks,' he added, staring after him. 'Poor devils. I don't think we've done much to 'elp their kind.' He hesitated, then resumed his composure. 'Make most things 'ere, I do. The miners is always looking for replacements. Things they've broken or lost. Anything you can find in any smithy's I can do. And a few other things as well.'

There was another pause, during which he gave Tom a long, hard stare, as if he was unsure whether to go on. Then, taking him by the arm and apparently reassured, he went across to a large, dilapidated box hidden away in a corner. 'Includin' these.' He bent down and removed a slender, sharp object that reflected the red glow of the forge. 'Includin' these. You might wonder what they are. Well, I'll tell you. They're the 'eads of pikes. And what will they be used for? Well, I'll tell you that, too.' His face took on its broad grin again. 'Well, you could use them things for 'unting kangaroos, couldn't you?' Replacing the weapon in its box he straightened, looked piercingly into Tom's eyes and went on. 'Or a man could use somethin' like that for other things, too, couldn't 'e?'

He was deadly serious now and his voice took on a hard, almost impersonal tone. 'I makes the 'eads. And a local carpenter, 'e makes the 'andles. For those that wants to use 'em for other things. You understand that, me boy, I think.'

Tom nodded. Yes. He understood all right.

The blacksmith became jovial again. 'Well, you'd better get on your way. You don't want to be late gettin' to the Tavern. It's a popular drinkin' spot and you don't want all the grog gone by the time you get there, do you?'

Tom laughed, his hand again absorbed in the blacksmith's. 'No, I don't, that's true.'

They walked together to the door and soon he was picking his way through the tents, huts and stables towards the hotel. The blacksmith was right. It was easy to find. Past the bakery and turn left. Besides, someone had conveniently hung a sign on a nearby tree, showing in bold print, The Tavern.

He had no difficulty, either, finding Ben Logan. He appeared pretty much as Martin had described him. Wary at first as Tom introduced himself, he relaxed quickly once Martin's name was mentioned.

'Can't be too careful, here,' he said in an accent that could be nothing but Irish. 'Always better to discuss things in private. The traps don't seem to trust us Irish. I don't understand why. We like everyone. Except that is,' he went on, laughing quietly, 'except for the English.'

He led Tom outside and they sat on a stump well clear of the hotel.

Yes, there was something about these Irishmen. A directness, a blunt earthiness a man felt he could trust. Martin had been correct about that. In fact, he seemed to be pretty much right about most things.

'Now we can talk, laddie. There are about fifty of us, waiting here in Creswick. Ready for some spark to set us alight, you might say. I'm with my mate, Martin, reckonin' the fire will come among you fellows at Ballarat first. We have the same problems here, though. The same everywhere, aren't they?'

There was no need of a reply. Tom simply nodded and waited for the Irishman to go on. He did not have to wait long.

'You tell my mate, Martin, that once he gets the rest of the weapons we need, we'll be ready. He's got them comin', I know.' Suddenly he broke into a smile, the leather of his face softening. 'Ah, but we had a time of it when he was here on the field, Martin and me. Meetin's. Rallies. Men vowin' to go to jail rather than surrender. Troopers rushin' through the camps and run off their legs. Men from all over, there were, laddie. Flags flying. Languages no man could make sense of. But they was united. And most of 'em are still here. Yes, you tell Martin that once the fire's lit and we have our guns we'll be ready.'

Tom left at about four o'clock the next day, hoping to return to Ballarat by nightfall. However, his horse being slightly lame, he had to settle for a clump of trees and sleep in the open again, still some distance from the town.

Sunrise saw him on the move early. At about eleven o'clock, he could see the distant streaks of dust that surrounded the diggings. However, coming upon a large, grassy clearing, he dismounted, left his horse and decided to relax for a while himself. Silence was broken only by a small flock of gnawing cockatoos at work on a fallen tree. Unused as he was to this quietness, he decided to walk on, entering a stand of wattles. Bees fussed and buzzed among the leaves. To his left, a dog sidled away and above a ridge an eagle hung briefly in the clear air and slid out of sight.

But, in his wandering, he came upon something unexpected, a single secluded mound of earth, hidden away in a small hollow. Over its surface shadows moved smoothly and from its flanks weeds had been carefully removed. Clearly this was a well tended grave, framed by the dark trunks of wattles weeping copper rivulets of gum. Silence was now flooded with questions. Who was buried here? Why should a grave be hidden like this? The mystery became more tantalising when he noticed at the head of the grave and almost clouded over by green hanging leaves, a small jar of flowers. They were faded, reduced almost to crumpled sheets of paper.

Tom stood for a few moments, looking down. His thoughts drifted back to that other grave, the one that housed his father and he wondered whether it had been invaded by weeds. He had not revisited the site and did not know whether his mother had either. Indeed, they had rarely discussed his father after the funeral. For a moment guilt slithered into his thinking but this passed and he began to retrace his steps.

Why he bothered looking back he didn't really know. But he did, after he had walked about two hundred yards, to see a young woman approaching the grave. There was about her an obvious sense of secrecy. Apart from her long red hair, she was almost indistinguishable from the trees she crept through. In her drab grey skirt and stopping frequently to check if she was being observed, she was like some furtive animal. There was a slight ripple as she pushed aside the branches concealing the grave and stooped to throw out the faded flowers and replace them with new ones. Finally she stood up. For a couple of moments, she remained there, motionless and looking down. And then she was gone, a slim shadow receding into the trees.

Tom waited for a few moments and then he, too, turned away. But before he had moved very far, something else caught his attention. He had not been alone watching this strange ritual. Crouched about a hundred yards away and hidden beneath a fallen tree was a man. Clearly, watching intently as the girl disappeared, he had not noticed Tom. His attention next moved to the trees concealing the grave. Then he, too, was gone.

Slowly Tom picked his way back to his horse, feeling a strange and unaccountable need to be secretive himself. He could make nothing of this small drama and soon, as the tents of the Ballarat diggings began to emerge and he was immersed in the daily dramas he knew well, the event faded. But not completely, and over the next few days the grave, the gliding figure and the stationary watcher were to creep back often into his consciousness. Not as often, however, as the explanation and its aftermath. They were to haunt him for much longer. For the moment, however, his task was to report back to Martin Jacobs.

There was a sense of comfort, of familiarity, as he returned the horse and picked his way on foot back to their claim. A few men he knew waved. Others peered out from their shafts. Shanties bubbled with noise and the small party of Chinese nodded and smiled. He waved in return, thinking back to the help they had given him in burying Joe Tyler.

When he arrived at the tent, Martin was seated with Frank Burgen. A horse, presumably Frank's, stood chewing what feeble grass had been left undisturbed. Both of the men were keen to hear of events in Creswick.

He gave them a detailed account of his meeting. But he kept the story of the girl and the grave to himself.

10

Feathers

The routine of daily work took over, of course, as it must. However, the picture of the girl and the mystery surrounding her appearance remained. As, too, did the memory of the secret conversation with the agitator in Creswick.

However, there was another personal issue that nagged: his relationship with the Welsh bullocky, Dan Morgan. He didn't dislike him. There was no reason for that. He was easy enough to talk to, easier than his own father had been. Certainly less critical. No, his irritation, if it could be seen as that, came from the fact that the bullocky was obviously forming a relationship with his mother. For some reason, inexplicable even to himself, he held on to some sort of loyalty to his father. And, each time he saw his mother, obviously comfortable with the bullocky, this irritation niggled.

On this particular day, seeing Dan Morgan arriving at the store, he decided to return to the camp early, his excuse being that he wanted to look at what was happening to the land a few miles west of the town. He had heard, or at least he said he had, of new claims being taken up and wanted to look at prospects there.

He rode slowly away, surprised at the rapid changes taking place in the landscape. Much of the country was being cleared. Many places that had been thickly covered with stringybarks and red gums were now open grasslands cloaked with large stretches of kangaroo grass and bracken fern. On the edge of one clearing, he came upon a small group of miners he knew. They were busily splitting timber for a new shaft they were sinking on Canadian Gully. In the distance, he could hear the thump of axes and knew that other miners, too, were out chopping and carting.

In a small gully a mile further on, he saw a simple wooden hut. Around it a rough fence had been erected and by the back door there were vegetables growing. There would be many more like this, he thought, once the squatters were forced to give up their hold on the land. And forced they would be.

On one slope, he even encountered a man planting potatoes. Close by, a little girl, in a spotless white dress, was skipping, counting as she did so. Two older boys were climbing a tree. The girl laughed and waved. The boys were too busy to notice his passing. Their father, straightening from his work, called out a greeting. Tom waved back. He knew this man. Knew, also, that his wife had died of a fever and that he was staying as an employee of one of the emerging mining syndicates. 'No choice,' he had said once. 'Three kids to support and I can't afford to leave.'

He had not forgotten that comment. You'll get your chance, he thought, as he rode past. Fairer times are coming for honest battlers like you.

Some areas he rode through were relatively undisturbed. Here kangaroos and emus roamed at will, darting off only as he came close.

'There'll be more than me to frighten the devil out of you,' he muttered at one point as a family of emus burst away. 'The bloody squatters'll be coming soon with their cattle and their sheep. There won't be much room for you then, will there?'

On a bend of the track, he met a small group of Chinese. There were six of them, six men bent in a solid group, walking and chattering in that high-pitched way that annoyed so many of the European diggers. He noticed their intensity and their short shuffling steps, characteristics that made them easily identifiable. It was as if they were never quite sure whether they should run or walk. They certainly ran enough, though, when the Europeans took after them, scuttled like startled rabbits if they were seen fossicking over mullock heaps left by other miners. And earlier, Tom might have hounded them too. But now, after his experience by the shaft and the intervention of the Chinese diggers, he felt something else, a curiosity, a desire to learn more about their strange customs, a

126

wish to understand their secrecy and their strong sense of togetherness. He had seen them often, smoking inside their tent, had listened to their conversations, conversations that, to him, were more like the meaningless jabberings of exotic birds. And he had felt the power of the silences that came upon them when they were forced to rub against other miners in the streets. Now he felt a strange sense of kinship.

The six moved towards him with the lassitude of men who had come a long way. They were really small dusty mounds on skinny legs, so heavily laden were they with equipment. Seeing him, they stopped. One, a man of about sixty, was obviously distressed. He was short, emaciated, and his face was lined and gaunt. His loose-fitting clothes might once have been white. Now they were grey with dirt. Poor devil, Tom thought. If I'd walked as far as you have I'd be worn out too. Needing a place for my bones to rest.

The man switched on the automatic smile peculiar to the Chinese he had met and asked in broken English how to get to the diggings.

Tom did his best, instructing him as clearly as he could to follow the bullock tracks. It made little sense until he bent down and pointed to the clear ruts of the wheels. 'Follow those,' he said, slowly and deliberately. 'You won't get lost.'

The man smiled, nodded, his pigtail bobbed and he led the group onwards. Probably, Tom thought, the Europeans crowding on Canadian Gully and Eureka wouldn't even blink if they did get lost. But he would.

Yes, he had changed his view of these strange Orientals who knew so little English and yet had taken up their shovels and bent their backs to help him bury a dead mate. And then, having done so, had simply smiled, nodded and gone their way.

He also admired their tenacity. He knew that many had walked long distances to take their chances on the Victorian fields and guessed that this struggling band had done the same. Dan had told him recently about a group of ten he had met on the track through the western district and had described their determination, their willingness to persist through rain or blazing sun, plodding and surviving with no help from the settlers or other travellers.

A long, dangerous trip it must be, Tom thought, watching the group slowly being absorbed into the grey of the bushland. Rocking and tossing on the sea in leaking boats and then confronting the harsh conditions of the Australian bush. And all the while being rejected or shunned by the Europeans. Many argued that they simply benefited from the back-breaking work of others by fossicking through the tailings of abandoned shafts. Also, some believed they would be bringing diseases. Also, their food stank and no one could understand what they said. Even Martin had shown his disapproval. The battle for rights on the goldfields, he maintained, would be fought for hard-working Europeans, not these invaders from completely alien lands. Democracy was something they would never be able to understand.

Tom waited until the party had completely disappeared before moving on.

By a shallow creek, he came upon a semi-naked Aborigine, a man of perhaps thirty years of age who stood by a tree, a spear in his right hand and looking directly towards the water. It was his stillness that captured Tom's attention. He was more a growth from the earth itself than a creature able to move upon it. To an observer, there was something mesmerising in his attention, the tenseness of his body and the long, gleaming weapon. Tom had heard many times of shepherds alone at dusk, knowing that they were being watched, yet unable to make out anything except trees and shadows around them. Others, he knew, had been found murdered in land that was quite open. A trickle of fear ran down his body, but he felt also a shaft of admiration for the confidence and the intensity. The man was naked from the waist up. In the bright sunlight, his skin glowed, the muscles on his arms stood out, smooth and taut. Across his chest were scars. And about him there was a sense of confidence, that of the hunter at home in his territory. His utter focus and stillness gave him the appearance of a statue.

Now, looking across the shallow pool, Tom saw a single kangaroo grazing quietly, moving back and forth in slow, rhythmic hops, stopping to look around, then lowering its head again. The tension of the moment was inescapable. And, hoping to see more, he crept forward. Suddenly there was an eruption of movement and the kangaroo crashed away through the undergrowth. The Aborigine turned, straightened, waved angrily at Tom, pointed to where the animal had been and disappeared. Not like the 'roo in a wild rush, but melting quietly into the shadows.

There was a simple, primitive dignity about all of this that kept him surprised and motionless long after the man had gone. More than surprised, in fact. Try as he might, peering out into the hollow that had been filled by the black warrior, he could not hide a sudden pang of guilt. Guilt that he had intruded, blundered clumsily into something where a European had no place.

No. This man was not like those others he had seen lounging like inscrutable shadows around the town or making themselves drunk in secluded corners. Nor was this the frightened boy clutching out at his hand as the two hung above the shaft. Here was a man comfortable in his world, confident in his ability to survive and showing anger only when that world was blundered into by an outsider. He wished that he could call the stranger back, set the kangaroo in its place and let things resume their ancient course.

Finally, on the edge of what he assumed was Yuille's Swamp, so large was the area, he encountered a group of about fifteen Europeans, men and women. They were gathered together as if bent on one common task. Behind them, a long shambling row of wattles cast uneven shadows. In front lay a shallow creek, a sickly, torn ribbon that unrolled itself lazily through a huddle of reeds and into the swamp about two hundred yards away. One of the men looked up as Tom approached, then, as if reassured, turned again to the gathering.

On a slight incline, half hidden behind a pile of rocks, stood three Aboriginal women. One held a small child tightly in her arms. She seemed oblivious to the fact that the baby was crying. Her breasts stood out, full and glowing brown. The other two were much older and stooped, their shoulders covered by what Tom thought were roughly sewn possum skins. All three were watching closely what was happening below. But where the hunter had portrayed confidence in his stillness, these three seemed almost overcome with fear. Their eyes never shifted from the group below.

Tom dismounted, tethered his horse and walked over. He guessed, from their clothing, that the men were miners. They all wore heavy, grey trousers and bright shirts. Some had impressive-looking hats perched firmly on their heads. The common uniform of diggers. The women, he supposed, were their wives. They were following closely a movement to their left and took little notice of his approach. It was a halting kind of movement, almost a stumble that riveted their attention. Clearly, someone was being brought, or rather dragged, forward by two men. The group parted and the three spilled out into the clearing, stopping to confront the watchers. On the faces of the audience, for that was what they seemed to be, there was an air of excitement. So intent were they that they did not respond as one of the Aboriginal women shrieked and ran off. Nobody spoke.

A spectator himself now, Tom peered through the group towards the three central actors. The two men, rigid as statues, held between them a girl. She might have been seventeen or eighteen and her face was white with fear. Down her shoulders poured a mass of red hair. What had been a neat grey skirt and white blouse were covered in dust. Her terror welled up and burst out in a series of incoherent cries and convulsive tears. But no arm lessened its hold. No word of sympathy crept out. At a precise moment, one of the women stepped forward and gripped the prisoner's hair. There was a sharp animal cry of fear and for a moment the woman paused.

Tom turned to one of the men. 'What's goin' on here?' he asked.

'Ah, lad, punishment, that's what's going on. A tarring and a feathering. Not nice. But it has to be done. We haven' got any tar so we're using molasses.'

A few of the crowd laughed at this point and, from somewhere close, another voice chipped in. 'Aye, a tarrin' and a featherin'. Ain't never seen one before.'

'A what? What the hell are you talkin' about?'

The first speaker was quite matter of fact now. He was like a school teacher explaining something important. 'Yes. A young girl. Eighteen perhaps. She works in a hotel on Bakery Hill. A few months ago, her brother raped a woman in the bush near Buninyong. A party of miners took off after him, chased him and finally cornered him. Not far from here either. The young bastard drew a gun and wounded one of 'em. When they caught him, well, they hanged him. Hacked him up and left the remains.' Satisfied with the adequacy of his response, the man looked back at the girl and her captors.

'But that girl over there? What has she got to do with that?'

A new speaker broke in, gripping Tom briefly by the shoulder. 'Poor be damned. Mad, if you ask me. Gathering up the bits and pieces of a bastard who'd just raped one of her kind and burying them. No need for sympathy there, boy. Buried 'em somewhere in the bush, she did. That much we knew. Took flowers there, too. We had no idea where until a few days ago. Then one of our lads saw her on the track, followed her and saw what she was at. This is punishment, lad. That's all. Nothing you need do.'

The mystery was now solved, the identity of the girl and the grave revealed. His response was panic, a panic that hardened into anger. Not the cold, calculating anger of his father. This was much more. A blind, uncalculated upheaval.

He lunged out, pushing the man beside him to one side. 'Stop! You can't do this! She's done nothing. This isn't justice.'

His outburst raised only a ripple.

The man quickly recovered and with two others he gripped Tom, holding him fast. 'We told you, laddie. This is only punishment. It's got nothin' to do with you.' The eyes staring into his were cold and the mouth taut. 'Nothin'. You keep out of it.'

His struggles persisted but the arms were like iron. 'Bastards, you are. Punishing this girl for something she had no part of. Bastards, the lot of you.'

No one was listening now. There was a shout and on the edge of the clearing the girl toppled at the feet of the two men who had dragged her forward. Sunlight glinted on a tin and a brown, slow liquid poured down. Her hair, that smooth rush of colour that had caught Tom's attention and slid so smoothly through the light, now hung in ugly thick strands, blotched and caked where the molasses had fixed itself. Her blouse had been ripped away, revealing her throat, shoulders and breasts, all heaving beneath a sickly brown scum. Only her grey skirt, the one that had drifted so silently through the wattle branches, remained intact. Her face, round and contorted with terror, shook and her eyes sought frantically for escape.

Then, on a signal, one of the women brought forward a bucket. There was an outburst of laughter and from its gaping mouth there tumbled a shower of feathers. Some sank and settled like slow falling snow at the girl's feet. Others clung to her body. For a moment, all movement ceased. Arms fell away from their hold and she collapsed. This was the sign for the crowd to make one last assault. Shouts, whistles and curses rang out. And above this discordant ecstasy she screamed. It was long and high-pitched, a scream that reached a crescendo and then fell back to a lingering wail.

The job was now complete. The audience drew back, some silent and some muttering. One or two of the women lingered on, looking almost fearfully at the victim.

The Aboriginal women stood in full view now, their eyes wide open.

Hands gripping Tom fell slack. 'There, lad. Had to be done.'

A black, cold surge of anger ran through him. Wrenching himself free, he pushed his way forward. No one endeavoured to stop him now. Like the girl, he could be passed over. Tension and excitement evaporated and the crowd began to disperse. Taking off his coat, he wrapped it around the pitiful figure. There was no resistance, just a helpless acceptance. Then, reaching down, he stood the girl on her feet. She did not look up but clung in his arms, her tears and her trembling unchecked.

'There, look at her now!' he thundered. 'Satisfied, are you?'

There was no response. Just a slow turning of heads, a residue of interest. Three older women remained, picking a few drifting feathers from their hair. A fourth, much younger, picked up the bucket while the men trickled away, one or two of them breathing heavily as if they had been involved in some frenetic activity.

Soon the clearing was empty, except for the Aboriginal women, who stood as if waiting for permission to leave.

No word came from the weeping girl as Tom lifted her on to his horse. Molasses continued to slide down her skirt and some of the feathers fluttered free.

It was dark when he arrived back at the store and deposited the still trembling girl into his mother's keeping.

11

A mystery solved

Martin Jacobs sensed that something was wrong. His partner's silence told him that. True, the work went on as usual. But Tom's movements were almost mechanical, detached from what was going on around them. And in the evenings, he would wander out into the darkness, say nothing to those he knew quite well and finally return to the tent, lock himself away in thought and then fall into restless bouts of sleep.

He began to fear that the lad was simply losing confidence, both in himself and in the cause he had committed himself to. And, indeed, there was much truth in this, although not for the reasons he might have suspected. What reduced Tom to silence was the realisation that the men who had humiliated the girl were miners like him. Like Martin. Miners who had pledged loyalty to a noble cause. Men Martin had told him were the very metal needed for revolution. Men worthy of great deeds. Those same men he could see, in the semi-darkness when work had finished, going about their usual tasks or yarning by a fire. Tomorrow would see them grey, anonymous shadows among hundreds of other grey shadows, all going about their honest labours, following the same routines that governed his own life.

What troubled him most was the sinister pleasure the men and the women found in tormenting their victim. Some of the women, he felt, would have been happy to see her stripped naked. And the lust of the men and the delight they took in her frantic efforts to escape were as strong as their avowed intention to wreak revenge on her.

He remembered, too, his own excitement as he had lifted her on to his horse. The warmth of her body as she clung to him on the ride away. And her bending and yielding as he lifted her down outside his mother's store. How different all of this was, he thought more than once over those troubled days, from the kindness his mother had shown. She had been quick to take charge when he arrived and by the time he left, soon after, she was heating water to wash the filth away and preparing to wash the girl's clothes.

He wondered, in the course of the next few days, what had happened to her: whether she had stayed with his mother or had simply disappeared, afraid of further acts of cruelty. There was, too, a sense of guilt that he had not been able to intervene. Also, and it troubled him to think this, what would Martin have done?

Certainly, all around him circled as it had always done. Work flowed and rattled. Miners nodded and shouted to him as they descended into shafts or scrambled out in the evening. There were the same tired eyes, the same drooped shoulders, the same intake of fresh air as men surfaced at dusk. No indication of men guilty of involvement. No mistrustful glances at him. And over everything there circled the same cloud of dust. Here, as always, was the rough, simple purpose of men labouring for gold. But he sensed that something within him had changed. Something had been loosened.

There was, also, a real problem that helped turn his attention, the need for a third partner. The shaft now was too deep for them to work it by themselves. Martin had asked Frank Burgen to join them but he had refused. He was, he said, working with a larger syndicate, one that had bottomed at over ninety feet into promising material. There was nothing like the discovery of a buried creek bed to ignite hope and he, understandably, did not want to leave. No one would leave a syndicate that looked as if it was on to something. His refusal disappointed Martin. However, Tom had been grateful, without being sure why. They would find someone else.

So, gradually, he let himself be drawn back into the rhythm of the slope. Then, on the following Thursday, he received a shock.

Early in the morning, even before the cry of 'Joe, Joe' could galvanise men into evasive action, a party of police and soldiers descended on a claim and carted off two miners. Their uniforms, blue for the police, red and black for the soldiers, always made them conspicuous on the slopes. Up until the last few weeks, the sight of the colourful procession had either infuriated the miners or amused them. On one occasion, a miner, laughing at the bright glow of the soldiers' uniforms, had suggested that he could supply them with red lipstick, to complete the picture. And one of the soldiers had laughed. But no one laughed now.

Licence hunts were more intimidating. They occurred often and at irregular intervals. And with the police there came many more troopers, armed with muskets and fixed bayonets. One could taunt police officers armed with truncheons and pistols that were notoriously inaccurate, particularly when they came with only minimal support from the soldiers. But it was very risky now when larger detachments of troops accompanied them. There was nothing comical about the flash of sun on sharp steel or muskets that could kill over hundreds of yards.

As one would expect, rumours flourished: brief comments passed in a bar were transformed into half truths, half truths into gospel. And, by this time, miners were quick to make judgements about the authorities. Harsh judgements that, in these clouded times, turned out often to be accurate. Miners who had been to Melbourne came back with information that harsher conditions were to be imposed on the diggers. Hence the increased presence of the troopers.

Clearly, the theatrical show of weapons today, the shouted instructions, the handcuffing and the parading of two popular men down Main Road, were intended to cow the observers. The authorities, nervous about the rumblings among the thousands of men here and elsewhere, were going to make sure that the miners would know the consequences awaiting them if they took to arms.

Most watched in grim silence or shook their fists. Only a few shouted obscenities at the police and the soldiers. Whatever their reaction, the miners now kept their distance. However, it was a relief for Tom to sense the old anger still present. This was the righteous anger, the anger that had both cause and target. It was good to let himself be drawn back to it.

He stood by the windlass, waiting for his mate to appear from the tent. The arresting party was already out of sight and around him the day was beginning to take its usual shape. Barrows began their torturous journeys between piles of clay. Buckets lurched and clattered. Voices took up their nondescript cries and shouts. And even a few children emerged, scampering between tents. But, amidst the confusion of sounds, one stood out. One that captured Tom's attention.

'Bloody Miller. Bring the bastard close enough to me and I'd give him a taste of this. Him and Commissioner Rede. I'd ram it up their arses if I had the chance.'

Curious, Tom glanced across. A bent old miner was holding aloft his pick. And the voice had a ring of familiarity. Where had he recently heard it?

'Honest battlers, those two. Germans. They won't even understand what they're supposed to have done wrong.' The miner maintained his statuesque, defiant pose then slowly lowered his pick. Noticing Tom's interest, he stared across. Here was the hard, creased face of one of the men who had justified the treatment of the girl on the edge of Yuille's Swamp. There was a flicker of recognition and the voice took on a sharp edge. 'Don't worry, lad. The day of reckonin' is coming. You saw how us miners can dish out punishment.'

Tom stared back. 'Yes, I saw that.'

The stranger shrugged and spat theatrically into the clay at his feet, and Martin emerged from the tent.

At the end of the day, they decided to head down to the small hotel they often frequented. It took longer now. Main Road was becoming more and more cluttered with buildings that almost fell over one another in their rush to find a place. Stores stood where a few months ago nothing existed but deserted shafts or piles of clay. Grocers fought for space with concert halls, barbers rubbed shoulders with blacksmiths, the Hedlington Hotel vied with Charlie Napier and the

Washington. John Alloo's Chinese restaurant attracted the regulars and the curious. And everywhere, a man could get drunk. At odd spots, the road would take a brief turn. Here, the interests of commerce and mining had clashed and commerce had been forced to yield.

'Things are changin', lad,' Martin muttered as they came to their hotel. 'And we need to make sure that when this rotten administration is swept away, we can direct what happens next. There's plenty here who'll want to twist things for themselves. Can't have that happen.' At the door, he paused and pointed back at the tumble of buildings and the road. 'Ah, yes. Hardly the same as it was a few months ago, is it? And with a bit of a nudge, they'll change even more.' His fists clenched for a moment and he looked directly into Tom's face, almost as if he accused him of imposing the injustices on the fields. 'And when that happens, as it will, well, we need to be ready, lad. Ready to grab the tiller and make things go in the right direction.'

He had not finished yet and when they sat down he went on, this time, slapping his companion on the shoulder. 'And ready we'll be, me boy. But now for a drink, eh?'

What the right direction would be, he did not say. Did he even know? And what plans were afoot after the assault and destruction of the administration? These were basic, important questions. But, in the midst of turmoil and the expression of lofty principles, Tom Douglas did not ask them. Commitment to a cause and loyalty to Martin were enough. Particularly when that commitment was so readily reinforced by comments passed so freely in the bar.

For some time, the two sat in silence, listening and watching the comings and the goings around them. There was a pattern here that rarely changed. A pattern that Tom welcomed. There was reassurance in the rhythm, the yarns, the laughter, the complaints and the crude jokes made at the expense of police and officials. There were miners he recognised now. Pubs were beginning to attract a regular clientele. And the familiarity gave Tom a sense of confidence: here were many others who shared the same suffering, the same hard work and the same hopes. Often, even in silence, this solidarity was conveyed. Also, many, like him, were waiting, though some of them perhaps were not at all sure what they were waiting for. But waiting and expecting they were.

When Martin broke the silence, there was a thoughtful, almost fatherly tone in his voice. 'There'll be a revolution here, Tommy. I've no doubt about that. But revolutions can fail. Fail if there isn't firm leadership. Look at these lads. Waitin', they are. Men burning with a cause. Waitin'. But needing someone to lead 'em.' He stopped, waiting for the words to register. Then, looking far off, as if conjuring up figures from the shadows, he went on, 'Never been to France meself. But me grandfather had. A tough old character, he was. Had been a sailor and ended up stranded in France for a while. Told me about his time there.' His voice now was gathering intensity, as if he was reliving a personal experience.

Tom waited, bemused. What relevance did the experience of a man long since dead have for the battlers in Ballarat now?

'He went there during the troubles of the 1790s. Told me all about it. Only a lad, I was, of course. A dangerous place, he said. The citizens of Paris had taken up arms, brought the Bourbons down. Bringin' 'em down, well, according to him, that was the easy part. After that, well, madness set in, lad.' Now Martin was there, in the heart of Paris. His voice was like a taut rope. 'Madness. Violence in the streets. People were murdered, beheaded. The innocent along with the guilty. It was fine, talkin' about liberty and equality, he said. But, putting them into practice, well, that wasn't so easy.'

Again the pause, this time to allow Martin to catch his breath and his composure. He took a long, slow drink before continuing. 'He didn't stay long in the city, I can tell you. Glad he was to leave. But long enough to see the city tearin' itself apart.' Again, a pause, but this time, to make sure he had his young companion's full attention. 'And why do I tell you this, lad? Well, to show that revolution by itself isn't enough. Leadership. That's what's needed. And unless strong men take charge when things blow here, the same might happen. We don't need a Napoleon Bonaparte, here, laddie, do we?'

Whether Tom Douglas had even heard of Napoleon did not matter now. Martin had made his point. But he had not quite finished yet. 'Like I said, there are enough hotheads here to take action, but they'll end up runnin' around like roosters with their heads cut off. That mustn't happen, my lad. Must not happen.' Martin pointed directly across the table as he said this, sweat gleaming on his forehead and his hands trembling slightly. 'Cool heads are what'll be needed. You can see that, can't you?'

The answer came almost as a whisper. 'No, the right men must take charge. That's true.'

But who were the right men? That was the question. And Tom felt an uneasiness as he looked across at the flushed face opposite.

Nothing more was said. There was time, now, to refocus on what was happening around them. More men had come in and the bar was filled with greetings, laughter and the smell of sweat and beer. To be swept up in this was often reassuring. But today Tom had something particular on his mind. He hoped that Dan Morgan, who often came here, might be sitting in his usual corner. He would probably know something about the girl. Unfortunately, it looked as if today the bullocky was not here.

Frank Burgen was and, while he waved to both Martin and Tom as they came in, it was clear that he was in animated discussion with two other men. He was watching, also, the miners and tradesmen who came tramping into the bar. Occasionally his fingers would drum upon the table as he indicated a particular individual.

Martin had noticed this also. 'He's a cagey one, all right, Tom. A shrewd businessman. He'll be lookin' out for some new possibility. Some new dealer he might come to an agreement with. He's always been like that. He'll be pointin' 'em out to his wealthy mates there. Did pretty well on the Californian fields, he did. I've never quite found out how. But he's cunning. I know that. And he'll be lookin' out for news that might help us, too, I know that as well.'

Talk swelled around them and they let themselves drift along with the general conviviality that beer and cheap grog would always evoke among labouring men.

Suddenly, Tom looked up to see Dan Morgan coming directly towards them. His steps were quick, not measured and slow as they usually were. And he was leaning forward, clearly agitated about something. Shouldering his way past the men standing at the bar, he made a brief comment of greeting and then motioned Tom outside.

In his corner, Frank Burgen was again quietly tapping on the table.

Once outside, Dan spoke quickly and quietly. 'There are two people here I think you should meet, Tom.' He said nothing else but turned abruptly and led the way out along the road.

Some distance from the hotel and almost hidden between two shops stood Dan's cart. On it, almost huddled together on the back seat, were two figures. So heavily concealed were they under heavy cloaks that they almost blurred into one. There was no comment from either as Tom and Dan clambered aboard. All that stood out were two single flames of red hair welling out from beneath their bonnets. Their faces were nothing more than brief sketches.

The bullocky took the reins and flicked them over his pony. 'Don't say anything yet, Tom. Wait until we're well away from here.'

He drove quickly but carefully, stopping only when they were out in the open country. Then, jumping down, he tethered the pony, helped the two figures to alight and waited for Tom. Now he was again, slow, deliberate and patient. Taking his pipe from his pocket, he lit it and stood back as little rivulets of smoke curled away. 'Now, madam, it's up to you, I think.'

There was a slight movement. One of the cloaks was drawn back and Tom was amazed to see, peering out from its folds, the face of Madame Hortense. She of the flowing costume, the theatrical gestures and the extraordinary voice. The famous actress come to teach the miners and businessmen of Ballarat the values of culture. But there were no gestures from the stage today. Gone were the paint and the facial contortions. This was the face, the unpretentious face, of a very ordinary middle-aged woman. A woman who, after a flicker of a smile, stared at him with genuine seriousness.

'You may not remember me, Tom,' she murmured. 'That is your name, I believe. I came to you as Madame Hortense. That's not my real name and I'm not French. Your mother, I think, guessed that. Who I am and what my real name is do not matter.' Even the voice was plain. No fake lilting. No foreign affectation. 'And this, this is my daughter.'

The second figure came forward, almost reluctantly. A small hand was raised cautiously, slowly. A bonnet was removed and the same flurry of red hair came tumbling forward. But the cloak remained, fixed in its place. He could not conceal the surprise he felt. This was the girl he had wanted to save at Yuille's Swamp. And had failed.

Her voice, high-pitched and almost childlike though it was, carried the same seriousness as her mother's. And it was far removed from the terror he had heard that day. 'Yes. You remember me, don't you?'

She was not pretty. Her face was round and the freckles that ran over her cheeks gave her an impish, if vaguely comical, appearance. But there remained that vulnerability, that fragility that had excited him on their ride back to the store.

Before she could go on, her mother placed a hand on her shoulder. 'I wanted to thank you. I have already thanked your mother. Both of you have been very kind.' Tom was about to speak but she held up her hand. 'But there is something else I would ask of you. And I have already asked your friend whether he would take us. My daughter is too afraid of returning there by herself. You will understand why, I think. Would you accompany us back to,' and there was a brief pause here, 'to my son's grave?'

Tom glanced across at the bullocky. He had not moved during these revelations. But behind a cloud of smoke there was the hint of a nod.

'Yes, Madame Hort— Yes, madam, I'll do that.'

The mother smiled. 'I thank you. I wanted to visit it before we set out for Melbourne. We do not wish to stay here longer, longer than is necessary.'

Tom waited for a moment, expecting more explanation. But it was not forthcoming.

He helped the two to board again and Dan guided the cart out along the Creswick Road. Presumably they had no fear of being recognised now, for their faces and hair were clearly visible. Few travellers paid any attention to them anyway. Women were appearing more and more often on the roads these days and where a few months ago excited shouts or whistles might have greeted the sight of these two, today there was silence.

Under the direction of the girl, Dan stopped the cart near the spot where Tom had entered the bushland those few days earlier. It was almost sunset now. Long shadows were already creeping out from the trunks of the wattles and spilling out over the clearings. Far off, a single strand of smoke marked an early campfire. But here quietness prevailed. A kookaburra lumbered away as they approached. A dog stiffened in a small clearing, watched and trotted away.

Mother and daughter were cautious now. They looked around as they walked but did not endeavour to recapture their hair or hide their faces. The girl led the way, stopping frequently to peer back. Finally, they reached the secluded corner where the rough curtains of branches and leaves concealed the grave. She drew them back so her mother could push her way through.

The two men remained at some short distance and Tom found himself peering back into the advancing shadows. Then he and Dan stepped into the small clearing also. The girl was holding her mother's hand. On her face was a weary sadness, as if she had come a long way and her work was done. Her mother stood almost fiercely upright, her face quite impassive. Then she turned towards the two men. Tears suddenly broke out and coursed down her cheeks.

'I know what he did,' she half whispered. 'Melanie, here, has told me. And I cannot excuse him. It was a dreadful thing he did. I came to Ballarat some time ago, knowing that he'd already been in trouble with the law and was wanted by the police in Melbourne for theft. He and my daughter, the dear loyal girl you see with me now, had come here seeking work. And,' there was a dull resignation in her voice now, 'I hoped he might escape capture and find honest work. You might judge me harshly, but I…I was his mother. And a mother, well, she wants to defend her children, doesn't she?' She was looking directly and pleadingly at the two men now. 'I came to try and help him after Melanie wrote and told me that he had been unsuccessful. But I had little money. That's why I became Madame Hortense. I didn't know how long I'd have to stay. I have, in fact, been an entertainer, you see. I dared not use my own name, of course. The police would have used me to find him then.' She paused again, turning back to the mound of earth now disappearing into the shadows. 'But, as you see, I came too late.' She faltered again, but quickly regained her composure. 'I must thank you both again. I just wanted to visit the…the place where his remains lie. Before we return to Melbourne.'

Dan moved forward to help her back through the branches. But she motioned him away, at the same time struggling to contain her tears. Soon they were back on the road.

The mother climbed quickly back to her seat. Clearly she had done what she wanted to do and was ready to leave. Her face conveyed no feeling. Her eyes were fixed ahead. Any sign of tears was gone. This blankness was more unnerving for the two men than any show of emotion would have been. Neither could think of any words of comfort. Neither had the courage even to speak.

In fact, all movement seemed to stop. It would start again only when she indicated it was time. And eventually, drawing the cloak more tightly around her shoulders, she nodded almost imperceptibly.

Then, in a voice that seemed to fall like cold, clear water, she murmured, 'Thank you. Could we go now?'

Relieved, Tom turned to help the girl climb up. Again he felt the unsettling closeness, the muscles of her waist tense as he lifted her and the yielding of her body as he released her. 'I suppose,' he asked, hesitantly, 'I suppose that…that I will not see you again?'

He imagined, even in the half-light, that there was a faint tinge of pink between the freckles. Perhaps even a hint of a smile. However, before she could answer, her mother leaned across, taking her daughter's hand.

'No, Tom, it would be too dangerous for Melanie here now, after what's happened. We must return to Melbourne. I've rented a small cottage near the bridge over the river. It leads into the centre of the town. And, with all of the traffic there, we may go unnoticed. It's not a pretty area. But we'll be safe there.'

Tom could not clearly see the girl's face. But her voice carried, perhaps, just a suggestion of regret. 'Yes, I'm sorry. My mother's right. I can't stay in this town now.'

They made their way in silence back through the falling darkness, arriving at a small hotel on the Melbourne road.

'This will be safe enough,' announced the mother as she alighted. 'I enquired earlier. The innkeeper takes us for two travellers returning to Melbourne after visiting my brother who's a blacksmith on the edge of the town. Safe enough anyway for one night. Until we catch the Melbourne coach in the morning.'

There was no hesitation now. Just a matter-of-fact voice and a quick word of thanks. The women disappeared quickly, the mother waving briefly, the daughter pausing and smiling up at the two men.

Soon the cart was again bumping, occasionally gliding over those few smooth sections of the road, back towards the camp. Night, now, was a heavy, patched curtain, through which scattered light peered out. Here a half-open tent, there a swinging lantern, over there a huddle of mushrooms moving together. At one point, they slid past a long pool of yellow that oozed out from a cheap hotel and washed a partly built fence. Propped against one wall of the hotel stood a woman. Tom guessed she might have been forty. Her breasts and waist were tightly, cunningly held in place. Her hair fell provocatively down over her face and almost mechanically she would sweep it back, revealing the nakedness of her neck and shoulders. Her eyes followed the advance of a thick-set man who was swaying towards her.

Dan withdrew his pipe 'Hard for women out here, Tom. Too many end up like that.' His hand pointed to the prostitute and the pipe made a narrow trail of red. 'Probably honest when she came here. Not much left for them now, though, is there? Once they're reduced to this.' The pipe was returned to its rightful place, there were a few puffs of smoke and the journey continued.

Tom made no comment. But he looked back. The woman had circled the man with her arms and he was leaning forward. No. There was not much left now, was there? Nothing tonight, in fact. If the miner had no money.

Again they were floating through broken patches of light and the camp was quite close. Suddenly Tom was aware of the bullocky turning towards him and again removing his pipe.

'Your mother, Tom, is a pretty remarkable woman, survivin' here and makin' a living for herself and the wee Susan. But I suppose you know that?'

The answer was slow in coming. Partly because Tom had never really considered his mother as being remarkable. More because of the old irritation surfacing within him. Eventually, he stumbled, 'Yeah, I guess she is that. Pretty strong, I mean.'

On their return to the camp, neither man said much. However, as Tom jumped down, the bullocky stretched out his hand, placing it on his shoulder.

'And I know that she, well, she's worried about you too, lad.'

Tom had half expected this and made to move away. But the hand remained fixed on his shoulder.

'And I am sorry, Tom, lad. About the girl.'

There was a slight nod. 'Yeah, I think I am, too.'

'But Melbourne isn't so far.'

'No, perhaps not.'

'And there aren't many bridges over the river. Not yet, anyway.'

'No.'

'And red stands out.'

'Yeah.'

'And you remember her name.'

'Yeah. Melanie.'

'That's right. Melanie. And a nice name it is, too.'

12

Of news, roads and religion

Commerce along the roads now, although frenetic at times, was taking on a more predictable character. More families were settling in the area, intent, it seemed, on making Ballarat their home. There were more women, of course, and while some brought the concerns of their husbands with them into the store, many now spoke with a degree of confidence about their own prospects and also about the possibilities for the whole community.

Mary particularly admired those single women who came into the store, made their purchases and then spoke about their hopes of making a life for themselves in the area.

One, a bouncy, Scottish woman of about thirty, told her that she intended to start a dress-making business right in the heart of the town. 'There are enough lassies now in the town needing fine things to impress their husbands,' she said, in that lilting voice which sets Scottish people apart, 'and I shall be the first one they come to, won't I?' With that, she bought the few items she needed and skipped out into the sunlight.

There were still plenty of miners who came in, of course, buying, talking among themselves, or occasionally letting their eyes wander up and down her body. Once, this attention had embarrassed her. More than that, had unnerved her. But now, she saw this attention as pretty much a harmless game played out in the safety of the store.

She had been repelled by the clumsy advances of her husband and frightened by the groping hands of the sergeant. Entrapment by her husband she had endured: there was no real choice. The sergeant she had escaped. To both of those men, she, the woman, was not important, rather the plaything, the outward show of their mastery.

Although, with the bullocky, there was a measure of caution still, she felt herself coming more and more to welcome his embrace, the strength of his arms around her and the gentle touch of his hands as they surrounded her face. She had known closeness with her father. But this, this intimacy with a man, was something quite new.

Everywhere, there were changes, some thrust upon her, some she welcomed.

For her daughter, life was changing too. There were other children in the area, children with whom she could now play. On one occasion she went off with a family to see a visiting circus and came back determined that she would one day become a circus artiste. Mary well remembered her anxiety when Susan had become lost in the bush. But she was learning to give her daughter a greater degree of freedom.

However, there were certain rituals that she wanted to preserve, rituals that had stemmed from her own childhood. One was the Sunday evening walk with Susan along the Melbourne Road. There was usually no real destination. Mary would simply help her daughter dress in the best and cleanest clothes available, do the same for herself, and together they would set off. Her own mother had done this with her and it seemed important for Mary, now, to do the same.

Sometimes, Dan would accompany them, rolling along as she imagined him doing on his long, lonely expeditions. It pleased her that Susan seemed to welcome his presence. She had seen families strolling along the beaches of Melbourne when she and James had first moved there and had envied their apparent tranquillity. Now, for the first time, that tranquillity seemed to be hers. How long that would last, she had no idea. But she was learning to enjoy moments as they came.

Much remained secret from Susan. She did not need to know that when Mary ran her fingers through her daughter's hair at the end of these walks, she was repeating something her own mother had done, almost religiously, at the end of their perambulations. Nor that her small girlish face was so like her grandmother's. The same round cheeks, the bright eyes that always seemed surprised, the hair that wandered and the glance that shot everywhere.

The biggest change for Susan would come at the beginning of the year, when she would be able to attend school. Mr Hastie, determined educator, had many times now encouraged Mary to send her daughter to his established school in Buninyong. However, Mary had been informed that plans were afoot to build a school on Bakery Hill. This would mean, of course, that Susan would not need to leave home. And, in the meantime, Dan had been able to bring from Melbourne a number of suitable books, had helped when he could, and Mary was pleased with the progress Susan was making.

In the midst of all these changes, a letter came, unexpectedly, from Mary's father. As usual, she had gone out to greet the coach, ready to welcome the weary travellers.

But this time, instead of throwing open the door to release them, the driver came across, thrusting forward a single letter. 'For you, Mrs D,' he announced, in a voice he ensured would catch the attention of all within earshot. 'For you. From Sydney.'

The shock, for that's what it was, held her riveted. So fixed that the laughing coach driver had to push the letter into her hands,

'There you are, me dear. And now,' turning to the curious passengers, 'remember, only ten minutes. We'd not want my masters venting their ire on me, would we?'

The letter was not long. It outlined concern for her welfare. Expressed a hope that her husband was treating her well and explained that, although he himself was not particularly well, he was still able to work. But that he missed her very much.

It was essentially her father. Short in his careful handwriting and wanting, she felt, to say more. Long out of date. But reducing her, when she was alone to read it, to tears. Having been through it a couple of times, she picked up the simple vase her father had given her, held it as one would a sacred object replaced it carefully, folded the letter and put it beside it on the shelf.

But, as she did so, a strange thought inched its way into her mind. A thought that troubled her more and more as she stood there. She had told her father of James's death, had written twice since then. So why was he not expressing sympathy now? Could the letters, all she had written, have gone astray?

Troubled with another possibility, but not wanting to explore it, or even give words to it, she let her eyes wander out along the road towards the sloping, green hills. Such a distance it seemed. And such a distance it was. But, like most of us when troubled by disturbing possibilities from the past, she immersed herself, as much as she could, in the present. And there were many developments happening, right now, that engaged her attention.

The town was expanding, creeping ever closer to her store. Shops and businesses were springing up where stretches of land had slept undisturbed. New buildings were replacing tents and, where there had been chaos, streets were setting down firm roots. At night, the lights of shops and homes stood out clearly.

Competition there was in all this, of course. But Mary now had confidence in the viability of her store. She had even established a small collection of children's clothes and toys. And the delight upon the faces of children who came in would spring up as a memory from her own childhood when, on the rare occasion that her father could do so, he bought her some small trinket.

The store remained, as it always had, a meeting place, a coming together of shared complaints, requests for information, a stage for general conversation. Mostly, of course, it was a place where people came for information about developments on the goldfields. Some of her customers would say that they did not need to read the *Argus* or the rousing reports from Henry Seekamp in *The Ballarat Times*. A visit to the Wider's Store gave them all the information they needed.

Clearly, the troubles among the diggers were stirring much interest in the widening community. It seemed that no one could escape them and, as 1854 hurtled towards its end, the huge chasms developing between the miners and the administration were becoming more evident. Rarely did a day pass without discussions about them.

One old woman, shaking her fist, in the midst of her buying, maintained that the diggers were merely gamblers, 'Ruffians, my dear,' and that the police must act firmly. And quickly. Adding, with a flamboyant wave of her arms, 'Ordinary citizens have a right to peace and quiet.' This outburst ended with a thump on the counter that went close to dislodging its contents.

Clearly, there was concern among many of the residents about the ructions. And some at least were not sympathetic to the miners.

Others, more distant perhaps, were confused. A few days later, a serious-looking young schoolteacher, speaking in a quiet voice that had almost a prophetic hush to it, warned that something dark and ill-defined was hovering above the town, mustering its forces for an assault. This sense of mystery impressed his listeners enormously. So impressed were they by the quality of his rhetoric and the confidence of his delivery that no one asked him what the something might be.

Some of the accounts were quite amusing. But, by now, few of the stories coming from the miners themselves had any real note of humour. It surprised Mary that a few actually defended the authorities. They dismissed the agitation as the work of French radicals and Irish troublemakers. But most argued that demonstrations were justified.

'And, Mrs Douglas,' one leathery old Scot remarked, 'it won't stop with mass meetin's. I can tell you that.'

Some of the stories were tinged with apprehension, others expectation. All had the stamp of anticipation. Something must surely happen. And that something, Mary realised, would involve her son.

Fortunately, none of the discussions within the store had ended in violence. But outside, and just outside, that was another matter altogether. And on a particular, ordinary-looking Sunday morning, she was to see at close quarters just how near to the surface a major eruption might be.

The bullocky had arranged to take her out for the day. A neighbouring family had arrived, happy to look after Susan. 'It's good for our daughter,' the mother had said, in that quiet confident voice experienced mothers have, 'to be with other children.'

And they had waited together. Entertained, for a time, by a group of travelling entertainers, who, inspired perhaps by this small audience, had stopped and performed for them, juggling, singing and carrying out acrobatic feats that entranced the children. Mary herself enjoyed their actions. But her real attention was drawn to the empty road, eager as she was for the arrival of the cart.

Mid-morning saw Susan depart with the family and Mary was left, standing alone by the door.

Time went on and, anxious that some unexpected event might have prevented him from coming, she went back inside. There, she busied herself setting boxes, pots and bottles in line, then turned her attention to the items of women's clothing she had put on display so proudly a few weeks earlier. This made her think of the unfortunate girl Tom had brought to her and to whom she had given some underclothes and a skirt. With the morning sun cleaning the world outside, she found herself shuddering at the memory of the obscene mixture of feathers and molasses caked together. More particularly, of the terror on the girl's face.

Suddenly, from outside, there came shouts. Not the shouts of excited or happy men. These were shouts of anger. Sustained shouts that brought her quickly to the door. Seeing her there, four men began scrambling away through the bush, leaving behind, like an abandoned parcel, the figure of a man groaning and clutching his stomach. Slowly, he struggled to his feet and stood bewildered as blood trickled down his face. Beneath the dust on his clothes Mary recognised the blue of a police uniform. As she approached, what struck her most was the almost childlike expression of fear and bewilderment on his face. It might well have been the face of her son, so young was it. And it was certainly the face of some woman's son. Had she not seen, so very recently, that same terror?

She helped the officer regain his feet, manoeuvred him through the door, cleaned him up as best she could and waited for him to relate what had happened.

'I thank you, madam,' he began, struggling to fit his words into any real order. 'I, I was sent, sent today. To check on an old shepherd who'd complained of bein' robbed on the Melbourne road. Simply doing my duty I was. Nothing more.' His eyes filled with tears, tears he wiped away as quickly as they came. 'Just doin' my duty.'

Then, putting on his cap, he turned awkwardly, reassured her that he was recovered and set out, walking slowly down the slope towards the town. Had Mary stood on any one of a hundred evenings outside the government camp and watched this same clumsy walk, she would have recognised the victim as the Turkey, the young officer who, with Sergeant Miller, marched out across the parade ground, stood beside the snub-nosed cannon and sent smoke and noise catapulting out over the diggings.

It was with a strong sense of relief that she saw the bullocky arriving some time later.

'Aye, lass,' he said, as they headed towards the bushland. 'There's bad feeling everywhere now. We can only hope that there are cool heads somewhere. The men of the Reform League are itchin' for trouble. I know that. Some of them, anyway. But there are voices of sense as well. John Humffray. There's a good man. The voice of reason. He wants change. Like all of 'em. But without violence.' The bullocky paused, brandished his pipe and laughed. 'A Welshman, he is. Like me.'

The horse might have been amused, whinnying and tossing its head, but Mary was not.

They continued, saying little, for about an hour. The town, the beehive slopes and the tents gradually disappeared from thought and around rose up areas of scrub largely untouched by the chip, chip, chipping of metal and the shouts of men. At intervals, a small creek would creep out from the trees and ferns would gurgle in the sunlight and disappear again.

Far behind, where men dug and troubled the earth, the Yarowee creek now slunk between channels and wept brown mud. Here was water that ran clear. Here, a long clearing would disgorge sunlight over green plants, not blisters of clay. Cockatoos, rosellas and galahs would erupt in a blaze of noise and colour, then flash away through the clear sky or settle back to peer back at them from high branches. And here was Mary's spirit rekindled.

Later on, they came upon a small tent snugged in against some stringybarks. A woman sat on a log close by. A man rhythmically ran a stone over an axe and suddenly, from within the tent, an old man appeared, playing the bagpipes. He marched a few steps, resplendent in kilt and high boots. Two children burst from the bushes, sniggering. The mother motioned them to be quiet and let the grandfather play on. That he did. Soon the scene was swallowed up, the sound hanging loosely among the trees and slowly fading away.

Some time later, they came upon another stream, this one hardly flowing. Between the banks a barrier of clay and logs trapped the water, forming a brown pool stretching for about thirty yards upstream. In more congenial times, the creek probably flushed itself clean of silt and the water remained clear. But now, it lay muddy and weary. Only by the far end of the barrier did a trickle of water find the energy to creep by and resume its journey. On one bank stood two large egrets. As the cart approached, one stretched its white, almost transparent wings and flapped away. The other remained motionless.

As they approached, Mary and Dan could hear angry voices. The words could have been spoken anywhere.

'Bloody licences.'

'Lockin' up 'ard-workin' me.'

'No taxes without a vote.'

The voice of protest had clearly invaded even this quiet corner of the district.

Then, above the discordance, a woman's voice rang out, higher but just as insistent. 'And what about the governor, Hotham? Don't forget 'im. A right royal welcome you give 'im just a few weeks ago. And us women. We 'ailed 'im, too. Betrayed youse all, 'e 'as. Betrayed us all.' Her robust figure seemed to grow larger as she stood, clutching in one hand, a pile of washing and the other clenched and held aloft. 'Done us all in, 'e 'as.'

Some of the men applauded or nodded. Others, even if they agreed with her, were clearly irritated. 'This is no place for a woman,' one of them muttered. 'Let 'er get back to the washing.'

The bullocky stopped the cart and he and Mary watched the meeting stutter to its end, an end punctuated by the usual threats. The men collected their hats, coats and whatever else they had thrown down upon the ground. As they began to break up, there seemed to be a tangible sense of frustration. It was as if they all wanted something to happen. As if their meeting deserved a better ending.

Almost as if in response, a voice piped up, high and urgent. Almost a woman's voice. 'Wait, brothers, wait.'

Men about to mount their horses paused, looking round and holding their reins. The four women stood up, surprised and waiting. From the nearby trees came a figure, an old man dressed in meticulous black. He tottered somewhat in his advance, but on he came, swept along by the urgency. In one hand, he held what appeared to be a book.

Mary started in her seat, grabbing Dan by the arm. Here, lurching forward with the zeal of any impassioned missionary, was Joe, the old hatter. In the afternoon light, while his face still bore the signs of his pre-reformed days, his eyes shone with a fierce glow and his voice carried clearly above the amazed diggers.

Unaware of the cart and its occupants, he forced himself onwards, a comical scarecrow in his persistence. 'No, brothers, do not leave. I have heard your cries. And I come with hope. Do not leave in despair.'

The book rose above his head. On all sides, repressed anger turned to laughter.

He continued his rushed descent upon them, oblivious to the taunts and the jokes now thrown at him. 'Brothers, friends, I share your pain. But know that the good Lord is with you. His will is mightier than the evils of repression. Vengeance is mine, says the Lord.'

Yes. This was indeed Old Joe. He who had cast away drink and embraced a new god. He kept on stumbling, righting himself and finally stopping in front of the tents. It seemed as if his pleas had been heeded. The exodus from the clearing was stemmed. The group reassembled around him. And he rose now, upright with the book brandished like a sword. At the same time, he launched into a fervent, if rather garbled attack on the creeping sickness of power and corruption. Faces lit up around him and the poor old fellow interpreted the glow as a sign of divine awakening. There were whistles and shouts of encouragement.

Someone yelled out, 'Go to it, Moses,' and one stout young wag, obviously delighted by the performance, whipped off his hat and sent it spinning over the pool.

This was too much for the remaining egret. It sprang off in disgust and flapped away through the trees.

The voice of the old man rose higher, bravely battling the laughter now erupting freely on all sides. He reminded them, his whole body shaking under its load of emotion and religious intensity, that the powers of prayer could lift them above the reaches of hell. That God would eventually rescue them and punish the unjust. This rhetoric brought an even more enthusiastic response from the audience.

Now, however, at the very climax of the show, he committed what could best be described as a serious theological blunder. Raising his hands and transported high on a wave of divine inspiration, he called upon the congregation to pray for the governor and his servants on the goldfields. 'We must ask God's blessing, in particular for Commissioners Rede and Johnston. That they be guided in their decisions. And for all those who serve. Police and soldiers.'

There erupted a chorus of laughter in response.

Undeterred, he went on, 'Trust. Trust in God, my friends. Great indeed is His power. Greater than the lust of men for gold. We must pray for all.'

At this point, his mission foundered. Perhaps in another place, with mortals whose hearts were not so hardened, he might have struck water from stone and turned men from their greedy quest for earthly wealth. But here was stone impenetrable. Laughter now had a rough, sinister edge to it. Whistles and shrieks of derision intensified. One man booed and, in response, a host of the Philistines descended upon him. The old fellow found himself hoisted aloft and heading in a direct line for the water.

Dan jumped down, intending to save God's messenger from a dunking. But he was too late. The divine voice was buried under a flurry of laughter. In a quick dash and a rush, men cast the reformed old hatter among the reeds and frogs.

Reaching down, Dan grabbed the old man's muddy hand and pulled him out. The face that appeared above the reeds did not exhibit signs of fear. It bore a consistent blank stare. The eyes seemed to be looking, if anywhere, at a point far away.

'Thank you, my good man,' he said with surprising aplomb. 'God's work will never be easy.'

It seemed, for a moment, that he was focussing on the cart and its occupant. But his eyes quickly settled on that mystical point far ahead. Clearly, he had not recognised Mary, even as she scrambled down and set about cleaning the offending mud from his clothes. She thought, as the mud and stalks peeled away, of those other clothes, that other body, smeared with molasses, huddled and humiliated as it had been on the floor of the store.

But there was something worse here. The girl had been clearly terrified but had finally become able to speak rationally. As had the young officer. But here, on the face she was looking at now, there was something unhealthy, almost unearthly. A strange calmness. Almost an acceptance. Perhaps this poor, ailing man would see himself now as a martyr. A man punished for the sins of others and yet determined to reclaim their souls, wrench them from the greedy quest for gold and set them on the path to righteous living. If so, he had her sympathy. But he might also be quite mad. And, if this was so, she recoiled.

Setting himself on his feet, he scrambled through the reeds and retrieved his Bible, relieved that he had had the good sense to throw it clear of the water. No. He did not want further assistance. This unfortunate incident had just been sent as a test by God. 'But, like Abraham and Moses, I will not be found wantin,' my dears. I must and,' with an authoritative wave of his hands, 'I will continue.' He thanked them both for their assistance, assured them that, in time, they would have their reward and scuttled up the bank. They watched him mount a small, weary pony and depart.

By this time, the drama was played out. The clearing was almost deserted. Only two men remained, silent and observant a few yards away. The washerwomen had resumed their work and the brown leather of the water was smooth again. Only a few crushed reeds showed where the future saint had fallen.

Disgusted, Mary watched the trees slowly passing beside them. 'How could they do that, Daniel? To an old man, a helpless old man?'

The bullocky pulled the cart to a halt.

'No, I don't want consoling. I'm too angry.' Then suddenly she collapsed against him. She had steeled herself against showing strong emotion ever since her husband's death. Even at his funeral, she had been an outsider. The coffin, as it was lowered, had been an island disappearing into the mist. And the minister's voice, as he read the obligatory words, was a distant wind, remote though clear. The wrenching away from her father had penetrated her defence. But James's dismissal of her sadness had forced her to hide her feelings deep within herself.

Yet the humiliation of an old man, all but a stranger, had released these feelings with such force that she had no control over them. The loss of her childhood. The loss of her parents. The long years of isolation with her husband. All, all came tumbling out.

She clung to the figure beside her. 'Daniel, you will try to save my son, won't you?'

The bullocky looked down, torn between pity for the woman beside him and an awareness of the chaos threatening to erupt on the goldfields of Ballarat. 'Aye, lassie. That I will.'

13

A meeting on Bakery Hill

In the days that followed, Dan Morgan thought a good deal about his current situation. About the developing relationship with Mary. More particularly about the commitment he had made to help her son. Sometimes, too, when he had the time to be a little more philosophical, he could look back over the preceding years and reflect on his whole life.

He thought of those occasions when he might have sold his team of bullocks and joined the thousands now digging for gold. He had heard the fantastic tales of syndicates that had stumbled upon extraordinary pockets of gold hidden in the deep darkness of clay and gravel. Golden Point, Canadian Gully and the Gravel Pits were full of the stories. And he had seen enough himself to know that there was some truth in them, the yarns of diggers parading the streets with gaudy women on their arm or floating with them on expensive gigs, others ostentatiously flouting nuggets of gold before the astonished gaze of storekeepers or bystanders. Indeed, he had once met a party of Americans on the Geelong Road, claiming to have unearthed six hundred ounces in a week. Oh, yes. The temptation was there. With gold bringing four pounds an ounce, anyone would think about taking his chance.

True, he was certainly getting his share of the one hundred tons of goods coming into the town from Geelong every week. But he knew that his contracts could not bring anywhere near the wealth some were getting from gold. Such riches were beyond the wildest dreams of a bullock driver.

Dan Morgan, however, was not a man of wild dreams. His small hut just outside the town was simple. But it sufficed. And as long as his stables could accommodate his horse and his yards the beasts that dragged his loads, he was relatively content. Besides, he had met on the roads too many of those who had not succeeded. Some were embittered, heading back to Geelong and Melbourne with nothing. Some carried only their swags. One Irishman he had come across near Bacchus Marsh had gone out the next morning and shot himself. Some who had decided to stay were forced into labouring jobs or dangerous employment in the deeper mines.

And he knew something of working conditions in deep mines. He had seen, in his childhood, the green valley of the Rhondda scarred and chewed away by the advancing coal mines and his own village smeared with constant smoke and dust.

He had seen, too, the effects of mining on people he knew. Men of forty years of age stumbling and shuffling along the street, sucked dry by their years in the mines. Others, who greeted him on his way to school, coughing uncontrollably as he went past. And the black flag flying after an explosion, the screams of wives and the lines of men carrying coffins to their resting places. Oh, yes. He remembered all that, only too well.

But most vividly, he recalled his own father bending his back after a day's work cramped underground and telling him that he must not follow him deep into the earth. 'Look for something else, Danny boy,' he had insisted. 'Anything.'

Most frightening for a boy of seven had been the violent death of his father. He recalled the swinging lanterns, the grey, grim figures carrying his father's body up the garden path and into the small kitchen of their cottage. The sight of the half blown-away face and the blood sliding down the front steps had remained with him ever since. That was the price one paid for involvement in a strike that slid into violence.

But he had heeded his father's advice. Never once did he enter a mine. But work for a young boy was not easy to find. He could not stay at home. The forced poverty of his mother made that impossible. So he had taken whatever labouring jobs he could find. Marriage, for a time, seemed to give him a sense of purpose. But when it became clear to his wife that he did not want children, life took on a rocky, unsteady path. He had not worked out, in the times of reflection later – and there were many of those – why he had been so insistent about it. He guessed that he feared the responsibility. Or was it because he did not want to see children of his subjected to the poverty he had endured? Anyway, it didn't really matter in the end, did it? The marriage collapsed and he was again thrown back on his own resources.

Perhaps his wife had trusted that he, like most husbands, would change and eventually want a son or a daughter. If that was so, then her trust was ill-placed.

Then, luck took him to Portsmouth and the chance to work his way across the ocean. Anywhere would do. Sydney Town was the destination of his ship. So Sydney Town it would be. And finally, luck brought him to Melbourne and a businessman who suggested he should try bullock driving. He had known nothing about the cantankerous behaviours of bullocks, but he had learned quickly enough. And he had found a living here. Lonely, dangerous at times, but one that gave him an income.

Yes, it was a strange mixture of memories that circulated today as he walked along Main Road. The past. The present. Linked, somehow, together. And, somewhere perhaps, with a meaning.

He was not there because he was dissatisfied with his life and was looking for a job with one of the new mining syndicates. He knew that. Nor was he heading for Bakery Hill because he wanted to join the protesters of the new Ballarat Reform League who were meeting there. He was sympathetic, of course. Most people were. The corruptions swilling out of the camp were plain for all to see. And certainly he had been encouraged to take an active part in the diggers' protests. But the death of his father had shown him what could result from open conflict with authorities. Violence, or the threat of it, sickened him and he recoiled from the upraised fists and the knots of angry men continually threatening rebellion.

No, he was attending this meeting for one reason. Mary had asked him to. What he could do to turn her son from actions that might involve violent confrontation, he did not know. But he had said he would do what he could.

So here he was picking his way through the tangle that made up Main Road, heading for a protest meeting on Bakery Hill. And, troubled though he was, he was amazed at the transformations taking place. Canvas was being replaced by timber, shingles by gleaming iron on many of the roofs.

New hotels, like the Victoria, the Charlie Gardiner and the Red Hill, stood out boldly on strong foundations. Flags and signs invited all to come in and buy: a huge boot here to entice those needing new footwear, a red shirt fluttering over there to encourage wives to buy for their husbands. Obviously, no stone had been left unturned. No trick had been overlooked in attempts to enthral prospective buyers.

Here, in fact, on this single road, were all of the trappings of a growing local economy. He earned good, solid money from it. Why not Mary's son Thomas also? If he could be turned from his present risky involvement in the rumblings along the slope. Ah, but the turning. That would be the problem.

As he pressed further, he was amused to see that there were still many of those innocent-looking shanties that had advertised lemonade but really specialised in extraordinary concoctions of alcohol. Each, as he remembered, had its own recipe and he imagined that they would not have changed very much.

He had been caught once, long before his misfortune on the Bacchus Marsh Road, and had woken up under a tree a few hours later. Angry, but curious, he had returned and confronted the owner, asking what the drink contained.

The latter, a round, red-faced rogue, had not been at all put out by the question. He had simply beamed across his makeshift counter and laughed. 'Oh, that, my man, that is what I call the knocker of Ballarat. Jamaican rum, opium, metho, cayenne pepper. That's what's in it.' Then he had slapped Dan on the shoulder and added, roaring with laughter as he did so, 'And a dash of water. Nothing else like it. A powerful brew, eh? Probably the best you'll find here.'

Powerful? Yes, it was certainly that. And Dan had not tried it since.

However, he was amazed to come across that very shanty, still standing, still maintaining its veneer of innocence, still advertising coffee, tobacco and lemonade. But it was much larger, with what looked to be a small cottage behind. Clearly, he thought, there must remain a market for the knocker of Ballarat.

The same miscreant stood as he had on that afternoon, beaming upon all who were there. Today, however, he was not alone. Beside him was a young woman. With her long hair falling down over her half exposed breasts, she was leaning towards a customer, smiling innocently into his face. Mary Douglas would have recognised her as the temptress who had fascinated the males in her store the day the coach had also delivered the extraordinary Madame Hortense.

Smiling, Dan continued down the road. Even its surface had changed. Compressed by thousands of wheels, it glowed now, like the roads and streets he had travelled over in Melbourne and Geelong. Even a small detail like that smacked of change! He knew that in the winter it would run with the brown, yellow mud disgorged from hundreds of mullock heaps and that water and mud would combine in an assault on the surrounding shops. He had seen already, last winter, a blacksmith's shop and a bakery succumb and he guessed that a similar fate would overtake countless other businesses when the rains came again. At the moment, it had the appearance of an ordinary road or street in any town.

However, what surprised him most today was the strange, orderly calm that prevailed. This was not the frantic Main Road that reeled from the sound of cradles and tumblers or choked under the dust thrown up from barrows, carts and the thousands of tramping feet. Only a few figures lounged or wandered from tent to tent. Several boys ran freely between mullock heaps.

But the pockmarked hide of Golden Point was virtually empty and many of the claims on Red Hill were more like deserted rabbit burrows than working shafts. Horses that usually plodded their circles at puddling machines stood in their chains, flicking away flies. Warrneepe and Mount Buninyong stood unclouded against the horizon.

The reason for this unusual quietude soon became clear. As he began to go up Bakery Hill, Dan found himself swept up into a slow-moving tide of people. They came in small groups, locked in quiet conversation. They came alone, speaking to no one. Or they came in lines. Hundreds of men, a few of them accompanied by women, were moving like pilgrims towards a rough stage that stood on a grassy knoll.

Six months ago, Dan had taken Mary and Susan to see one of the circuses that occasionally came to the town. The mass of people assembled there had been united by good humour and the grey, billowing tent had rocked with laughter and camaraderie. But there was no joviality today. Talk, if there was any, was of licences, greedy squatters or the lack of political representation. The bare stage had the appearance of a scaffold.

He had hoped to encounter Tom Douglas there, but he looked in vain for some time. However, finally, he came upon Mary's son, with Martin Jacobs and the Californian, Frank Burgen. Together, they all moved closer to the stage, waiting for the meeting to begin.

A few minutes later, a small group emerged from the ranks and climbed the few hastily constructed steps. Around them, the crowd of diggers stood in the open sunlight or slouched in whatever shade they could find. Women whispered to one another or stood silently beside their menfolk.

There were some people, Dan noticed, who either watched from a distance or bunched together and hurried past. Some, braver than the rest, instructed the miners to get back to work. Others, more daring still, accused them of deliberately fermenting trouble with the police. One old man, brandishing what looked like a walking stick, mounted a fallen stump and accused the diggers of bringing the town into disrepute. He was quickly helped down and scurried away. Most accusations were, in fact, ignored. Or perhaps the perpetrators were too far away for the miners to hunt them down.

Whatever their reactions, the diggers and their supporters soon turned their attention back to the stage. Few took any notice, either, of the boys who had crept unnoticed into their ranks and were either assiduously seeking out any unattended pockets or scampering about among the onlookers. And no one seemed aware of half a dozen black children who stood apart, restlessly kicking at empty bottles or throwing stones down the slope at a flock of cockatoos

These aggrieved miners were here for something much more important. They had no time to respond to a few ignorant locals or the misbehaviour of a few adolescent boys.

Many did take the time to look out for ferrets. They, Dan had been told, were spies, men often disguised as miners, who would come to meetings and report back to the police. If detected, it was the usual practice to take them away and 'deal' with them. He hoped no one would be rooted out today.

However, just as the meeting was about to begin, six diggers quietly descended upon an inconspicuous individual, took him away behind a small hut and presumably 'dealt' with him, the slamming of boots and the occasional cry of pain being quite audible above the murmur of the crowd. The motley collection of boys gathered around, shouting their approval and soon after, a skinny, dust-covered body staggered away down the slope and the six assailants merged back into the crowd.

One of them, flushed and conscious of the attention and the approbation of those close by, shouted out, 'Bloody spy! That's what we do with his kind.'

There was a quiet chorus of approval and attention returned to the stage.

The first speaker to rise was, Martin Jacobs informed him, a German, Frederick Vern. 'A good man, Dan. A fighter for the cause. A man to be trusted.'

Vern was young, tall and spoke with passion and confidence. His heavy accent might have lost a few in the audience but his anger and his complaints were theirs. They listened, therefore, with growing enthusiasm. His arms pumped upwards and outwards with each attack. The administration stinks with corruption. Licences should be burned. Miners must resist with every weapon available any attempt to arrest their comrades. This was stirring stuff. The melody was well known by all. And the diggers shouted in agreement. Excitement swelled, heads nodded and fists were clenched as if battle had already begun.

Attention then turned to the next speaker. They clearly expected him to deliver the same call to arms. They were to be disappointed. The miner who came forward now was older, thicker in build and looked out over the assembly with a kind of benevolent sympathy. His hands were extended as if pleading for attention. This was not what men baying for trouble wanted. And very quickly mumblings began to seep upwards. Clearly, this man's views were well known already.

Undeterred and squaring himself to withstand any objection, he began. There was no dramatic gesturing here. No voice rising and falling with anger or passion for a cause. Here was the voice of quiet authority. Yes, injustices and inequalities existed. There was no doubt about that. But, and the moans that came now showed many expected to hear this and had probably heard it before, authorities must be persuaded by reason, not force. The moans now turned into shouts of anger.

Very few of the listeners, Dan noticed, too few, spoke out in favour of the speaker, who stood there, surrounded on all sides yet as if surrounded by no one. If a man could be lonely among thousands of clenched fists or staring faces, this was that man.

'A Welshman, John Hummfray,' muttered Martin. 'I've got nothin' against your kind, Dan. But he's no fighter, this one. He won't be there if the goin' gets tough. A few too many like him in the league.'

Many in the audience seemed to share this view. All listened politely enough at first. But, as his message became clearer, there was a shuffling, a murmur of dissent and finally a collective shout of disapproval.

'Reason be damned,' called out one dark-faced miner. 'The commissioner, 'e don't believe in reason. We've tried that. A good belt in the lug is what 'e needs. And if you go on talkin' like that, I'll come up there and ram this pick down your bloody throat.'

Whether the unfortunate John Hummfray heard this particular threat or not, he made one final plea for peace and negotiation and then sat down. There were a few who applauded his effort. Most continued their shouts of disapproval.

There was excitement in Martin's voice now. 'Yes, young Tom. Things are warming up. Won't be long now. The men have heard enough weak talk. A few more weeks, I'd reckon. One spark. That's what we need. Just one and they'll be with us. Even those waverers among the league might be turned. We just have to wait. And be ready when the time comes.'

Others speakers took over the stage and slowly the excitement grew again.

Then there came a universal cry. 'Great Works! Give us Great Works!'

In response, a red head, a flourishing beard and a flamboyantly clad figure materialised, followed immediately by a voice that rang out above the tumult. 'I, Raffaello Carboni, miner from Urbino, Italy, I hear you, my fellow sufferers. And I share your pain, your anger.'

There was an instant hush. Clearly, the star performer had arrived.

Martin Jacobs nodded approvingly. 'Yes, Great Works. He's our kind of man. He'll put his back to the wheel, Dan. No need to worry about him.'

Martin and Tom were focused on the stage. Their attention did not waver. But Frank Burgen, Dan observed, seemed more interested in the faces of the men close by. His eyes did not show excitement. There was about them a kind of dispassionate probing. As if he was recording and storing something away.

Carboni now stepped forward, claiming the sunlight and raising his hand. He wanted peace, like everyone else. Like Hayes and Hummfray, those two respected members of the League who had just spoken. But men must be prepared to fight the dogs that lay in the shade and preyed upon honest men.

'We must,' he shouted, 'be prepared to die. But die like soldiers, defenders of freedom and justice, if that is required of us.' A great swell of agreement spread out over Bakery Hill. 'And I,' he continued after a pause, 'I agree with my colleague, Mr Vern. I move that we, we diggers undertake to burn, to burn these cursed licences,'

Theatrically, he took from his pocket a sheet of paper and brandished it high above his head. Dan noticed that he did not set a match to it. But in the ensuing pandemonium this did not seem to matter. When order was more or less restored, the motion was put and a forest of hands rose to support it.

Then there followed one triumphant outburst. Men shouted. Hats were thrown into the air. Shots rang out. Men embraced or locked arms. And, finally, as if unable to contain the force of its emotion, the great crowd began to break up.

As they dispersed, men sketched out hasty plans.

'Burn licences.'

'Lay siege to the camp.'

'Gather arms for the coming strife.'

The chorus rang out all over Bakery Hill. At various points, small groups of men huddled together and spirals of smoke showed clearly that licences were in fact being destroyed. Faces had the seriousness one would expect to find at a religious service. Only when all offending documents had been destroyed did any of the groups burst into a collective show of triumph or rebellion. The whole area was filled with bodies, moving or still. And groups like restless islands that would suddenly explode into activity, to be replaced by others as the ritualistic burnings were completed.

And in the midst of it all, Martin punched the air with his clenched fist. 'Yeah, boys, things are movin' now.'

Suddenly, he wrapped one arm around Tom's shoulder. They stood there, two statues, following the action spurting up on all sides. Martin needed only a flag now. In his mind, he was already the leader of the revolution. Supreme on the edge of the barricade, he stood with his trusted lieutenant. And trusted lieutenant Tom Douglas was. Faith restored in the cause and surrounded by so many good men prepared to fight against injustice, he himself was ready to take his part.

But Dan, conscious of the young man's excitement, thought of the promise he had made Mary. Yes, there would be reason for a mother's concern. If not now, then soon enough.

Almost mechanically, he looked out over the crowds leaving but stopping once more to focus on the calm figure of Frank Burgen. There was something unusual about a man who could remain so detached here. But detached he would have appeared to any casual observer, standing amidst the moving tides around him, arms folded over his chest and his eyes seeming half closed. You might have thought he was actually quite bored. But Dan felt that there was little that had gone on that the American had not filed away. There was the kind of silent observation one sees in a good journalist. And Dan rather admired the dispassionate demeanour. But he was also troubled.

More so when Frank looked directly across at him, nodded coldly and left.

14

Guns

Some report had to be given to Mary. There was no way Dan could avoid that, wish though he might that he could. She had known of his intention to attend the meeting, had in fact encouraged him to do so. But knowing what to say, without raising her anxiety, would be difficult. He had seen a body of men galvanised into a single will, anger and frustration harden. And most alarming, her son like a rebel with a cause ready to ride into battle. Any mother's alarm would be justified. But Mary Douglas was not anyone's mother. Not to Dan Morgan.

So he came the following evening.

Mary had closed the store. Susan was already in bed and Mary sat opposite him, waiting. Only a candle protected him from her gaze, and that gaze was calm and fixed on his face. Her long dark hair, proudly free now, floated down, and he wanted to run its coolness through his fingers. Her lips, slightly parted, seemed to beckon. And the cream smoothness of her neck was a velvet needing the softness of his touch. Such was his desire to escape. To lose reason. To bury himself like a swimmer in some wild current. To have her arms drag him deep, beyond all thought. But those eyes never wavered. They were the eyes of a mother, not some eager lover. The eyes of a mother, worried yet patient for news.

He did his best, knowing all the time that every movement he made, every sign of obfuscation or evasion, would be picked up immediately. Mary Douglas was much more observant than many, including himself, had recognised initially.

Yes, he said, as confidently as he could, there might be confrontation coming. But there were some calm heads and voices. John Hummfray

171

was one, he added quickly. 'A Welshman like me. Must be good, eh?' He was relieved by the glimmer of a smile. But the eyes quickly regained their cool focus. 'Sense might still win out, Mary.' His voice was quite mechanical now and what he could say next without giving away his own lack of conviction he had no idea.

Mary said nothing. Her nod was as mechanical as his words.

Yes, he would speak to Tom again. His words seemed to come from a long way off. Almost as if they had an existence of their own. They were being smothered by his memories of the meeting. The images of the massed miners rising and shouting out their defiance, the icy defiance on the face of Mary's son and the intoxicating language that had worked upon the listeners, rose up like accusing hands, defying him to say more. And so he stopped. Mary was too astute anyway to be easily deceived and he was too honest to drift too far from the truth. So he waited, knowing that he had largely failed to convince her.

There was a long silence, the kind that you expect to be filled at some stage and feel you know what the filling will be.

When Mary finally spoke, her voice was not at all upset. It was flat, conveying little other than the words themselves. 'Oh, yes, Daniel. I know you'll do what you can.'

Was this acceptance? Surrender to what was inevitable? Resignation? An attempt to reassure him? Or perhaps a final attempt to encourage him to keep trying? There was no way of knowing. But the words seemed to reinforce the heavy sense of responsibility he had laboured under ever since Mary had told him of her concerns. Was it irritation pricking at him, now or frustration at his own helplessness? He did not know that either.

He wanted only to lose his hands in her long hair. Lose all thought in her closeness. Forget everything in the warmth of her body. But the sad acceptance in her eyes held him. He remained still, as she was. The silence was something impenetrable. A vast dark distance and yet she was so close, so close he had only to extend his arms.

Suddenly, Mary stood up and walked to the window. The

moonlight coiled down her hair and settled on her neck. She looked even more desirable there, in her proud isolation. And at the same time quite untouchable.

When she turned, her voice was a wave, perhaps more a tremble of sound coming through the darkness. 'Only, only, he is so like his father.' Once more, she looked out.

Dan could not move, could not rise. So large, so tragic was she.

Next, he was aware of her scent and the closeness of her coming. First a shadow and then a presence in his arms. She was not his lover. She was mother, child lost, woman ever hopeful. Woman eternally suffering. And they sat together. Sharing without words, understanding without reason.

For how long they remained there, they had no idea. But by the time they stirred, the moon was no longer peering in through the window, the breeze had gone and the only sounds were the squabbles of a family of possums entrenched high in a red gum.

Finally, Mary spoke again. 'Thank you, Daniel,' she said. 'I don't blame you. I know that my son must make his own way. I'm afraid, that is all. I'm frightened for him.'

She was like some captive bird, trembling for release. And to release her, he held her more tightly, running his fingers down through her hair. Feeling the fragility of her against him, the melting of her to him.

He had held her like this once before, after she had explained the disappearance of her daughter. Had felt her relax in his arms. But tonight her body remained tense against him. And as he left, he knew that his reassurance had not really been successful.

That same evening, with the same moon peering in through a window away in the town, the same story was being told in the commissioner's office. But if you had listened, you might have been forgiven for thinking that the speakers had attended different meetings. Seated at a table were Commissioners Rede and Johnston. Both were impressive in uniform, both were leaning forward, both were intent in concentration. Commissioner Rede occasionally looked down at a pencil he was playing upon the table. His colleague never let his eyes wander from a civilian standing before him. Slightly apart, as if set below the two in importance, a police officer sat, his arms folded and his eyes flicking from his superiors to a point in the semi-darkness. Occasionally his hand would caress the side of his face and then, as if correcting himself, he would lower it.

Clearly the centre of attention for the three of them was the civilian. The lantern showed him as a tall shadow, little else. He seemed quite at ease. His voice was clear, his delivery unhastened. There was nothing particular: many Americans were on the fields now. Accents that might have seemed arresting a few months ago were commonplace.

If he was annoyed by the fact that he was forced to stand while his listeners sat, he did not show it. He was calm, though observant of the reactions of the men before him. And by the nodding of heads, he knew that he was telling them what they wanted to hear. Occasionally they would look across at one another and smile. To find one's own suspicions confirmed is always affirming.

Yes, he explained slowly and confidently, there certainly was trouble brewing. Yes, the American and the boy, Douglas, were dangerous and needed to be watched. Yes, Vern and Carboni were inciting violence. But no, the Welsh bullocky seemed to be clean.

Heads nodded, glances were exchanged and the three officials rose together.

'Well done,' exclaimed Commissioner Rede, extending his hand. 'Keep watching. Keep close now.'

'Yes, indeed, well done,' added Commissioner Johnston, and then, eager to appear magnanimous, 'You've earned your pay this month.' Finally, even more determined to appear magnanimous, 'And you'll be paid well in the next month too.'

The police officer simply nodded, somewhere lost in thought, his fingers drumming on the table.

When the civilian had left, the three sat silent for a while,

Commissioner Rede already planning the urgent message he would send to the governor requesting more troops, Commissioner Johnston lamenting to himself the lack of adequate police and the third, still drumming on the tabletop, plotting some action of his own.

Plots were being hatched elsewhere tonight too. Beneath the same moon, far from the road, but within a mile of his mother's store, Tom Douglas stood beside Martin Jacobs, facing a band of miners. There were about forty of them. But so still and so intense were they that you might have seen them as one single body. All stood in silence, a solid chunk of darkness, more threatening than the moon shadows floating across the clearing. All were waiting for their leader, Martin, to speak.

He was ready, suitably calm, suitably close, yet suitably remote from his followers. For followers they now clearly were. He had long prepared for this moment and had been patient over many months. Time after time, he could have recommended action. But the men had not been ready, had not hardened enough. Until now they would have shied away from violent action. Oh, they might have rattled off the right words, vowed their intention to confront the authorities. That was easy. To be swept up by the moment. He had seen and heard brave gestures often enough on other fields. But to feel anger and frustration in the belly and to accept the fact that action was the only cure, that was something else. And a leader had to know when the illness was bad enough to call forth the remedy.

For him and for these men, that time had come. The meeting on Bakery Hill had told him that. What he had to do now was to set his men on a path that they could not retreat from. Bridges must be burnt behind them. That is what drives a revolution forward: desperate men galvanised into action, trusting their leaders and knowing the past offers no escape.

He could sense the tightness in his own body as he stood there, the tightness of anticipation, not that of fear. Yes, he was ready.

Beside him, Tom was waiting also. There would be no retreat for him either. Whatever storm might be gathering, he was prepared and committed. There had been two voices, two competing voices clamouring for his attention. One, that of his father, instructing caution: it was cold, iron and intransigent. The other, that of his leader, calling him to shoulder the wheel of revolution and strike out against injustice: it was fire, flexible and all-consuming. Now there was only one that he would follow. And the energy of Martin Jacobs flowed like a current through him.

The group tightened even more and Martin lifted his arms to speak. 'I thank you for comin', lads,' he began. 'It's a disgrace that men must meet like this. Like dogs afraid of the light. But this will change, is changin' already. Something big is comin'. You're aware of it, like I am. The meetin' on Bakery Hill will lead to bigger things now. You saw it, like I did. And we are ready.'

A few men broke in, eager to express their agreement.

Martin raised his hand again, at the same time glancing across at Tom. 'The licence hunts have got worse. We've all had to put up with 'em, haven't we?'

No need to wait now for confirmation. The nodding of heads was sufficient.

'Men are bein' thrown into jail for not havin' their licences with 'em. Honest, hard-workin' men are bein' treated like criminals.' He paused, riding the silence of their pent emotions. 'We don't need any more evidence, do we, to show what the authorities think of us?' Again the pause, filled this time by sharp cries of agreement. 'No, that's right, lads. We've seen 'em at work. We know their views, and we've suffered enough to know they won't change. Unless we make 'em. Many of you have families, wives and children. What future for them if we don't act? None of us wanted violence. But it's been forced on us.'

He waited. But the silence that came was the silence of men who had gone beyond doubt. The reality of violence no longer daunted them. Martin had tried the waters and the men, his men, had not wavered. He struck out again, confident, and his voice rang out into the night. 'We're goin' to have to fight, lads. I think you know that. And we're ready.'

Again, there was no sign of retreat from his listeners.

'Our mates from Creswick will join us, too. When they're ready. And what do they need to be ready, boys?' He paused, raising one arm and pointing out over the crowd. No ringmaster could have done better. 'Guns. That's all they need. We have 'em and they'll have 'em, too.'

Completely in command now, Martin motioned to two men standing together on the edge of the crowd. 'And guns are what these two lads'll get for 'em.'

The two shadows slid forward as he said this.

'Joe Carmody and Robert Barnes. Scots they are. Creswick men. By the time these lads, and those I'll send later, have done their job, we will not be alone. Our comrades from the Creswick field will be armed, too, armed and ready. Then we can take on Commissioner Rede and his dandies.'

Men were eager to know more and questions bubbled up through the darkness.

'No, lads. That's all you need to know. We don't want information fallin' out accidentally later. And we know the traps have big ears. These comrades of ours, for that's what they are and what all of the brave lads of Creswick are, will know exactly what to do, when I tell 'em.'

Comment faded and he went on. 'Now, boys, I know that the reform lads will ask you to join 'em. They're gettin' stronger and most'll fight if they need to. But remember, we might be all fightin' the same cause, but there are different ways of fighting. So don't be swayed. Vern and Lalor are good men. Men worthy to be followed, I'm not denying that. But others in the League might weaken. Might settle for less. We know what we want. New government. No royal toadies spruiking out of Toorak and damning honest men. And we know that we're goin' to have to take up arms and fight for our rights. And I'm asking you now to be patient. Be patient and remain loyal to one another. We're brothers now. And our cause is just.'

Silence hung again. This time the silence of soldiers knowing that battle was inevitable. And that they were ready to take their part. He had not given out his battle plan as yet. That would come later. What mattered at this stage was that they were ready to fight. He had succeeded.

Almost humble now, he concluded. 'And I'm asking you to remain loyal, loyal to me. You've trusted me this far and I won't let you down. Some of you'll be wantin' to know more, I know. Be patient, lads. We don't want information reachin' the ears of the camp, do we?' He was relieved that no one did in fact question him.

Instead, the darkness was charged with activity. Men crowded around Martin and Tom. Eager voices rose, exhorting all to stick by their mates and to their leader, Martin Jacobs.

And so, quite quickly, the men broke up and set out towards their camps, this band of honest, determined but untrained miners, waiting for the spark that would ignite a blaze fierce enough to destroy corruption and leave in its ashes space enough for a new order to be established. A bright utopia for all working men and their families. Martin stood at last, victorious.

But the victory had come at a cost. Tom was amazed to look up at his leader and notice his hands quivering. Even his body, usually rigidly upright, was slumped. And his voice was heavy with weariness as he spoke to the two Scots.

'I'll be brief. There's a ship, a brigantine, already in Hobson's Bay, the *Queen*. On her there's a friend of the cause. We'll call him Jack. Passes as a businessman and I guess he is, if you don't look too hard. And our friend Jack has just what we need. And he's waitin' for us to take 'em off his hands.' He had regained some of his energy now. 'They're not Enfield rifles, that's true, but Colt navy pistols. Already paid for. By some friends of mine in California. In the hands of brave men they'll give the red-coated troopers somethin' to think about.'

For a moment he looked directly at Tom. 'Now, Joe and Robert here will take off for Melbourne in the morning. Pick up the guns from our man on board the *Queen*, bring 'em back and hide 'em in a hut a mile out of Creswick. Nothin' could be simpler. Our plans can be revealed once everythin' is set in place.'

Again he focused on the two Scots. 'I trust your men as I do me own. But at this stage the less who know the better. Those bastards, the traps, have long ears.'

He stopped suddenly, as if anticipating a question. There was none. Turning to Tom, he continued. 'You might be disappointed, lad. But you'll be needed here. This is a job for the Creswick boys. Besides, these two jumped ship to take to the diggings. An added incentive, you might say, for 'em not to be caught.'

If he expected a smile from the two Scotsmen, he was disappointed. Turning directly to them, he fixed the lantern on their faces. 'Now, our man's expectin' you. A messenger was sent two days ago to let him know you'll be contactin' him at midnight the day after tomorrow. No earlier, now. Bein' sailors yourselves, you'll know the brigantine when you see her. You probably know where she'll be standin'.'

There was a nod and a brief reply. 'Aye, man, we know 'er. Go on.'

'Good. Now, I don't need to tell you to be careful. These bloody traps expect trouble, as you know. Snoopin' around has become a habit for them. Get yourselves out to the *Queen*. At midnight, remember. Jack will expect you then. You know where the hut is. Well hidden, it is.'

Joe Carmody nodded. 'Aye, man. I could find it with me eyes shut. Buried in 'ere, it is.' The 'ere was his head and he tapped it lightly. But there was no smile on his face as he did so.

The younger of the two, the one Tom remembered as Robert, turned, ready to leave. But the other clapped his hand on Martin's shoulder. 'Don't worry, man, we know what we're up against. We'll plant them guns away, safe from pryin' eyes. You let us know when the time is ripe and our lads'll be along. Good lads, all of 'em.'

Martin stood square in front of them. 'I don't doubt that, lads. But we're all bein' watched, now. Probably you and your Creswick mates as well. I wonder, sometimes, whether there's a rat somewhere among us, passin' information back to the traps. If so, we'll deal with him later. But be careful.'

There was a quick handshake and the two departed.

Martin watched their silhouettes absorbed among the trees. 'Well, Tommy, lad, there's no turnin' back now, is there?'

'No. Whatever happens now, we're in it, for sure.'

Martin was almost whispering now. 'Secrecy's the thing from now on, Tom. You, Frank, the two Scots and I know the details, where those guns'll be stored. Nobody else. Let's keep it that way, eh? There'll be two others sent out later this week. To the same vessel. They'll pick up the last of the guns and bring 'em back to the hut.'

Although two days were to be spent on the road, Joe Carmody and Robert Barnes left very early the next morning. Rather than return to Creswick, they had camped by Yarrowee Creek. They were to be merchants. The bags they carried were to be used for transporting trinkets for Mary Douglas's store on the Melbourne Road. All they knew about her was that she was a widow and the mother of the lad they had met the night before. But they might be called upon to explain the empty, bulky saddle bags and that story would be as plausible as any other. And they could indeed pass as two travelling salesmen, Joe sharp-eyed and tall, with a slight limp that had in fact come from contact with a falling mast in a storm off the coast near Sydney town, but which would be explained as the result of a fall from a horse, Robert shorter and thinner, but with a restless energy that his companion felt might need watching, should trouble occur on the road. Or at the port.

Pre-dawn gave to the slopes, the shafts and the windlasses a gaunt, empty appearance. The kind of emptiness they had seen month after month on other fields. The emptiness of expectation. Soon, both at Creswick and here, men would be abroad, stretching, coughing, eating, preparing for the day's work underground. Occasionally, they heard a man stirring in his tent or hut.

By one of the tents a digger sat, smoking. He looked up as they slid past. 'You're on the move early, lads,' he said, in what they took to be an American accent. 'A long way to go, 'ave you?'

'Aye, that we have,' replied Joe. 'We're 'eadin' off to Melbourne, to bring back goods for a store on the Melbourne road.'

The seated man waved and they rode on.

'Practice, Rob, for any nosey trap we might meet later.'

His companion laughed. 'Yeah. Dunno 'ow convincing it sounded, though.'

Soon, over the whole area there hung a soft fur of grey and pink. Dawn was not far off. By the time the sun did appear, they were clear of the diggings and out on the open road. At one point, they came upon a store.

'Could be the wider's,' Robert announced, reining in his horse.

'Yes, lad, it could be. Remember what it looks like. Wouldn't want to deliver our goods to the wrong place, would we?'

Mid-morning brought its usual heat and they dismounted under some stringybarks.

'I can't get used to this landscape,' muttered Joe. 'Cold Scotland might be, laddie, but it's comfortable. Friendly, you might say. A man can feel safe there. 'Ere a man don't feel safe. It's like as if the land wants to squeeze the last wee drop of life out of you in summer. And, if you survive that, drown you in the winter.'

Robert gave off patting his horse. 'Aye. And it ain't too generous with its gold, neither. At least it ain't to me.'

Soon they were back on the road, now a clear, if rutted, line cutting its way through the heavy and intimidating grey-brown of the bush. Monotony was relieved, however, by the number of travellers they met. And by midday, as they approached Bacchus Marsh, they found themselves part of a steadily moving caravan of vehicles and pedestrians. This gave them greater confidence. They might well, in such a varied collection, pass as harmless and anonymous buyers and sellers.

In the town, they rested their horses, ate what food they could buy and watched the traffic moving in both directions.

They spent some time talking to a schoolteacher and his wife bound for Buninyong and the Catholic children there. The husband, thin and wearing thick-rimmed glasses, spoke with a distant kind of eagerness, as if he was already poised outside his classroom. The wife, small, plain and silent, bore in her face the apprehension common to many women following their husbands into the unknown. Joe felt a real sympathy for her. His own wife, reluctantly, had followed him out to Creswick twelve months ago. And had died there from pneumonia. Her agony had lasted a week and no doctor had been there to ease her pain. Nor any other woman to sit with her.

Had he been able, he would have turned this young couple back. But he knew that men on a mission are not easily dissuaded.

Early in the afternoon, they came upon a bullock team. The driver told them he was Welsh and was returning to Ballarat with some equipment for a new syndicate. They, in turn, related their tale and were surprised at his response.

'Mary Douglas. That's the one you're talking about. Oh, yes. I know the lass. Hope to marry her soon. If she'll have me, that is.'

His booming laughter all but displaced a crow from its perch above them and when they left him he was stirring his beasts into action.

Joe laughed as the wagon tottered away. 'Must be keen to get back to the widow. Anxious to know whether she'll take 'im on or not. Good luck, bullocky!' he shouted. Above the grating and the heaving, he doubted whether he would be heard.

At night, they tethered their horses a few hundred yards off the road, covered themselves with their blankets and tried to sleep.

In the morning, stiff and restless, they rose, ready to move on. They did not rush, however, having decided much earlier that their chief requirements, apart from their own cunning and luck, were horses that were fresh.

So, steeling themselves, they dawdled through the morning and the afternoon, coming in sight of Melbourne and its port after dark. There was no sharp line dividing the town from the surrounding countryside. Buildings strayed out among trees. Tracks seemed to start and then, for want of any real destination, simply gave up and lost themselves in open land. It was slow going through the darkness. But gradually the town took on a firmer shape and they could move more confidently.

They knew, everyone knew, that all manner of contraband was being shuffled to and from the ships that came into Hobson's Bay. Cheap grog for the hotels, arms for the miners, nuggets stolen and bound for a better price in London, equipment headed for the black market. Anything, in fact, that was better kept out of the sight of authorities. Sensibly, those carrying out these nefarious activities usually did so at night. But sensible and suspicious authorities were also aware of this. If they were not careful, now, the whole plan would come unstuck. And they, if arrested with weapons bound for disgruntled, some would say disloyal, miners, would receive little mercy.

As they picked their way through the shacks and warehouses along the shore of Hobson's Bay, they were assailed by the scents, sounds and sights of the sea. Things that were familiar to them both: gulls carrying out their universal squabbles, a chain rattling, somewhere drunks muttering in a foreign language, boats like animals asleep, prostitutes prominent in sickly pools of light. Nothing new here.

The *Queen* stood where they thought she would be, about three hundred yards offshore.

Knowing that boatmen could usually be found in any shoreside hotel, they tied their horses up, some distance away from one of the hotels and walked towards it. The noise alone was enough to guide them. The laughter, shouts and clinking of glasses could be found in any number of ports they had visited. The building was crowded with sailors, labourers and a few uniformed soldiers. It was not difficult to find a boatman. They usually drank together. But to get one to row them out into the bay was.

Many of these men had probably taken part in shady deals

themselves and were cautious now, or cunning. Most gave them a blank stare when they asked. Picking up goods from a ship at twelve o'clock at night had a familiar ring to it. And they were generally quick to refuse.

However, one agreed to let them take his boat and row it out themselves. Having paid him, they trudged down to the shore and climbed into it. The wily old boatman took the stern, pushed it away and stood watching as the two miners pulled out through the shallow waves.

Behind them, the shore spilled its upturned boats, crates and ropes. Huts and warehouses blurred in the darkness and at odd moments a dribble of light crept from an opened door.

At one point, Joe stopped rowing and pointed. 'Look,' he whispered, 'a clipper.'

Far out in the bay a large vessel stood out, her three masts thin and clean, her sails furled and her bowsprit pointing seawards.

'You'd think she was keen to get back on the sea, wouldn't you, seein' 'er there swinging on 'her anchor? Great, thunderin' things, they are,' he went on, gaining enthusiasm. 'Nothin' else like 'em. I've done me time on clippers, lad. Seen the sails close to burstin' and the 'ull creakin' as if it was groanin' in pain. Oh, yes. You were never far from the edge of danger on them. Fast and wild, they are. Fast and wild are their captains, too.' His eyes lingered for a moment and then he took up his oars again.

Soon they were under the bows of the *Queen*, its three masts cutting across the moon as they swung closer and its rigging gleaming like web cast out by some gigantic spider.

'Careful now,' muttered Joe.

They waited for perhaps five minutes, feeling their boat tremble slightly. Above, they could hear ropes creaking and beside them the swish of water against the hull. Nothing more. It might have been a ghost ship, swinging there slowly on its anchor.

Then Joe whistled, twice, softly. There was an anxious wait and he whistled again. No response. So they waited for a few minutes, hearing only the water slapping the hull. This time, as he whistled, a shape appeared above, leaned out, retreated, reappeared and a rope ladder slithered down the hull. The two men rowed slowly, carefully and a gentle nudge brought the two craft together. Above them now hung the bowsprit, a single finger pointing ahead. Like print on a dirty page, the name of the vessel stood out clearly and beneath it some seaman, perhaps while cleaning the hull, had scratched the shape of a bare-breasted woman.

Next, a rope was lowered to them. Robert leaned forward, tying it to the bow. For a few seconds, blackness filled the space above. Then the figure came again, indicating that they should climb up.

Once on deck, they heard a man's voice. 'Come with me.' He led them across the open deck and down a flight of rickety, narrow steps.

A candle was lit and they found themselves in a small cabin. Somewhere not too distant, someone stirred, snored and bumped against his bunk. In the pallid light, they could make out a bearded face and eyes that turned briefly upon them and then away.

'Now,' the stranger said, quickly and coldly, 'we must be quick. You don't need to know my name. Nor I yours. I've been paid and our business will be done when we finish here. It's a dangerous game, this.'

Joe bristled and shot back, almost in a whisper, 'More so for us, laddie. You could have brought the goods ashore yourself.'

There was no response. Hands were already carefully prising open a box. Soon all the pistols, fifteen of them, lay on the table.

The stranger transferred them to the saddlebags, along with powder and balls. 'Now, follow me.'

Joe and Robert gathered up the heavy, bulging bags and climbed upwards. A raised hand stopped them at the top of the stairs, then motioned them on. Nothing more was said and, as quietly as they could, they clambered down and into the boat. The hawser slid up and away from them and by the time they had pushed off, the deck above them was clear.

Quickly they began to row towards the shore, noting the boatman's shed and the distant point where the horses were tethered.

About halfway across, Joe stopped rowing and pointed to a spot well away from the shed. 'I don't trust that bloody boatman. We'll land well clear of 'im and walk back to the 'orses. There's money for men like him, 'andin' over 'ard-workin' lads like us.'

He took up his oars again, keeping his eyes on the beach and the small shed. Suddenly he stiffened. 'There. See that. The bastard's put the police on to us.'

In the half-light from a lantern, they could clearly see three men about three hundred yards along the shore, all in uniform, all armed. As yet they had not noticed the boat sliding between patches of moonlight.

'Now, lad. Quick and quiet.'

The boat surged ahead, lurching slightly a minute later as it scuffed through the sand and came to rest. They could not have been more cautious in their approach. However, there was a shout, the lantern began swinging and three shadows came running towards them. Another shout followed, then a flash of light, then an explosion and a splash in the shallows beside them.

'Quick, lad. Get those bags up or by Christ we've 'ad it.'

The waving column of light was getting closer. Desperate now, the two threw the bags across their horses, mounted and galloped off, careering away from the shore.

Another shot followed and there was a tinkling of glass. But now they were clear, weaving their way through the tangle of warehouses set around the docks.

'Bastards,' muttered Joe. 'Never met a boatman yet that I could trust.'

They rode hard now, cutting through the shanties and huts that stood like grotesque toadstools along the streets. Finally they slackened off, relieved to feel the country opening up before them.

As the moon slipped finally from view, they were far out on the

Ballarat Road. The stream of light that heralded dawn gave them warmth, but it also was a reminder of the dangers they now faced. Travelling on the open road and in broad daylight, they could not easily hide away saddle bags full of illegal weapons. Everyone knew that troops were being sent each week to strengthen the garrison at Ballarat and travellers were often stopped and searched on the road. So they moved out of harm's way if any large group came towards them.

By the middle of the morning, they were within sight of Bacchus Marsh and about a mile short of the town, they dismounted, led their horses well clear of the road, unsaddled them and settled down to get whatever sleep they could, taking it in turns to watch. Sleep was virtually impossible, however. Each crack of a branch was a trooper. Each whinny of a distant horse the sign that they were to be overrun and captured.

Late in the afternoon, they mounted again, knowing that night would bring them a measure of safety. By dusk, they were on the track leading on to Creswick and, soon, under the cover of the darkness, they could almost relax. Occasionally, they saw pricks of light bobbing towards them along the track. They would dismount then and move well away. At one point, they heard a clatter of horses. That alarmed them. But it was only a party of miners. Some of them were carrying lanterns. A few were obviously drunk. They trotted past and disappeared round a wide sweep in the track.

Both were tired now. However, they knew that they could be at the hut by lunchtime if they persisted.

Dawn brought them one real cause for concern. As they rode into a small gully, they saw ahead a group of ten soldiers, riding comfortably towards them. Scrambling off their horses, they made for a thick mass of wattles. Fortunately, the troopers rode on past them, but they did not move until even the sounds of their horses had faded.

'Christ, that was close,' Robert muttered, trying to laugh.

'Aye, laddie. That it was. The sooner we get these to the 'ut,' tapping the bag as he remounted, 'the better I'll feel.'

The hut was well hidden, a blister hidden among trees. Only those familiar with the scribble of a track that lead to it would be able to find it.

But Sergeant Miller was familiar with it. As the two weary Scots flung open the door, he stepped forward. Beside him and with their pistols drawn, were six police officers.

'Welcome 'ome, boys. Those bags look rather 'eavy. My lads'll 'elp you out there.' The humour disappeared quickly. 'You'll be 'hung for this, of course. They'll be a grand 'anging by the time we round up the rest of you, won't there? Now, boys, we'll pack these two off to Buninyong and on to Melbourne. We've got to keep this secret for a bit longer. Commissioner Johnston, 'e was insistent on that. We'll get the others, Jacobs and 'is mates, when we're ready. We 'ave our plants among those traitors on the Bendigo and Creswick fields. They can 'ave it put around that the guns are safe 'ere. And they are safe, aren't they, lads?' looking at the two hapless prisoners as he said it. 'Safe enough with us, that is. And we won't 'ave to wait long. Things'll 'appen soon enough now. I've no doubt about that.'

15

Bentley's Hotel

In the heat that ensued over the next week, tempers on the field simmered, Tom and Martin remained ignorant of the disaster that had occurred and the authorities continued their prodding and their poking, hoping that enforcement and harassment would be sufficient to dissuade open rebellion. Frayed tempers went along with increased excitement and many waited now for a final spark to ignite the diggings.

Not everyone, of course, waited with the degree of enthusiasm that Martin did.

Many in the town feared that the ruffians on the goldfield would have their way and the whole community could be caught up in the conflagration. These people hoped that the authorities would gain control, crush any resistance and allow the town to settle back into its sensible rhythm. To them, the unruly miners were not really part of the established community at all.

Then there were men like the Reverend Thomas Hastie, trying to steer a middle course and at the same time show compassion for the diggers and their families. His faith dictated that he preach love where there was hate, justice where there was inhumanity and compassion where there was indifference to the plight of the poor. And he had visited the town and the diggings often enough to see the impact of injustices on poor, honest miners. It was there, like the dust on the streets. A wife fearful in her tent after the arrest of her husband for not carrying his licence. A young man hauled off because he spoke in the street about the corruption of officials. All of it obvious, even to a casual observer. And his services and visitations throughout the area meant he was certainly no casual observer.

But there were times when the poor themselves were the perpetrators of injustice. When, fearful of going under themselves, they would turn upon their neighbours. How, then, could he simply blame the wealthy? Were they all evil?

Any number of incidents revealed the moral dilemmas confronting him. Only a week ago, for example, he buried a young miner, killed in a rockfall while working deep underground for a large syndicate. He would not forget the distraught, terrified face of the widow as the coffin was lowered. Nor the comments of his colleagues as they stood bunched together by the grave.

'We told 'em, Reverend,' one of them had muttered, pointing far off towards the mines on the slope. 'Told the managers that the timbers wouldn't 'old. But they wouldn't listen, would they? Not them. All they want is pay dirt dragged up by the sweat of us labourers. The wealthy 'ave it all. 'Elped along by the police and troopers.'

He could not but share the anger and grief here.

But during that same week he visited the family of a grazier who had drowned saving a young worker from a dam. On another occasion, he learned of a young woman being helped financially by the manager of a syndicate after the death of her husband. Was the poor man's widow more worthy of sympathy? Did death somehow have a different significance because those grieving were wealthy? Were the tears of the poor different from those of the well-off?

His sermons were directed to all who came to church. How could he reconcile the chaotic currents sweeping through the community and deliver words of comfort when those conflicting currents ran through him as well? Few knew of the torments a man of faith must endure in a society like this. But he persisted. And his vision of saving the children of the poor did not fade.

However, on the diggings themselves, every rumour of injustices committed against the miners was taken up and used to fuel further resentment. Each shanty reverberated with the stories. Here, soldiers had been pelted with eggs and rocks as they marched to the camp.

There, a miner had been dragged from his hut and hauled off, leaving his wife and two children open-mouthed and desperate. Over there, someone had been bashed and left in a street, 'as an example to others who might disobey lawful instruction'. The tone of these never varied, the message was constant. Honest men were being harassed and provoked by corrupt officials.

The most disturbing tale, repeated often and in many places, was of military reinforcements being rushed from Melbourne to protect property. Nobody listened more closely, nobody listened with more excitement, nobody fuelled these rumblings with more skill, than Martin Jacobs.

'Commissioner Rede might well be settin' the fire of revolution himself,' he announced one evening, 'and when the time comes, we'll be happy to set it alight for him.'

Then, a few days later, early in October, it seemed as if that time had come. With the field in full swing and the sun and the heat fuelling tempers, shouts erupted from one corner of the diggings.

'Bentley's been acquitted.'

The news swelled out among the diggers, swept through tents and shanties and within an hour anger had reached boiling point.

'What? Bentley acquitted?'

'Yes, the bastard.'

'Our mate Scobie murdered at Bentley's hotel and the pub owner walks free.'

'Acquitted by Bentley's mate, Magistrate D'Ewes.'

Tom and Martin stood together by their shaft. The windlass trembled in the wind but they knew it would not be used any more today. A deadly silence settled for a while, punctuated by angry denunciations of the police and the judiciary.

'By God, Tom, somethin' will come of this.'

Somebody, somewhere, decided that Bentley should be confronted in his lair. Quickly, the decision to advance on his hotel was transmitted along the slopes. Men appeared at the doorways. Some tumbled out of their tents, pulling on trousers and boots. Others scrambled like rabbits out of their holes. And a few, the unlucky ones working at depth, were forgotten and had to be hauled up later, complaining that they had missed the fun.

By early afternoon, activity was grinding to a halt on the slopes of Canadian Gully, the Gravel Pits, Eureka and Red Hill. Soon lines of miners, some still with the dust and mud clinging to them, were making their way towards Bakery Hill and the Eureka hotel. From a distance these were lines of ants converging and forming moving colonies.

'Yes, Tom, this could be it.'

Frank Burgen joined them and they let themselves be carried along by the current of men.

Martin could feel the excitement pulsating among the miners and was confident that they had almost passed any point of return. Until now, their anger had been largely fragmented, coming together only on odd occasions. These had fuelled his hopes, of course. But each time they had been squashed and the diggers had retreated behind harmless whingeing.

Today, things had changed. With the acquittal of Bentley, the powder keg had been opened. The corrupt magistrates and the court officials had done that. Now it looked as if the spark was about to be thrown. He was not sure what direction the fire would take or what wind would propel it onwards. But it was coming. And if the actions of the diggers were fanned into open rebellion, so much the better. He knew, also, that a revolution needed firm control. The failure in France had taught him that. Only men like Frederick Vern, Great Works and perhaps Peter Lalor could help him take control of the situation and hammer those ideals into permanent reality.

So Martin strode on, more confident than he had been for many months. It just needed a nudge now, to see events finally explode and revolution burst out on the field. Each man was carrying his own lighted taper. Only one needed to drop or throw his and the keg would erupt.

Tom, who was struggling to keep pace with his partner, could feel the quickening in his own body and, at the same time, a pricking anxiety that would not go away. He was approaching that thin line his father had always retreated from and had warned him about so many times.

'Survival, boy. That's what matters. No use raisin' your fists against an army. You stick things out, lad. That's what you do. And you look for the chance to make your move. And it don't mean committin' suicide.'

His uneasiness became stronger the closer he came to Bakery Hill.

By now, the army of miners was rapidly advancing upon the Eureka hotel. Its shingle roof and weatherboard walls were already clearly visible. The sight seemed to increase the energy of every marcher. Each had his own story, real or imaginary, about the evils perpetrated there. They were swapped in haste. And in the swapping, anger and determination took on extra fuel.

One man had been belted up outside the back door for condemning the administration. Another had got himself drunk and been thrown out. Quite a few had been seduced by prostitutes into drinking too much and had woken up in the morning badly out of pocket. Most knew that Bentley had received special consideration from the commissioners over business transactions. And all knew that Scobie, honest Scobie from Scotland, had been murdered as he knocked on the front door of the hotel and that Bentley, the murderer, had been acquitted by a corrupt magistrate. What was wrong with a man and a mate arriving to have a drink at a hotel even if it was a bit late at night? Bentley had certainly opened his door to any of his wealthy cronies who came around after closing time. The time had come to teach him a lesson.

At one point, the three men were surprised to see the bullocky, Dan Morgan. It seemed as if he had been looking for them for he pushed his way through the crowd and greeted them.

Then, waving Martin and Frank on, he grabbed Tom by the arm.

'Tom, lad. I must talk to you,' he said, standing his ground against the tide streaming past. 'This is no good for you. There could well be bloodshed 'ere. You can see the police against the wall.'

Bristling anger swelled and Tom tried to move on. But the bullocky's grip tightened. 'Too dangerous, lad. Listen to me. I can tell you what'll happen next. I've seen it before.'

Tom swore and endeavoured to push past.

'No, you bloody well will listen. I've seen men killed, boy. Wives made widows because their husbands were shot or hanged, taking action like this. Yes, I've seen it all on the coal mines in Wales. Do you want to see your mates killed? And your mother left grieving for a son who threw his life away?'

The bullocky, sensing the resistance and the anger, was almost pleading now. 'Give this up, Tom. I promised your mother I'd keep you out of danger. And that's what I intend to do. She's agreed to marry me and I don't want to see her made unhappy by the death of a foolhardy son. Get out of this, while you still have a chance.'

Tom's voice, as he strained to release himself, was that of a small, defensive boy. 'You're not my father. You might've had her in bed, but that doesn't give you any rights over me. These are my mates. Martin's my mate. No, my leader. And I'll stick with them.' That thin line, the one that had saved his father, was now snapped. Tom pushed and slid free.

Curious, some of the men had stopped. Comments of support for the young miner rippled out.

'The lad's old enough to decide for himself.'

'If you don't want to join us, clear off. Leave the boy in peace.'

'He's one of us.'

Free now, Tom had rushed on. Already lost in the crowd, he was set on rejoining his mates. But, around Dan, resentment hardened. Resentment that quickly changed to something more menacing as an old, hard-faced veteran shuffled through a gap in the crowd and pointed.

'A spy, that's what 'e'll be. And we know how to deal with 'is kind.'

That was the trigger. Three of the bystanders broke free from the circle and came forward, their fists clenched and their bodies tensed and leaning slightly ahead.

'Oh, yes,' the old miner murmured knowingly, smiling into Dan's face. 'We 'ave a simple way of dealin' with scum like you.'

The man stepped back, nodded, and the three rushed upon him. Their faces were now close to his, their eyes set in a stare, their lips drawn back. Among the onlookers, there was an air of expectation.

Anxiety and fear drove Dan now. He pulled back, only to be shoved again into the arms of his attackers. Wrenching free, he lashed out, catching one on the jaw. Blood flowed quickly down the man's cheek but that was the last punch he was able to give. Another grabbed his head, straightened it and drove a fist into his face. He slumped forward. Again his head was jerked upwards. Again he slumped forward and this time he was allowed to collapse to the ground.

'There, that'll keep you quiet,' he heard as he doubled up at their feet.

By the time he had struggled upright, only a few stragglers remained. One or two paused. Most moved on. There is never sympathy for a spy.

He spat blood from his mouth and looked at the grey mass ascending Bakery Hill. Only those very close would have heard his half whispered, 'Oh, boy, you'll die, snared in madness like this.'

Tom said nothing, when he caught up, about the bullocky's attempts to draw him away and the angry exchange that had ensued. Already the rhythm and the excitement generated by this army of angry men were propelling him forward.

Close to the hotel, the rhythm changed, slowed, and the men formed a loose circle. Those far behind strained to see the reason.

'This,' someone shouted in a voice that carried the echo of the Highlands, 'this is the very spot. Here our mate Scobie was bashed. His head splintered by Bentley and his thugs.'

Silence gripped the audience, the silence that engulfs pilgrims as they stand before the site where a saint has fallen.

The voice continued, this time intimate in tone. 'Don't worry, James, we'll 'ave our revenge. Punishment is comin'.'

There were nods of approval, but little comment as eyes looked down at the sacred spot. The pause was finally broken by the speaker himself. With one lingering look back, he began to walk directly towards the hotel. Slowly gathering itself together, the crowd fell into step, regained its rhythm and arrived within a few yards of the hotel. Before them stood a small contingent of police, clearly nervous before this huge assembly

'Good God,' exclaimed Martin. 'Those poor bastards aren't even armed. Rede doesn't expect trouble, does he? Well, trouble is coming, Misters Rede and Johnston, I can tell you that. There isn't any doubt about it now.'

For a time, there was uncertainty, filled with the upraising of fists, threats against the hotel owner and the answering call by the officer in charge to disband. This uncertainty gave Martin a strong feeling of alarm. Amidst such harmless sparring the momentum might be lost.

Eventually, the gathering was called to order and the speakers, well known to most of the diggers now, rose. All, Thomas Kennedy, Timothy Hayes and Peter Lalor, exhorted the miners to stand as one and demand a reopening of the Scobie case. Shouts of agreement rang out, rumbles of wild assent that tumbled out over those closest and reached those furthest away.

When Peter Lalor asked for money that could be offered as a reward for information leading to the arrest of the guilty, a hail of coins rained down at his feet. There was something charismatic about this young Irishman as he stood there, arms extended and red hair dancing in the wind. Also a quiet sense of control. He did not have to shout to gain the attention of the multitude. Men listened. Even those who might not have agreed with his earlier calls for moderation were silent now.

Martin watched as the events were played out. Clearly excited, his fists clenched, unclenched and his face glowed. 'Oh, yes,' he exulted, gripping Tom by the arm, 'there'll be action soon. All over the field.

And when the wave breaks, we must be ready, boy. The time is almost upon us.'

So intent was he that he could not remain fixed in the one spot, although his eyes were fixed on some event far away. Some utopia where justice and equality ruled unchallenged.

However, as the passion and the coins descended, so too did the mood of the miners. Shouts of approval continued. But to Martin, hauled back from his dream, there was a sudden and unexpected change here. Something anticlimactic. The fierce anger that had bound them together seemed to be evaporating, slowly, but inexorably. Indeed, parts of the great assembly were breaking off. Individuals were emerging, coming forward, dutifully placing their money in the boxes, rubbing shoulders and then moving away. And in response the thin line of uniformed men seemed to stand more resolute. Yet was it not uniformed authority the men claimed they despised so much? If a small contingent of unarmed men in uniform could intimidate them so easily, what chance was there for them to confront the authorities and bring about the changes they said they wanted?

The great tide of anger and energy that had promised so much seemed to be collapsing on itself.

Martin shook with frustration. 'Oh, no, it's happenin' again. Look, Tom. Look at 'em. Paying their money and leavin'. Are they never going to roll up their sleeves and take real action? There's more at stake here than revenge for Scobie's murder. Can't they see that? Damn them all. They're not worth fightin' for. If they had the heart of our own men, they wouldn't be stoppin' at this.' He was battling now to retain control, stamping his feet and waving madly towards the crowd. Then, shaking his head in disbelief, he turned away, ready to leave.

Tom was amazed, also, at the change in the public mood. But he was confused, too, by Martin's reaction. The slumped shoulders and the look of near despair were there for all to see. Could a leader lose heart so quickly?

However, the fates must have heard Martin's lament and, sharing his disgust, they visited something totally unexpected upon the miners: a projectile that soared above their heads and smashed through one of the impressive windows of the hotel. Glass shattered above the police and the explosion electrified the mood of the miners. A boy, throwing his arms in the air, congratulated himself on his aim and his mates cheered. Picking up another stone, he took aim and threw, and the gaudy light above the front door disintegrated. His actions were to thrust events catastrophically forward. He had shattered not only a window and a light. He had broken that invisible circle that protected property. And his had been the first taper tumbled into the powder keg. The spark to ignite revolution on the Ballarat goldfield had come.

For a while, the men had difficulty seeing this. Many, in fact, stared in disbelief. But soon the groups were re-established, hardening into that mass of energy Martin had admired earlier.

He stopped dead, gripped Tom by the shoulder and turned back. 'There might be a chance yet, Tom.'

On all sides, excitement rose. And again there followed a moment of uncertainty. All seemed now to be holding stones. All seemed to be waiting for the order to fire. And it came soon enough as a voice, from deep in the crowd shouted out, 'Let's burn the bloody place.'

At first, there was only a mutter of encouragement. But it quickly became a wild, discordant chorus that hardened into action. Tumbling, righting themselves, falling and straightening again, the miners were now bent on revenge. Nothing would stand against them. Although the police stood their ground as best they could, they were quickly pushed to one side and the mob began a wholehearted assault. Some stormed through the building, hurling aside furniture and wrenching doors from their hinges. Others descended on the bar, grabbing bottles of grog, the same fiery liquor that had seen many of them in earlier days reduced to insensibility and left penniless in their beds or out in the road. A wild laughter rang through the corridors.

Bentley's hotel was doomed.

The men were careful, though, not to set the place alight until they had smashed all they could and taken all they wanted. Once started, the flames spread quickly through the weatherboard building. Men fanned it with their rage and excitement. And to their delight, at one point, Commissioner Rede appeared at a window. His fists were raised in defiance, his words, either lost in the storm, or laughed at, warned of dire consequences.

He was greeted by a torrent of abuse, stones and, from somewhere, a volley of eggs. Presumably, a few of the more inventive miners had penetrated to the kitchen. Fortunately for him, the adult males had less skill than the boy who had cast the first stone. The angry commissioner stood for a moment, shouting into the melee, but was forced to retreat. Soon the whole building was throwing out flames and black smoke. Outhouses caught fire and the Washington Bowling Saloon began to tremble as the flames licked its walls. The auction mart, the concert hall and the half-completed billiard room were forced to surrender to the advancing fire, and soon Bentley's empire lay in ruins.

At the height of the inferno, a figure was seen frantically riding away.

'There goes that swine Bentley!' someone screamed out. 'Keep going, murderer. There won't be much left when you get back.'

Before long, there was not much left. The twisted buildings fell upon themselves. The police left, relieved that they had not been murdered in the madness. Miners emerged from the smoke, carrying bottles, items from tables and pieces of furniture. Some were silent. Many were flushed with their own audacity and shouted to one another or held up whatever they had looted.

But quite quickly the energy subsided and the men began to disperse, some in small groups, others alone. A few, perhaps, wondering what they had unleashed and what the consequences might be.

Martin Jacobs had no doubts. 'Tommy, my boy. The time has come. Look at 'em. They're committed now. Guilty as hell. And us saved by a bloody rock hurled through a window. There's no goin' back. Just a need to watch, wait and be ready. Things'll happen now.'

Tom remained silent, looking back at the smoke.

'Yes,' murmured Frank Burgen, almost to himself, 'you're right there. Things will happen all right. And all we need to do is be ready.'

There were a few who remained at the scene, after the flames had done their work. One was Dan Morgan. He had done what he could to stop the blood oozing from his nose, and his arms were crossed over his stomach. His body was slightly bent and his breathing remained shallow and painful.

His whispered 'Oh, Mary, my love, I've let you down' would not have carried to any of those around him. His slow, stooped departure would not have been noticed by anyone.

The other was the minister, Thomas Hastie. His face was blanched to a pasty grey and if you had observed him closely you might have detected tears creeping down his cheeks. No one would have detected his internal self-condemnation. He, too, felt he had failed. Failed to dissuade any of the miners to turn away from violence. But, where Dan Morgan had been beaten up, at least his distinctive black costume had protected him from retaliation. The crowd had simply separated around him, half listened or ignored him completely and continued their march. The thorns of his own helplessness were as painful as any blows that might have fallen upon him.

16

Meetings and a surprise

The smoke did not clear above the wreck of Bentley's hotel for many days. Travellers paused on the Melbourne road, curious about its destruction. Locals came out, some sympathetic to the hotel owner, others arguing that Bentley's hotel had been a disgrace and deserved to be destroyed anyway. For the diggers, the significance of its destruction was clear. They had flexed their muscles: they had made their first real assault on corruption.

Martin Jacobs worked without rest now, keeping his ear to the ground, listening to every piece of information, fabricating new rumours whenever he thought it necessary, watching the movement of soldiers and police and each day going from claim to claim and encouraging his men. The anger he saw, heard and fuelled could be stiffened into action: in the heat of conflict, the miners could be transformed into warriors. Never had his hopes run higher.

There was no meeting he did not attend. Each time a group of angry miners assembled on Bakery Hill, he was there. He heard Vern call again for the burning of licences and he heard John Humffray call for moderation. He stood with the thousands who assembled on the twenty-ninth of November to hear the report of the delegates who had met with Governor Hotham in Melbourne. And when he heard that the governor had not yielded to the miners' demands for the dismantling of the commission and the granting of votes to the diggers, he secretly rejoiced. Even small concessions might have satisfied some of the miners.

What he wanted was a new social order, something the authorities would never countenance. They would respond only to force. And if that is what was required, then that is what they would have. The governor's refusal would only stiffen the miners' resolve. Of that he was sure. He was confident, too, that any careless move by the commissioners would be sufficient to provoke the men to action.

He took great interest, as well, in the particular happenings around him on the slope. He watched as troopers arriving along Main Road were pelted with rubbish. He viewed, almost with excitement, as the commissioner ordered more licence checks. And, when Peter Lalor called the men to take up arms and establish their military base on Eureka, he could not contain his satisfaction.

Now the moment was at hand. The storm was rumbling and he welcomed its closeness. The dark shadows would burst with the flashes of lightning and the clouds would disgorge their fury. Then, in its aftermath, the new day could dawn.

On the evening of the first of December, he called upon his men to come together at the clearing they had used before. This would be no ordinary meeting. This was to be a council of war.

Again, a guard was posted. Again, with the darkness blanketing the bush around, Martin rose to speak. More were here tonight, he noticed, peering out into the clearing. A credit to the work of his lieutenant, Tom Douglas. Each comer brought his own resolve, his anger, his expectations. But together, they had the resolution of a small army, so united were they. In the gloom and the silence there was an air of excitement, a pressing closer to hear what the commander had to say.

He began humbly, almost hesitantly. 'Lads, we've waited for this moment. Now it's here. You've all seen the troops marchin' in to the camp. And you've seen the boys of Eureka buildin' their defences. Hundreds of men are there, now. Peter Lalor and Vern at their head. The troops will attack soon. I reckon Sunday mornin'. Cunning old Freddy Martin here has been snoopin' around the camp. And he says that more troops are stationed on the Eureka lead, ready to join the redcoats at the camp. Those bastards wouldn't respect the Sabbath, would they? Not given the ways they've treated the honest men here on the field. Yes. Sunday it will be. A good day for slaughter, eh?'

There were a few muttered words, even a nervous laugh from one or two. Most remained silent, waiting.

'The time for action is here. Unity, lads. That's what we have now.' His confident voice folded over them all. 'Change is comin'. More than change: the chance to build new lives for yourselves, your wives and your youngsters. But,' and he held out his hands, as if to comfort them, 'but it will need sacrifice. From us. And I know that you have the will to see this through and make that sacrifice.'

His voice became almost matter of fact, businesslike in its precision. He had waited a long time to be able to outline a firm plan and now he must show nothing but confidence. 'Now, tomorrow night we'll meet at Johnson's flat. You all know where that is. Well south of the barricades and far enough out in the bush to avoid bein' seen. Then we'll set up near the stockade. When we know that the government troops have attacked the Eureka boys and been thrown back, as they will be, I've no doubt about that, then we move on the camp. Young Tom here will rally our mates in Creswick. They know I expect them to be ready tomorrow night. The Eureka men will sweep up to join us. And final victory will be ours. A bit like draughts or chess, eh?'

He did not really expect a response. For a moment, there was a heavy stillness. And into it poured the breeze and the sad call of an owl. They distracted no one. All eyes, those hard points of light reflected in the glow of the lanterns men had brought with them, remained fixed on him. He knew that he was succeeding. These were practical, simple men. They needed simple, practical instructions.

He did not feel the need to tell them that the miners from Creswick had made it clear that they would not ride across in support until the camp was firmly in rebel hands. Only Tom and Frank needed to know that. He had been hopeful that Tom might convince them to come earlier and had sent him across the day after the two Scots had departed for Melbourne to take possession of the guns. But he had been unsuccessful. At least the guns, according to Frank, were safe. And, whatever he felt now, he knew he must control his men until the diggers from Creswick arrived. Patience and self-belief must not fail.

If Martin felt uneasy about this, he kept it well hidden. And around him the confidence of his followers was palpable. Men pressed forward, eager to know more.

He folded his arms, leaning forward as he went on. 'Once the men in the stockade have shattered the redcoats, the road'll be open to us. You've been patient, lads. But victory's close now. The Eureka boys will do their part. We'll hold the camp until the Creswick lads come ridin' in. After that, we'll see what the toffs in Toorak have to say. Our own government, lads. Free of interference. Land for honest men. Votes for all. No more licences. And a fair go for all. They are our goals.'

He paused and raised his hands. 'Victory for the miners of Ballarat.' He felt as if he had been rehearsing these words for many months and now, with the darkness and his men behind him, he could release them. 'Victory for the miners.'

Applause was sporadic at first. But it quickly grew in intensity and ended in shouts of support and cries of 'Victory, victory for the miners of Ballarat.'

Martin rode the wave of sound, his body trembling with excitement. If the guards out in the darkness were alarmed about the din, they did not show it. They, too, joined in the chorus.

He waited, then raised his hands again. 'We'll meet on the slope south of the stockade at one o'clock Sunday mornin'. An early start, lads. But the beginnin' of a new order. So, no sleepin' late, now.'

There was general laughter at this.

His voice, when silence was restored, was quiet but decisive. 'Secrecy, lads. Remember, no one must know of our plans. No wives. No sweet lass you might be, er, actin' up with, if you know what I mean.'

Laughter broke out again.

'Yes. Clearly you do know what I mean. But our success depends on us keepin' things to ourselves. Victory, comrades, it will come if we stand up when the time arrives. And that time will be tomorrow night.'

There were no wild cheers as he finished. No throwing of hats. No extravagant promises. Comments were measured, handshakes firm and faces showed nothing but resolve. He was relieved to see this. His followers now clearly saw the magnitude of the task ahead and were not retreating from it. Many of the miners simply came forward to shake his hand. Some paused to encourage Tom, also, thanking him for his efforts.

Martin was well pleased. He had roused their spirits and he had kept them buoyant. True, he had not informed them that Bentley had been convicted of Scobie's death and been sentenced to three years' hard labour. Any more than he had about the firm decision of the miners from Creswick. But there are things a commander should keep to himself, lest the confidence of his men be washed away.

It was enough, now, that the men were committed to the fight and were loyal to him. He watched as they faded away into the darkness. And wondered, at the same time, whether the revolutionary leaders in Paris, those years before, weak though they were, had felt the same pride before their assault on the Bastille.

Within a few minutes, the bushland had gathered up its secrets and presented once more its bland, inscrutable face. No subversive meeting had ever taken place there. Only a solitary lantern remained, lighting the faces of the commander and his lieutenant as they sat together, screwing down the last details of their plan.

And the following night, a solitary lantern played over the faces of Mary Douglas and Dan Morgan as they sat together in the store, Dan with his hands over his face, Mary leaning forward as if trying to comfort him. He had explained already the cause of his injuries and had been quick to dismiss them. There were things, he had said, of much more significance, things like the determination of her son, things like the enormous threat of violent confrontation, things like his fear that he could not protect her son from it.

They were silent now for a time. A silence he broke, slowly and with a heavy resignation. 'No, I've failed, Mary, love. The lad won't be moved. I'll go on trying' but I fear time may be running out. We understand the anger. Men have been treated badly. We've all seen that. It's just…'

Mary interrupted, taking both of his bruised hands and placed hers gently over them. There was a weariness in her voice, as if it was coming from a great distance. 'It's not your fault, Dan. There's something stronger here.' She paused, looking away as if seeking the words she needed among the items stacked around her. 'The cause. Yes, I think that's part of it. But there's something else too. You know, his father used to tell him that the most important thing is to survive.' There was an unusual bitterness in her voice as she went on. '"Survival, that's the thing, boy." I can still hear those words. And I think that Tom is trying to prove to his father that that's not true. That there is something bigger, something more worthy than just surviving. And the miners and their troubles? Well, perhaps they give him his chance. The sad thing is,' and her voice was trembling now, 'the sad thing is that I may lose my son because of it.' Her eyes met his and she held his hands more firmly. 'But you must not blame yourself. Who else could I turn to? And I couldn't have turned to anyone more, more worthy. Oh no, my dear. You haven't failed.'

He spread his large, rough hand over hers. 'Thank you, Mary. I will go on doin' what I can.' He made an attempt, now, to smile. 'And perhaps, in the end, there won't be violence anyway and your son can still prove he's right. And your husband wrong. Let's hope so, eh?'

'Yes, we can still hope.'

And they sat together for some time in silence, with the breeze tapping the roof and the lantern sketching its own thoughts on the walls.

Finally, Dan rose to leave. Embracing her, he sensed her weariness and the warmth of her body. At least, if he could not help her son, he might be able to protect her.

'Oh, Dan, I wish all of this was over.'

'Yes, I know, my love. But I'll do my best. Things might right themselves without bloodshed.'

'Perhaps.'

He rose with some difficulty. His ribs had been too painful to ride across this evening, so he had walked through the scattered bushland.

However, before he could leave, there was a knock on the door: a quiet, almost apologetic knock, as if the person did not really want entry, or felt uncertain about a welcome this late at night. He walked to the door, opening it cautiously. Framed there and edged in silver moonlight, stood a stranger. Or at least, a stranger to him. But not a stranger to Mary.

There, anxiously holding his hat and looking uncertainly around him, was the young labourer who had stood with her father the day she was married to James. Not so young, of course, but still slightly stooped and leaning slightly to the left, as he had always done. There was a brief smile on his face, a smile that eroded quickly as his eyes met hers.

'Thomas?'

'Yes, Mrs Douglas Jones. Thomas Jones. I was a friend of your father's. More. He was almost a father to me.' A coldness came creeping now. And a silence he was reluctant to break. So anxious was he, in fact, that he dropped his hat and knelt clumsily to pick it up. Only his eyes were firm, fixed on Mary's face. Then, in a tumble, came out news that her father had died. 'He knew time was short, Mrs Douglas, and instructed me, the day before he died, to let you know that he loved you very much. And that,' the emotion in the voice almost choked off the sound, 'and that he wished he had not given his permission for you to marry. I think,' the voice was stronger now, 'I think he knew, feared, that you would not be happy.'

There was a pause now. And the visitor seemed to retreat into the darkness, as if unsure of whether he should say more.

Mary held out her hand. 'Go on, Thomas. I'm grateful that you have come. There's something else, I know.'

'Yes, Mrs Douglas. I, I don't want to say this. But he was sad, I know that, that you hadn't written to him. Not,' he went on quickly, clutching his hat more firmly, 'not that he ever asked me to mention that to you. No. But, well, I have told you. Now. He feared that, well, that you no longer had feelings for him, that he had lost you.'

Mary felt a guilt. Then an anger. Then a confusion that seemed like a whirlpool from which she could not escape. She was aware of the closeness of Dan but wanted to push herself away.

'But I wrote many times before my husband's death. He took the letters for me to the coach here in the town. To be taken to Melbourne and then to Sydney. Many, many times I wrote.'

Suddenly, a coldness swept through her. And with it a sickening suspicion. 'At least he said...' And she could say no more.

'I am sorry, Mrs Douglas,' she heard from a great distance. And, before she or Dan could intervene, the man was gone, riding quickly towards the town.

The bullocky hesitated, then moved as if to embrace her. But she pushed him away, rigid and silent. Then, looking nowhere in particular, she moved forward and picked up the precious vase, the one tangible link she had with her dead father. Her face tightened and she raised her hand, ready, it seemed, to smash it against the wall.

Only a quick lunge forward from the bullocky prevented it. 'No, lass,' he said quietly, taking the object from her, replacing it carefully and closing his arms around her. 'He wouldn't want you to do that. You wouldn't want to do that.'

Her whole body was trembling now, clutching him desperately. Then, as if in silent resignation, she relaxed and they sat together.

Finally, she rose, freeing herself from his arms, weary but determined, telling him that he could, that he should, leave now. That she could cope. That for a time she preferred to be by herself. Reluctant, he rose, kissed her once more, closed the door behind him and set off, walking slowly, painfully, down and away towards his hut. Thinking about the sadness welling up in the woman he loved. The storm threatening to unleash itself. And the commitment he had made. Her wish to be alone, he understood. And, for a time, as he walked, he felt that same need.

About a mile from the store, he had to leave the road and cut through a small area of cleared ground. On it the stumps of trees showed where timber cutters had removed wood quite recently. Few ever came here now. However, tonight, on the far side, a campfire was burning. It stood out, a scarlet ball against the grey box trees and the piles of discarded branches the loggers had left. At another time, he would have stopped and made himself known to anyone there. Not tonight. There was too much to think about.

He skirted the fire, noticing in passing that two men were seated there. They had apparently eaten together and were clearly silhouetted against the flames. He was on the point of plunging back among the trees when suddenly he heard the names Jacobs and Douglas mentioned. Curious, he stopped to listen.

'Oh, yes,' he heard, 'Jacobs and Douglas, we'll 'ave 'em soon enough. And you've done well, Frank. Earned your keep, you might say. The lad Douglas, I'll look after. I've a personal reason for accountin' for 'im. There's some unsettled business I 'ave with 'is dead father. 'Ad me brother executed, 'e did. Murdered would be a better way of puttin' it. You don't need to know anythin' about that. But I can tell you I'll look after 'is son. You see that scar, don't you? Everyone does. James Douglas gave me that. Somethin' else to settle there with that 'othead son of 'is, too.'

This figure Dan recognised immediately as Sergeant Miller.

The other, from his strong American accent, could only be Frank Burgen. 'Yes. I think my job's done and your men have paid me well enough. Captain Thomas will have his men ready to march in the morning. The barricades, such as they are, will topple like a pack of cards. My man tells me dozens of the poor wretches have deserted already. I almost feel sorry for those that will be there when the troops come stormin' in. You don't want me to deal with the lad? We don't want him breaking out and getting through to Creswick.'

The sergeant was quick to respond. 'No, 'e's mine. We know where 'is mates'll be waitin'. When the lad breaks out, I'll have 'im. You can be sure of that. Jacobs and his men will soon turn tail when the stockade falls. And we'll 'ave no difficulty 'auling in Jacobs. The government don't 'ave much sympathy for those that commit treason.'

'Good. I think our business is done, then.'

'Yes. That it is. And what will you do now?'

'Well, there are mining companies in California that can, well, use a man like me, I think. Always problems with striking labourers there. I've made arrangements to sail early next week.'

'Good. Very good. We wouldn't want to see you shoved down some mine shaft, would we?'

They both laughed at that, stood up and shook hands. Their parting was quick, perfunctory and final, the sergeant riding down towards the town, Frank Burgen mounting and, without looking back, heading out and away into the darkness.

Dan remained hidden for a few minutes. Then anxiety goaded him into action. He struggled through the undergrowth, regained the road and made for his hut, there, in spite of his pain, saddling his horse and riding down towards Tom Douglas's camp.

By the time he reached the slope, the moon had shaken itself clear of the distant hills and stood high above the tents and the claims, a disc of silver that spilled its light down upon the slope, the same moon that had glazed the body of his father, the night of the strike, all those years before. The same moon that had given his father's eyes that sickening silver stare as he lay in the kitchen.

There was little movement on the slope. A few men sat talking by a fire but most seemed asleep. Even the stockade seemed at peace. And Dan found it difficult, even in the bright moonlight, to establish where its perimeter was. The walls, if they could be called that, seemed to wander through the camp, holding here a blacksmith's shop, and there letting a few tents creep out unprotected. At various points, he could make out individual figures, presumably guards set to alert those inside if any attack came.

But an outsider would not suspect that anything untoward was about to happen. To the casual observer, this Sunday would be little different from any other. The miners within the stockade would heave a collective sigh of relief, light their fires, put their pistols and pikes to one side; some might even go to church; others might turn their backs on the stockade and return to their ordinary labours.

Dan, however, was no outsider. He knew what was to come. What he did not know was that already the storm had formed over Bakery Hill and that Captain Thomas, with over a hundred and seventy infantry, one hundred cavalry and a troop of armed police, stood ready to unleash it.

Panting heavily, he stumbled up the thin track to the tent he knew was occupied by Tom and Martin Jacobs. However, as he pulled back the flap, he noticed that it was empty. On both bunks a few items lay. But there was no sign that either had been there all night.

He turned, threw back the flap and went outside. How in this tangle of mining equipment, shafts, tents, timber, shacks and windlasses, could he find them? Whether they were with the miners in the stockade or somewhere else on the field he had no idea. All he knew was that he must try.

17

A December morning

As Martin Jacobs gathered his men on the small, rough, cleared area known as Johnson's Flat and headed for their vantage point south of the stockade, night was already tottering towards the uncertain grey of pre-dawn. The sky shuffled a few recalcitrant clouds towards the western horizon and scattered stars stared unblinking down at the camps. Sunday clung to the vestiges of yesterday's heat and any person awake early in the distant town would imagine this day would unfold like any other Sabbath.

But he knew better. This would be a night and a dawn like no other any of them had known. And he linked those dark shadows moving beside him with images of past armies sallying forth on countless other nights just like this. There was beauty, a kind of tragic grandeur here: the half moon standing bravely among its bright stars, the breeze like a quiet, powerful breath all around them, the swish of coats against low hanging branches and the scrape of boots on gravel and clay. Beauty indeed. But a particular, precious kind shared only by countless generations of soldiers venturing forth to fight for some noble cause. The realisation gave him a sense of heroic endeavour.

There was work to be done, of course. And blood would be shed. He had no illusions about that. But thus far, events had fallen out pretty much as he had predicted. And, with the inevitable fall of the camp and the arrival of the men from Creswick, the government would have to capitulate and a new order could be established throughout the goldfields. What mattered was the courage to seize the moment. And that moment was rapidly approaching. However, he knew that he must remain diligent. Doubt must not be allowed to pollute the will of his followers.

Except for Tom Douglas, they were all on foot; he would need his horse shortly to rouse the Creswick men. But no one walked alone. There was little conversation among any of them, but it seemed important to each man to be physically close to a mate. Occasionally, half sentences drifted between them. More often, sounds were lost in the throat, forgotten in the very act of forming. Some of the more apprehensive were constantly fingering their pistols, as if the metal barrels somehow gave them confidence. Others held their pikes at the ready.

A young Irishman, well known for his quick humour and a source of entertainment in the local hotels, was anxiously playing with the bolt of his rifle, clicking it over and over until one of his mates stopped abruptly and muttered, 'For Christ's sake, Peter, cut that out, will you? You'll wear the bloody thing out before you get the chance to use it.'

Those close by laughed briefly and the journey resumed its solemn intensity.

A few minutes later, someone else muttered, 'I need a piss.'

There was no response this time.

As he walked beside his troops, Martin was filled with a sympathy and a feeling he thought must be love. The kind, he guessed, any military commander is expected to have for his men.

Close to the bottom of a gully, they came upon a hut. Beneath the harsh light of the moon, neat rows of cabbages stood in domestic rows. From the chimney, a thin streak of smoke rose slowly, and inside someone coughed, rolled over and began snoring. Here was a sight the men had viewed, heard or ignored hundreds of times in the preceding three years. Yet some stopped, as if encountering it for the first time.

Further on, a dog slid between two tents, growled vaguely at the men passing and settled back into its patch of darkness. Inside one of the tents, a figure stirred, brushed against the canvas wall, swore and went back to sleep.

In such simple ways, the fabric of their own lives was being revealed to these novice soldiers. And beneath the constant gaze of the moon that fabric was suddenly taking on new significance.

Once they had cleared the last signs of life and entered the open grassy stretch of land before the mining camps and Bakery Hill, the forty men bunched more closely together. Like ocean travellers seeing the familiar coastline disappearing behind them, they were aware of their quickening senses and the unknown looming ahead.

Soon they were climbing again. When they reached the top of the next hill, they looked out upon the stockade and beyond that the distant silhouette of the government camp.

The sight of the stockade, only half a mile away now, washed away all private thoughts. It stood, defiant yet pathetic in its simplicity. Posts stood sharp and rigid as teeth. Beams lay in ragged lines. Tents were blisters of white in the moonlight. The scattered huts, some only half enclosed by the rough barricades, seemed no more secure than wooden boxes. And above floated the flag, the one to which Peter Lalor and his men had sworn allegiance.

Beneath the metal grey of sky and framed as they were by the immense hump of Bakery Hill, the hastily constructed defences seemed extraordinarily inadequate.

'My God,' one of the men whispered, leaning on his pike and pointing down at the stockade, 'I hope there ain't too many soldiers acomin'. That won't 'old out fer long, will it?'

There followed an anxious silence, a silence into which Martin knew he must step quickly. 'They'll be all right, those lads. Stout-hearted, all of 'em. And well armed. And we're all fightin' for what we know is right, those brave men in the darkness down there and us up here.'

Some heads nodded. A few turned away. Nobody spoke. All settled down on the moist grass, placing ammunition and weapons beside them. There was nothing to do now but wait.

Above them, the sky was clearing away its stars. To the east, a grey smudge lengthened, throwing into clearer relief the jagged edges of the hills. Even the distant roofs of the town could be seen, and suddenly the moon, bursting through a thin bank of cloud, spilled a single beam of light on the Union Jack perched above the government camp. Taken by its strange, abrupt brightness, a few pointed across, cursing under their breath.

'Yes, lads, that's what we're up against,' Martin muttered. 'That bloody flag and the power behind it. Not for long, though. We'll see ours, the blue and white one down there, floatin' high above the camp soon enough.'

Had Tom Douglas been more observant, or less caught up in the general tension among the men, he might have noticed a change in the demeanour of his leader. Constantly on the alert, as if guarding something very private, clenching and unclenching his fists, sweating and breathing heavily, Martin Jacobs was struggling to contain his own anxiety.

Fortunately, attention quickly returned to the stockade. Within its blurred borders there was little sign of movement. A sentry shuffled from one corner of the yard to the next, peered out briefly, then shambled back inside a tent. A voice somewhere was wandering drunkenly though some half-remembered song. A horse whinnied and settled. There was no real sense of urgency. No indication that those inside expected an attack. Clearly, for them, Sunday was not a time for battle.

This apparent inactivity gave the watchers on the slope a sense of helplessness. Waiting for the unknown will always be unnerving, and Martin was very attentive now. He could detect the uneasiness in his lieutenant Tom Jacobs also. His silence had been almost complete since their march had begun and it could only be hoped that, with battle so close, the lad was not losing his nerve.

This was a dangerous time too. Anxious men, compelled to be passive, will often clamour for action or escape. Not all of the soldiers would have left the camp and if, when the battle began, his men broke to join the defenders of the stockade, his dream would be shattered. It would be futile to attack the camp with a badly depleted force. Vern and Carboni had confidence in the Eureka men, knew of Martin's plan and had agreed with it. It was imperative that his men be held in check. Also, he must prevent any of them from deserting. Who could predict their reactions once the hills unleashed flames and whining bullets? And which of them had ever witnessed the flash of bayonets or heard the agonised screams of dying men? Fear had a nasty way of transforming itself into panic. If even two or three, in the first few moments of the onslaught, were to throw down their weapons and melt away, God alone knew how many might quickly follow. So he walked among them, reassuring and checking for any sign of weakness.

There was one man he was particularly concerned about, a thin Scotsman, Charlie Kennedy. He had been a close friend of James Scobie. Martin had met him a few times and knew of his disgust that Bentley had been cleared. Revenge was what he wanted. And revenge could drive a man into ill-advised action. He was sitting by himself now, drumming his fingers on the butt of his musket and scouring the stockade for any sign of movement. Martin stood in the darkness for two or three minutes, watching him closely.

When he returned to join his lieutenant, he pointed across to the obviously troubled Scot. 'We've got to watch that one, lad. He's a good man and he'll fight. But he's hasty. There are a few of his Scottish mates down there. We'll need to keep an eye on him.'

Tom nodded, more aware of his own growing anxiety than anyone else's. At the same time, he noticed the urgency creeping across the sky. To the east now ran a clear line of pink, and the moon, having shaken itself free of the camp, was close to the horizon. Bakery Hill had shed its thin cover of mist and the creeks were already wandering, thin lines of silver. If the attack was coming, it must surely come soon.

Tension heightened among the watchers. But still there was no sense of urgency within the stockade.

'Remember, lads, the Eureka boys can look after themselves.'

Martin's comment, clear and precise though it was, received no acknowledgement. All eyes were fixed on a single line of armed, uniformed men moving down the face of Black Hill towards the stockade. There was something both hypnotic and chilling about the advance. For advance it clearly was. Precise. Mechanical. Purposeful.

'Gude God,' muttered Charlie, the Scot, 'there must be three hundred of 'em at least. You didn't tell us that, Jacobs, did you? I hope those fellows in the stockade have good eyes.'

Martin was quick to reassure, at the same time sliding closer to him. Below them, the attackers moved confidently. The growing light gave them the appearance of marionettes, each a single shadow, each joined to the next and all a gathering threat to the men within the stockade. The infantry, bayonets fixed, took up a position in the centre. The cavalry moved smoothly to the left flank and the mounted police marched to the right. On the high ground, riflemen bunched together, ready to cover the actual assault.

'Oh, yes,' Martin whispered, making sure no one else could hear, 'they've planned this out. You can see the weak spots in the defences from here. That's where they'll attack.'

He might just as well have shouted it out. The obvious gaps were plain for all to see.

Still there was no response from within.

The troops resumed their advance, this time in tightly closed blocks that vibrated gently as they moved. Uniforms shone in the pre-dawn. Bayonets gleamed. Rifles rose and fell, clean, cold reminders of what was to come. And fear gripped the men on the slope. No one, not even Martin Jacobs, had expected such a show of force.

But still the stockade slept on. And while the knot was tightening, disbelief turned to anger. Anger that bristled and sought an outlet.

Finally the attackers stopped about two hundred yards short of the barricades. It was clear that an onslaught would not be long in coming. An onslaught against poorly armed men with no military training and no expectation that a disaster was about to burst upon them.

Suddenly, Martin found himself looking directly into two eyes that blazed with anger.

'Aye, laddie, so ye've brought us to this, have ye? Look down there. There'll be slaughter there – slaughter of gude men. Gude Scottish lads too. Well, take your bloody plans and shove 'em up your arse. I'm off doon there to help. Or die with me mates.'

A thick arm waved, a pike flashed briefly and Charlie hauled himself to his feet. However, before he could launch himself down the slope, Martin was upon him. The fear he had confined to the corner of his brain galvanised him. He must act quickly. There was a sudden flurry. A pistol butt flashed twice. There were two thuds and a body rolled back and lay still.

Martin replaced his pistol and crawled back beside the crouching figure of Tom Douglas. His face was now ashen white and as he grabbed the younger man by the shoulder, his hand and his voice were clearly trembling. 'Go. Go now. Bring our mates from Creswick.'

Tom Douglas gazed in disbelief.

'Don't wait, now, damn you. Go! The attack may not come for a while. Our mates in the stockade will hold out until the Creswick men get here. Ride fast, lad. We might still succeed. Go, boy! Don't just stand there. Tell the Creswick men that everythin's worked out well here and that we are ready for them. Ride. Ride fast and tell 'em victory's close.'

The madness of this command was evident to Tom Douglas. But, swept along by the gathering tide, much like a man in the midst of drowning, he wrenched himself up through the sheltering brambles and ran towards his horse. Ahead lay the road to Creswick. But behind stood the man he had trusted, pledged his support to, now frantically waving him on. An ordinary man overcome by the same fear that possessed all of his followers. A man obsessed with an idea crumbling around him and commanding an act of insanity.

Before mounting, he paused and looked back. Over the whole area there was silence. The sickening feeling that something abominable was about to erupt. And it came, as he stood there, first in the sound of a single shot. A shot that brought men pouring out from tents and holes to defend the stockade. A shot that unleashed a sickening volley from the hillside above. Soon a line of red flames blossomed, died and blossomed again. Bullets thumped into the wooden barricades. Answering shots rang out from the defenders and the air recoiled under the hideous sound of men screaming in pain. There was a running now, a glare of light on bayonets, a rush of uniformed men on and then through the stockade.

Frantically, Tom scrambled on to his horse and began the descent towards the track. Then, like someone drawn to a nightmare, he stopped again and looked back. Flames were bursting from what had been a blacksmith's shop. In the shifting glow, the figure of a man could clearly be seen falling, writhing and lying still.

All around, men and women, aroused by the gunfire, rushed to any vantage point. Perhaps the only person not drawn to the chaos unfolding below was Dan Morgan. He had been riding through the mass of tents, shafts and equipment in search of Mary's son. And now, seeing him break clear, the bullocky had hastened to follow him.

But not quite the only person. Half a mile ahead, calm in his uniform, Sergeant Miller stood, shielded from view by a fallen tree. He had seen the opening of the battle and the departure of the rider. Now he had only to wait. Methodically, carefully he took his musket, feeling its cold metal in his hands. Next he unbuckled the powder flask, tilting it carefully and watched the powder, like black blood, disappear down the barrel. Finally, and with a tremor of delight, he placed the ball in place, gently tapping it in place. These were actions he could perform with his eyes closed. But there was something personal, almost delicious, about the ritual this time. Below, the rifles cracked, the flames erupted in sharp jets from the riflemen, and he knew that the end would not be long coming.

It all seemed an anticlimax, now, waiting for James Douglas's son to be within easy range. Looking back over the last few years, he prided himself on his patience. Now there was a legitimate reason to dispose of him: the boy was clearly a traitor. And with this final act, his revenge would be complete. In fact, the killing of the lad seemed now rather routine. The work of a tradesman. Frank Burgen had done his job. All had unfolded exactly as he had said it would.

Hearing the clatter of hoofs, he tightened his grip on the musket, letting its coldness rest against his shoulder. As he cocked the weapon, it took on a character of its own: efficient, impersonal, but, to a man used to violence, companionable. Light was now much stronger and the road seemed to flow towards him, delivering his quarry closer and closer. A slight pressure would bring the rider crashing to the ground. Such a moment should be savoured and he held back until Tom Douglas was about twenty yards away. Then, with the rattle of hoofs almost upon him, he pulled the trigger. But there was no welcoming explosion, no ball tearing into flesh. No cry of pain. Just a hollow click. The weapon, usually so reliable, had failed him.

The horse swept on and the sergeant stood in disbelief. Then an inexpressible rage welled up and he hurled the weapon to the ground.

However, before he could think further, he was aware that, two hundred yards along the road, the horse had stopped. Its rider, propped in the saddle, was peering down at the carnage. Then, unaccountably, the horse was turned. Tom Douglas was slowly coming within his reach again.

The sergeant remained hidden, unsure of what to do. There was no time to reload. If he was to succeed now, he must first wrench the rider from the saddle and kill him with his fists. Even a knife would have been useful. But at least he had his truncheon and, calm once more, he unclipped it.

Soon the horse was so close he could leap out and perhaps dislodge the rider. But before he could act, the horse came to a halt and Tom Douglas dismounted.

This was his chance. He waited until Tom Douglas stood in the centre of the road, head bowed, shoulders hunched over. Nothing could show more clearly a man's defeat. Nothing could equal the sergeant's sense of triumph as he watched. Beyond, the stockade lay in ruins. Flames licked the canvas walls of the tents, bayonets flared, bodies flung themselves out of shallow holes, women and children screamed, the proud blue and white flag was being hauled down and suddenly, above everything else, the wail of a dog could be heard, clear and chilling in the dawn air.

There was no need to wait any longer. The sergeant gripped his baton and crept forward.

As he was about to strike, Tom Douglas stood up and without turning, shouted into the empty dawn, 'No, by God, you've deceived us all, Martin. It's over. I won't bring men back to this slaughter. It's finished.'

'You're right about that, lad,' the sergeant said, almost soothingly.

The blow struck his victim on the side of his head and he fell to his knees.

Years of held-back anger cascaded upon him. 'This,' the sergeant roared, hammering again, 'this is for my brother. Your father gave 'im up to the troops so 'e could go free. Then watched as 'e swung and kicked on the end of a rope. The devil 'e was, your father. I've waited long enough for this.'

Blow followed blow. But Tom was young, toughened by months of work underground and he began to defend himself, lashing out with his fists and boots. Soon the bush resounded, not to the sound of gunfire, but the curses of two men locked together, each fighting to survive, each knowing that one of them would almost certainly die.

Beside them, the horse reared and plunged away. Still they fought on. There was no thought now. Nothing to guide them except primitive rage. Rage that was bringing them both to the edge of the road and a seventy-foot drop into a gully.

Only as the earth slid away beneath them were they aware of the danger. Then, like two crabs, they struck out, still embracing one another, both of them grasping at the crumbling clay. There was the sound of branches cracking. But only one fell through those branches. The other was hauled back, bloodied and confused.

Once the figure lay safe on the edge of the cliff, Dan Morgan was able to loosen his grip. 'You'll be right, now, laddie. I can't do anything to save the sergeant. But,' pausing a moment as he hauled Tom Douglas to his feet, 'perhaps that's a good thing, eh? But you're safe.'

'Yes, by Christ. Thanks to you, Daniel, I am.'

Painfully, slowly, the two mounted their horses and set out for the store. In the distance, lazy coils of smoke rose above what was left of the stockade. And they could hear, not the sharp crack of gunfire, but the wail, sustained and pitiful, of a dog.

'Yes. Thanks to you, Daniel I am.'

Slowly, to the people of Ballarat, normality returned. The miners continued toiling underground, commerce grew and within a few months a traveller could have passed through the town quite unaware of the events that had unfolded there.

However, if he was curious, he might have stopped at a store on the Melbourne road, looked up and noticed a freshly painted sign with the words,

General Merchandise
M. and D. Morgan, Proprietors.

Had he ventured inside, he might have heard one or two refer to it as 'The Wider's Store'. And, if sensitive enough, he might have detected in the voices a hint of nostalgia. Before leaving the town, he might have picked up a copy of the *Ballarat Times* and read an article by Henry Seekamp, that man of fiery temper and words. The words might have taken him by surprise. Or at least the extravagance of the language might have.

Later, he would have learned that the miner's licence was to be replaced by a fairer miner's right. Diggers were to be represented in the legislative assembly. And they were to have the right to vote in future Victorian elections. Mention was made of the leaders and their brave stand. But Martin Jacobs was not among them. Indeed, nothing more was heard about him. Nothing at all to indicate what had happened to him.

On his journey back to Melbourne, he might have met a young man travelling alone. And had he enquired, cautiously, cunningly about the object of the journey, he might have heard brief mention of a red-headed girl named Melanie.